Hugo Ulyss SEBASTIAN

OF LITTLE SIGNIFICANCE

To all who make their meaning to be kindness.

I

"My dear Mouse, you should know by now that ink dries far quicker than blood, " – Emperor Augustin, as spoken to his Veiled Hand.

Snowflakes drifted lazily through morning air. Some came to rest on a needled branch, waiting there to melt within a moon's time or to be shaken down in chunks by birds seeking refuge. Others would meet the ground much sooner, sticking to the white coat that stretched through gaps between trees, sheltering the earth and all that lived below from cold. Between the trees ran a road and on it slid a sleigh pulled by a chestnut mare in her shaggy, winter coat.

The sleigh itself was two trips short of a wreck, doubtlessly, a creation of a local carpenter working for a purse of silvers which would barely cover the cost of timber. Maximilian would have found it hard to describe the man's work as adequate and even less so the work done to preserve it. The sleigh seemed almost entirely held together by amateur repairs attempting to take back years of neglect and ill-maintenance. Uneven, one atop the other, attached by nails sunken so poorly they could serve as coat hooks, its boards threatened to abandon their station at even the hint of a bump. Not that it was a bother to any of the passengers. It was a local transport, running between farms and villages whenever the winter decided to bury the road. The peasants were bundled in dried up skins and scrappy swashes of cloth, huddling into two little groups in attempt to preserve as much warmth as their familiarity allowed them to – all tight except for him. He sat at the back, tucked within his coat, hoping that keeping his eyes on the horizon would dissuade the peasants from attempting conversation.

"By the gods, can't wait to drop my arse by the fire," spoke a man sat with two bundles of fur beneath his arms. His face seemed little more than two wiry shrubs of black and grey, one atop his head, one sprouting out his chin. From between peeked red cheeks.

The sleigh's driver turned for a moment, his face even redder than the other man's. "Will be there plenty soon my friend." One of his hands grasped the reins and the other a near-empty wineskin.

"I hope so, Gorgie. I hope so. You know, at least in summer I'd be able to tell, but in this snow... I'll be fucked if I know how you tell any of it apart. White, white, it's all white. You could be driving us in circles and I wouldn't know the difference."

"I guess we should be thanking the gods you're not in my seat." Gorgie took a long pull of his wineskin, but even with cheeks sucked in deep his eyes remained watchful, scanning the way ahead. The road, if it could even be called that, wove its way between spruce and pine that seemed to make up almost the entirety of the forest. Its outlines would hide without warning in the loosely packed snow, remaining unseen for stretches long enough he thought the driver had them lost. As of yet, that hadn't happened.

The red faced man shivered then lifted his arms about the two bundles. With a yank, he pulled them close. "You alright boys? Not too cold?"

The two bundles returned muffled replies.

"That's good boys, that's good!" With a fur wrapped hand, he clasped the two's heads and gave them a hearty rub. "It's good for the bones this cold I tell you – hardens them like ice and shakes the joints nice and loose." Satisfied with the thoroughness of his tussling, he looked to the other bench where three similarly bundled figures huddled. "How are your girls, Yoona?"

Yoona's brow lifted, eyes falling in a slow blink as if he had just awoken. He blinked twice more before his eyes moved from the road to the man before him. "Um, those aren't my girls, Bear. That's Mary and Ellinor."

Squinting, Bear examined the two more thoroughly as a grin opened a gap in his beard. "Oh, so they are! I couldn't tell with their faces all scarfed up. I guess we all look like chewed up, furry mounds when winter comes."

"That's right," agreed Yoona, "except you look like one all year long."

Gorgie snorted from the driver's seat. "They don't call him a bear for nothing."

Bear joined in, and while not particularly loud, he expressed the laughter thoroughly with his body, forcing the boys under arm into a tight hunch. "That's right! The Bear of Karlka! In a shield wall or if ale gets ya' in trouble, it's like having a bear on your side – that's what they used to say... gods... thirty years back. Shite, it's been a long time."

"You see, I always thought they called you that because you're fat, hairy, and lazy."

Muffled giggles escaped the bundles under Bear's arms only to be stifled promptly by a second chuckle – Bear's. His great mass dropped, bending the boys in half once more. Not that being crushed by their father could stop their amusement. Even with ears by their knees, the boys merry chortling continued as the sleigh slid its way between the trees. The driver took a long pull from the wineskin suckling it flat.

The sleigh's motion was beginning to squeeze Maximilian's eyes shut. *Maybe it's not the worst place to rest.* His eyelids were sticking – a symptom of not having slept for four days. A little rest would do him good, bring him back more lucid than he was at the present. He let his eyes drift, and tired they fell as if floating through syrup, their path interrupted by Bear's gaze. For a brief moment their eyes met. *Leave it be,* he hoped as his eyes continued drifting, knowing very well that it wasn't in a peasant's nature to do so.

The hairy man straightened himself, releasing his sons from the contortion. "Oh Yoona, if you were only half as good at anything as you are at chewing manure." His shoulders opened to include Maximilian. "Now, who is this – neighbour of yours?"

"Him?" Yoona tilted a narrow brow towards him. "I've never seen him before."

"Hurh, so just a traveller thinking it better to pretend sleep than talk with us lot." The man dropped two pats onto his knee. "What do they call you?"

Bastard, all of the sudden he wished the man ill for depriving him a moment's rest. Though he didn't need as much as most, the need for sleep still remained. If left restless too long, his mind would begin to blur the curtain letting the worlds merge into something *other*. But there was no rest to be found here for the moment, only futile conversation.

I'm Maximilian Aubridge, but no – not to you – to you, I cannot say that. Gregor, that's what he was for those four long days, a modest merchant from Dalre, but he'd rather die than be a sodding peppercorn peddler a minute longer. "Sparrow," he answered instead – something that was true. Many called him Sparrow, his friends, enemies, and underlings included. But the chance of either one of these riding inside this waste of a tree were nought. And yet, the man's face turned as still as the surrounding forest.

"I'm sorry." His sons, who were giggling just seconds ago, turned eerily quiet, eyes darting between their father and the stranger.

"What?" *Did I slip up? I should not have slept. I should have felt them,* invaded their minds in search of poor intents.

"I'm sorry." His red cheeks seemed tight as he took his arms out from behind his sons. It seemed all eyes were on them, the mare and sleigh being the only sounds that remained.

Sparrow's hands shifted within his fur lined sleeves, pointing his finger at Bear's chest. "What are you sorry about, friend?" The artefact began to heat up.

Bear's face creeped in closer, so close that they were trading air. He could smell the staleness of his breath and whatever fermented atrocity he chewed up that morning. Unblinking, Bear's eyes stared into his. Then a smile cracked through. "I'm sorry that someone would give you such a name!" He gave Sparrow's shoulder a pat hearty enough to send his body two inches to the side all the while laughing to the tune of a drunkard choking on his vomit.

Idiot. All he wanted was sleep, instead, he had to arrange his face into a smile, to exhale elaborately out of his nose, show teeth through parted lips. Yoona, and the women, and the two boys responded in kind, their faces lighting up to the well practised gesture. The driver went for a pull from his wine skin.

"So," Yoona turned his attention from the audibly amused Bear to the smiling stranger, "what's your trade, Sparrow? I don't mean for this to be rudeness, but it's just a coat like that will run a fair bit of coin. Wife's a tailor and I don't think she's ever put as much work into a bride's dress as whoever did into stitching that thing together."

"This? Found it on a hook – my predecessor seemed to have forgotten it before making his departure." Other times, it was his father's or maybe pulled off the back of a dead Reaver; if there was ever need to acquaint with thieves – which was rather often – it was a burglar's haul. But unlike those explanations, this one was true. It was his predecessor's, and that of several others before. For those who knew, and they were very few, it marked the Emperor's Veiled Hand – his glorified errand boy.

"Didn't he come back looking for it?"

"I certainly hope not. He died," which was coincidentally true.

The story seemed to pique Yoona's interest, "A predecessor do–"

"Did you kill the man for his coat?" Bear cut in with a grin stupidly wide.

"Apparently it was one of the gods. The Old Father, I suspect – the man's beard grew so long and thick he couldn't bear the competition." His real predecessor was put on a spike by Young Alfred, then King of then independent Swasia. They sent him back cleaned, clothed, and intact, seemingly untouched but for his face which was stuck in grotesque twists that marked four days of torture. *Nothing worse for diplomacy than a child tended by a loyal court.*

"Hurh," he chortled, "that does sound like the Old Father."

"A predecessor doing what?" asked Yoona much louder.

"It may not be the stuff of fantasies, but he was a researcher at the Archives. Just like what I am." The listeners' heads were at a tilt. While the explanation for the coat was within their grasp, research and the Archives were stretching their imagination so thin it showed in their befuddled expressions. *Hicks.* "I find out what happens, what did happen, and what will happen, then I write it down. A lot of writing and, if any of it is deemed adequate, it ends up a part of the Archives."

"The provosts do most the writing around here, and thank the gods for that. I'd take an axe or a shovel over a quill any day you ask," said Bear.

"What could you do with a quill anyway?"asked Yoona, his eyebrows and cheeks raised in self amusement. "Stick it up your arse and pretend to be a goose?"

Bear's grin was nowhere to be found. "I know my letters. Can't go into King's service without them. Not like you would know. What about you, Sparrow, ever served?"

Not in a way you would understand. What he had done in the past day alone amounted to more than the man's entire life. Even so, he gave an answer that would settle the fool down, "no."

"I thought so."

The conversation was replaced by the clacket of the mare's harness and the steady *shhh* of the sleigh sliding on snow; he couldn't be more grateful for that. *Maybe I'll need to find this Yoona a place in the court.* The sheer idea of the peasant in the Emperor's court put a smile on his face. *Maybe for entertainment.*

With the distractions gone, Maximilian Aubridge let his eyelids fall to a narrow slit out of which he started counting trees. Some came in groups and some stood alone, climbing far above the rest without having to share sun nor rain. A snowy owl sat on one of their branches. It gave him a little jolt – a little excitement that popped his eyes open. Her head turned over a motionless body of speckled white, amber eyes trailing the sleigh through the silent forest. She was hunting. His love of birds was no tightly kept secret, and a part of him wanted to stop, to wait for the dive, the glide, the violent grasp that trades death for nourishment. He considered stopping the sleigh – making them stop the sleigh – just to watch the spectacle, and then he thought about how ridiculous that would be. The sleigh stopped nonetheless.

"Whooaaa, whooooa! Easy! Easy." Gorgie soothed the shaggy mare as she bucked before a barricade of felled trees.

*

"Easy girl, easy," whispered the driver, soothing the mare's nerves down to a restless kicking of a hoof. The man's own hoof seemed to tremble far more, knocking the timber before him to a brisk beat. The trees were piled with purpose, there was no doubt about it, and they would have certainly backtracked if the barricade's makers weren't stood at its side gripping steel. From his bench with confidence feigned, the driver addressed them, "What can I do you for?"

"Did you hear that?" answered a voice scraped to husk. The face it came paired with resembled that of a starved hound more so than a man. "He's wondering what *he can do us for.*"

"Everything he's got," replied a voice far more melodic, "that's what he can do us for." A woman – secret supported only by the combed lock draping down the side of her hollowed cheek – stepped up to the man's side. "Come on, pork loin, you don't strike me as the kind to never had met toll collectors."

They were four, wrapped in tattered furs and cloth which counted more holes than fibres. Petty brigands not worth the executioner's fee, and that would only hold true on a good day. Today, they were a hump in the road, an uneven cobble that should pray to all things holy not to be worthy of Maximilian's notice.

"Well," the driver brought the reins onto his lap, leaning forth for a closer look, "last time I've met such an official looking bunch of officials, the price was far clearer – law of the land – five trolls, or the equivalent of if I recall right."

The woman bared a sparse collection of yellowed teeth. "I think your memory may be–"

"Because you're old, you fat, red faced fuck!" cut in a man on her right, spitting sprays out of his mouth with every ill-pronounced word. The man next to him gave a grunt, opening his mouth wide to show a spaciously toothed set of gums. The stench of each assaulted a different nostril.

The woman waited until his spit had settled. "Thank you for pointing that out," she spoke dryly. "Now quiet, please." The man looked to her then twitched a nod. He stepped back, mouth closing as far as it seemingly could – not enough to prevent yellow spittle from dribbling out in trails, slowly rolling down his lips into the clumps of tangled hair hanging off his chin. With the man back in his place, the woman turned back to the driver. "You're an awfully brave man to be negotiating with king's servants."

"I've been running these roads for a long time. Met myself many toll men, tax takers, road watchers, and booth guards. Wouldn't have a penny to my name if I didn't negotiate." The driver drifted to the side. The tapping of his foot quickened.

Yoona's waist was being crushed by the two women at his sides, the concern of neither being his wife seemingly forgotten. Opposite, unwilling to betray themselves in front of their father, the boys were trying to keep their fears tightly under wraps. The older one was more successful at stopping twitching in the face, though neither could help their racing eyeballs. Spastically, they glanced between the thugs and their father who, unlike them, seemed carved of stone – all that betrayed him was his foot. It was wriggling under the sacks, sliding back and forth with toes wriggling downwards in search of purchase – he was trying to grasp the blackened head of an axe.

You're going to get yourself killed. Brigands were drawn to woods, preying alongside any road significant enough for regular traffic but not to a point where the king or his lords would pay it mind. As long as the corpses were few and far between, there was no bother – the life of parasite and host carried on. *Give up your wooden beads – move along and get home alive.* More importantly, any further delays raised the chance of Maximilian getting caught at the crossing. His men should be able to hold it, but each passing hour was just another chance for a Nurhdvalian fool to cut his way into a song. What surprised even him though, was that he wanted these peasants to make it home nearly as much as he wanted to finish his task.

The owl hooted and the driver along with it. "You know very well us farm folk don't own much, and if you take it all, we may not make it through the winter. Now, take it for me – I've been doing these routes for years and know a bit about trade – I promise you that there is nothing better than return customers. That is of course, as long as these customers return warm and with blood still moving."

"Alright," said the woman after a moment's thought, "I'll tell you what we're going to do – we will empty your bags, strip your cloth, and pick all we need. Don't worry, we'll leave all we don't."

The contracts, they weighed down the breast of his coat, *if they find them… cunt.* It wasn't a possibility he could entertain.

"I'll pay our toll," he said, "hundred gold with scrap between – here and now. You crawl back into your hole and we go our way. Here." He reached for the purse at his belt and lobbed it towards her. It fell a yard short and disappeared in the snow.

The wolf man got to it in one gliding step, his knees sinking in as he pulled out the bag. He worked the knot with his teeth, jamming his hand in as soon as it could fit. A glitter of coins fell about as he pulled out a coin on which he began to chew. "It's gold," he mumbled with his teeth still feeling the coin, "the ugly bastard's on the back too." His protruding mouth showed a razory grin.

The woman ran to his side. The measured calm with which she spoke gave way to childlike excitement as her eyes and cheeks began to twitch. "Very good... very good... very good," she repeated over and over. Suddenly, she snapped back. The excitement seemed a surprise which caused her guard to drop, one she straightened promptly before speaking again. "What else you got?"

"That's none of your concern – your concern is taking the gold and leaving." *Take it and go. Nobody has to die.* Out the corner of his eye, he could see Bear, his hand now wrapped about the axe's handle. He tried to gesture him to calm, stand him down, but the man was already calm. He was prepared to act.

"You are being very rude," her voice now higher, cracked into a screeching inflection. She moved forth without a sideway glance. He could feel her breath on his cheek. He could smell it too as she stared unblinking, knuckles turning white as her fingers gripped tight onto the side of the sleigh. Her face hadn't seen its thirtieth winter, and though covered in dirt, it carried a charm – much of it in brisk hazel eyes still untouched by hunger which seemed to have melted all else. Were the circumstances different, her resolve could have been tested by court intrigue rather than steel. *Don't do it.*

With a feeler he reached out, slithering with ease through the unguarded fields which made up her mind. *Something's wrong. Something's wrong. Run. Take it. Run.* Her eyes twitched, black opening wide to consume most of the hazel. Fear burst its spores.

"Vulf," she said, turning back to her companion, "take the gold an–"

"Aaaaaargh!" Bear was already twisting the axe out of her skull.

The wolf man turned from the purse to the sight of his companion on her knees, twitching at the side of the sleigh.

Howling and dribbling mucus, he sprung forth spilling gold out of his grip. Sparrow rose with the artefact pointed forth. The wolf man lunged. Sparrow released. The man's protruding face collapsed in on itself sending teeth into tree trunks. A mist of red obscured where his head once was.

The other two were moving, blades descending in wild curves. Sparrow turned and flicked both wrists. The blades changed path – one meeting neck and the other cheek. Skin parted then flesh and bone. The spitter's jaw dangled loose, his hands attempting to remove the blade lodged above it. Over and over he tried, skin parting in trails of scarlet along fingers and palm.

His comrade fell to ground. Grip locked tight in a dead hand, he pulled both of them down. Yoona vomited. Sparrow turned to face the trees, siphoning whatever the slain had left into the little artefact – with it he motioned sideways. The trunks promptly obeyed, flying off into the woods to fall mere yards from the bow men.

Their strings rang like a detuned harp. Arrows filled the air. Broadheads found home in timber, flesh, and between Maximilian's ribs.

Fuckin–

A crack of the reins and the sleigh lurched forward, folding his knees over its backboard. He was in flight.

There was a gap between the clouds, a circle of sky so perfectly blue and calm. It looked just like it did back home. *Their arches hang open*, his folks would have said – soothing if it were true.

The fall felt so long but ended with a quick thump that emptied his lungs of air and put a stop to his heart. In the least, he was bound to become a prized piece.

2

"A little grain, that's all it takes. Fold it in while shaping or add it into the melt, it doesn't matter. If it's in there, the blade will outlive its third owner." - Gundisalvus Wigheard laid on his death bed, surrendering his secret to an apprentice.

After the first found home, he couldn't loose another. *Did it hit the little one?* He saw the kind woman's killer dive over the two boys – was it before or after the arrow struck? It happened so quick that his mind answered differently each time he asked. Sometimes, the father dove over the little ones as soon as the arrows were flying and had taken it himself. But the other times – the times he guessed to be true – the man was a finger short as it went under his armpit and sunk into a little one's back. It all happened so quick. The kind woman was standing then she was dying, axe in her head. Then wolf man's head exploded, then shaky and smelly were fighting. It was the wizard – his magic. Seeing it all, it took them so long to even put an arrow on the string. Then he was dead as if it never happened. But it happened, and there were bodies there to prove it.

Jonathen, the farmer's boy, was talking to himself between long breaths. What about, he couldn't tell, 'god' and 'what' being the only sounds that resembled real words. They repeated here and there as the boy began stumbling to where their companions lay mutilated, sprawled out besides the sleigh track in puddles of red slush.

On the other side, the three were standing frozen to the ground, staring at the corpses as if at any time they would disappear. Bern, folded to the side, spraying clear liquid out his mouth. Urkii, his brother, stood there too, still and silent until a splash of vomit brought him about. In a sudden jerk, he climbed out of their hole and thrashed towards the road, bow in hand, one leg sinking into the white with the other chasing after it. Each step ended short of the last sending him more and more off balance. Then he fell, but that only added his hands and bow to the motion. He no longer walked but lurched like a beast until he made it to the wizard.

"Bitch!" he boomed like a herald's horn and struck down with the yew stave. He struck again and again as cheek bone began to crunch, nose flattened flush and forehead shedded skin – a strip trailing as its tip emptied an eye socket. "You... killed... them!" He then moved on to pummel the body. The staff whistled through the air as it fell on the sorcerer's chest, spraying blood mist out of the mess that used to be the his mouth. The air turned pink and Urkii's face a scarlet painting of a monster. "Aaaar!"

"Urkii. Urkii. Brother! Stop!" He had now made it through the snow and was trying to get a hold of his brother but the bigger Urkii didn't seem to notice – red dripping down his brow, he just carried on swinging. "Do not desecrate the dead! They will punish us!" His brother was a foot's length taller and wider, and – despite the hunger – far heavier. It was like trying to stop a bull from grazing. With considerate effort, he managed to latch onto a shoulder only to be jerked off his footing. Back and forth, back and forth, he was a doll tossed around by a toddler.

Crack, the bowstring snapped. It coiled through the air with a mind of its own, determined to bite. Its end struck Urkii's face. The little pain it held was enough of a jolt to make an opening for Erkii to find purchase. Feet dug in, he pulled hard.

He thought his brother would resist, throw him off into a snowbank. Instead, he went limp. The yew stave fell to ground, and the big man fell back into Erkii's arms. It was as if they were kids again, holding the other back from a fight with one of the pig boys. *I killed someone's Urkii.*

"Fucking hell, that was something, wasn't it? Took me back that." Torgy was now standing nearby, loose and chirpy as if nothing had happened. "If I'm honest, there won't be any tears from me over this lot." He nodded towards Twick and Gesleg, one of whom still seemed to twitch. "At least now I know it won't be a hallucinating lunatic who slits my throat while I sleep. Now, I don't know about you, but I'm going to have a good look at our pickings." With that, he began digging for gold in the snow.

"Aye," replied Bern. If his stomach was in tumbles before, there was no sign of that now. "Retards should have kept to plan and not died." He dropped his cloak onto an unbloodied patch of snow and joined Torgy in picking pockets. His face was a wide, jagged canvas for a collection of scars that left gaps in the stubble covering its bottom half.

"What an ugly son of a bitch" said Torgy as he paused on the coin's obverse where one of the land's old kings was stamped. "Almost as ugly as you, Bern." He tossed the coin into the wizard's purse.

"Fuck you," barked Bern. He was picking through Vulf's pockets. The once unforgettable face was now a collection of unrecognisable chunks, none of which resembled a wolf. Eyes fixed on the macabre, the brute took a deep breath. "I thought you can't kill a werewolf?"

"Don't be getting any ideas, being ugly doesn't make you a werewolf... or maybe you can kill one by blowing up its head – dunno."

Bern's hands ran methodically up the corpse, from the boots up to the dribbling neck hole, picking out coins, trinkets, gems, and daggers out of pockets and sewn in stashes. "Who wants the sword?" He nodded towards the battered blade half sunk into the snow. "Good piece of steel that. You need one, boy – don't ya? Take it a present from uncle Vulf."

Jonathen didn't respond. He was the last to make it out of the trench and was now standing frozen on the skirts of the carnage.

"You're only offering 'cause you're scared of the she wolf," said Torgy.

"Ain't scared of nothing," Bern replied while tugging at Vulf's boots, "just thought boy could use a reminder he's a peasant no more."

"*Ain't scared,*" mocked Torgy as he pulled out another coin, "you're scared more than a dog in Erkii's bed. And speaking of scared, when are you two going to start searching that arsehole? Go on, don't be shy – Urkii's already made sure he's dead." He looked up from his excavation to find Urkii staring him down, blood drying to crust on the onyx of his skin. "And I'm glad you did! Can you imagine what would have happened if he was still alive? We'd be dead with our cocks blown off, eyeballs melted, and our legs stuck in the trees. I'm just fucking thankful we're still alive."

Why did it have to be a wizard. He looked down into the remnants of a face, the pulverised eyeball dangling in a vacancy carved into the cheekbone. That didn't bother him – he had seen worse. It was something else, something only the hairs on his neck could feel, that only his blood and bones sensed. The corpse before him brought on chills far worse than the winter air. "What if trapped?"

"What do you mean *trapped*?"

He thought of the words in the Nurhdvalian tongue – the firm sounds he didn't know his mouth could make till the summer passed. "What if he explode or we touch and have bad magic?"

Torgy looked at him for a moment as he tied the wizard's purse – he always tried to understand. "I've only seen one before. Much older, all grey and hollow looking. Unarmed but without fear, standing in the middle of the battlefield throwing fire with his hands."

"What happen?"

"To this day, I swear that I do not know. But I do remember Bern shitting his trousers, then running until the orderlies caught us and chained us for desertion."

"You shit your trousers," said Bern, dropping the weapons of their companions onto his cloak. The chunks of steel clanged as they landed. Torgy approached the cloak's edge with a hand on each hip.

"All things considered," said the rogue, eyes finding Erkii's, "if he were to explode he already would have while your brother was rearranging his handsome features." With a flick of the wrist, he dropped the coin purse onto the cloak. "And curses," he added as he moved towards

Gesleg's stinking corpse, "if that's truly what worries you then you're living with the wrong bunch, because I can promise that you've already been cursed plenty."

He's probably right. Yet, despite Torgy's sound reasoning, he was still terrified of even prodding the wizard with his toe. The corpse wasn't moving or making any sound, but the chill – there was something about it which frightened him to death. A feeling as if some great beast was hiding within. Staring into the mangled face, Urkii seemed to feel it too.

"Go on you big pussy," called Torgy with his face in a curl and nose held shut as he searched the reeking corpse, "I don't want to spend the night here."

La'Uth, please keep me safe. With the left palm open for the god, he placed the right on the body. A ruckus in the branches and something hit his shoulder. He let go, falling back onto his arse in time with a dusting of snow. Jonathen jumped in his boots.

"What was that?" asked the boy, frantically eyeing the disturbed tree.

"Squirrel or something just as scary," said Torgy without lifting his eyes off of Gesleg's body.

As it was, the sorcerer didn't explode, and so, Erkii began unravelling his thick coat. But the thick bear hide was stuck, pinned on by arrows, one of which was sticking out inches from his nose. There was intestine attached to its head, a little trinket pulled out of the wizard's belly. Gripping it with all fingers, he yanked back and forth until the wooden fibres gave way and the shaft snapped. The valuable barbed end went straight into his pocket. The other arrows were sunk from the side – he felt his way along the body until his fingers met their feathered wings. Urkii joined in on the other side, his large hand finding a shaft

22

just as Erkii was snapping one at its base. He tossed the last feathered end into the woods.

Together, they unhooked the thick hide from the splintered stumps, opening the coat to reveal a black blouse surrounded by a pool of blood collected in the crevices of the coat beneath. It was made of fabric Erkii had never seen before, smooth and shimmering, it felt light to the touch yet strong when pulled. Just touching it seemed an experience. The wizard's trousers were unusual too, and not because of the materials but rather their construction. Two layers at the knees, perfectly straight seams, and not a single hole in sight – they were trousers made far sturdier than any he had ever seen. They were a good sign.

The two of them began patting the wizard down, their hands moving up and down his legs, then torso, then arms. They were methodical, checking every crevice of the man's garb with care, only to find nothing. It made no sense. They began again, even slower than before. *There has to be something*. Only rich men throw gold like he did – like a child's bag of playing pebbles – there had to be more. If there wasn't, all of it was for nothing. He killed a child. Draw and release was all he did, and that was all it took. He didn't mean to. He wasn't even aiming, just pointing at the sleigh hoping it would hit the man with the axe. *He killed the woman,* Einsleigh was her name, the one who took him and Urkii in. It was a trade. He wished it hadn't happened – but it did – and there wasn't a thing he could do now. So, he went back to sliding his hands up and down the wizard's body as Urkii began removing his boots. They were dirty and scuffed, but the material and stitch seemed nowhere near falling apart – turned upside down and shaken, they gave up nothing.

"Flip him over," said Urkii in their home tongue. Bern flinched with a muffled slur, eyes stuck to their hands. Urkii paid him no mind, turning to the boy instead. "Jonathen, grab sleeve." It took pudgy faced Jonathen a moment to process what was being said, then he nodded and did as told. Blood spilled over the edge of the hide as they flipped the body, warm, red syrup mixing with the snow. The coat went onto the pile as the wizard's body settled in its new position.

Face in the white and back to the sun, it was far easier to see the four arrows piercing the wizard's side. Three splintered shafts – one on the left and two on the right – stuck out through holes in the fabric. The fourth arrow would have been all but hidden if not for a few stubborn fibres of the fletching which remained white. It was refusing to drink the wizard's blood. *Maybe we should listen.* Not that it mattered now.

They ran their hands down the wizard's sides one more time, trying to force all lumps and raises out of place. The only thing to give way was an arrow stump which splintered between his fingers. Urkii found a ring on the man's hand, a narrow band of unmarked bronze without a hint of care so unremarkable that Urkii tossed it to the pile without looking long enough to see it land.

"Nothing, it fuck," his brother growled, giving the corpse a kick as he fell back onto his arse.

"Well that can't be," said Torgy. He seemed more than happy to step away from Gesleg's body, adding a few bits to the pile on his way over to the wizard. "You Gharan boys trying to pull one over on us? Don't want to be turning out pockets... fuck." The last word lingered on the rogue's widening lips. "It's aluafir."

"What?" Urkii was back to kneeling, searching the corpse for whatever it was that Torgy had found.

"The thread – it's aluafir!"

"Fuck me sideways." Mouth drooping among dirty thicket, Bern now stood watching over his shoulder. Even Jonathen began to stir out of the daze.

"Alwefir?"

"Aluafir, Jonathen! Elder silver! We're rich!" Torgy was all but hopping in excitement, scabbard smacking against his thigh as he leapt at Jonathen, tackling him into an embrace. "We're rich! We're rich!" All worries and regrets which may have been keeping Jonathen down seemed to vanish, frightened off by Torgy's childish excitement.

Aluafir? Elder silver? It sounded strange, maybe something from Nurhdval that he hadn't heard of or maybe he misunderstood the words. But at least one part of Torgy's yelling was easy to grasp – *we're rich*. He began to inspect the blouse once more, the strange fabric, the shine, he kneeled besides it bringing his face up close. From there he noticed what he hadn't before, that most of the fabric was fibres of a deep, unyielding black – as deep as the night sky stretched between stars – and that all of the shimmer came from a thin silver thread which looped back and forth through the fabric in a patterns of crashing waves. There was not a hint of grey to it, no darkness, just a pure, radiant, shimmer. It was so subtle it could only be seen if one was truly looking and knew exactly what to look for. *It's beautiful.*

He realised he had been holding his breath. He released. The silver shimmer changed to deep scarlet turning the blouse to near perfect black. He pulled back and the shimmer returned. "It colour!" he exclaimed.

"That's how you know it's real!" Staggering Jonathen on the way, Torgy dropped to his knees. "You're blowing on it. Go on, do it again." Erkii did just that with the rogue joining him in the effort. The warmth of their frantic breaths turned the blouse to patches of black, some shimmering and some rooted scarlet.

"Our breath's not hot enough," he said with a jitter, "but put it near a fire for bit and it will stay that way for hours. Help me get it off." Before anyone had a chance to help, his hands were already working the blouse past the navel. Erkii propped the body up as Jonathen helped Torgy pull it past the armpits. Bern worked on changing boots instead but his stare remained with them at all times.

"Torgy," Erkii spoke as Jonathen struggled to work the blouse over a splintered shaft, "you happy. I don't want you angry, but if this not... not much gold. What we do?"

The blouse was now bunched up at the corpse's neck. "Don't worry about that – this blouse will buy us an estate." Torgy stood up and began wrestling the sleeves off the stiffening arms. "It will buy us land to farm." Jonathen joined in, tugging from the other side. "And a castle to live in. *Urgh*, there we go." The supposedly priceless blouse was now between them. They looked at each other for an uncomfortable moment before the boy forfeit his grip. "Right, we need to leave. Let's sort through this mess and get moving."

One boot on, Bern was the first to stand. "Why are you the one holding it?" He planted himself in front of Torgy, staring the other man down. "I'll keep it safe." His hand stretched into the air between them.

Urkii and he sprung to their feet but Torgy waved them away. "Bern you greedy fuck, this isn't the time, just... catch." Leaving a bloody trail in the snow, the blouse flew between Jonathen's arms and splatted into the boy's chest. Though not putting him at ease, the gesture had brute surprised – nearly as much as Jonathen who was now clutching a lord's ransom between his chest and elbows.

"Guard it with your life. And Bern," he said, looking at the bare foot sunken in the snow before him, "put your boots on. You're going to need all your toes when we have land to work." Bern took a hold of the other boot, but his eyes remained on the blouse. They followed it all the way to the trench, as Jonathen blew on it between grins, up until it vanished inside the boy's wraps. Then the rogue moved onto splitting coin.

Looking at the measly pile, there wasn't anything there that Erkii had use for. He already had a sword – a broad blade with a curve that he hasn't seen anyone carry in this land. Though a clumsy and dented thing, it had followed him all the way here. He would be damned before swapping it for Vulf's treacherous thing. There was no doubt in his mind that it had slit a child's throat on more than one occasion. Thinking of it, so had his own bow. *They would make a good couple,* he smiled, though it was a joke he couldn't quite swallow. Jonathen was the only one here who hadn't seen Vulf's true nature, doubtlessly making it easier to hang the man's sword by his hip. *The wolf woman will take it off the boy – maybe kill him too.*

Disinterested, he left the pile to begin moving corpses. They were going to take them home, not the most pleasant of tasks, but one which would be undoubtedly easier with the lightest, least smelling corpse – Einsleigh. Her tangled hair was caked in blood, the crusty mixture perfectly hiding the crack in her skull. At the edge of her mouth deflated a scarlet bubble.

*

"Erkii, we're not taking any bodies…"

"Alive."

"… if the four of us come back without any of them and start telling them all about how a sorcerer flicked his wrists and killed them all…"

"She alive."

"… we might as well ask them to string us from a tree. It was a Marshal, that's what we tell…"

"Einsleigh alive!"

"Belthar," Torgy was next to Erkii looking down at Einsleigh. The bubble had disappeared but with the hint given, the sparse movement of her chest was far easier to notice.

"Pass coat," he said, looking to Bern sat by its side.

"If she's not dead yet, she will be soon." Indifferent, the brute carried on inspecting a dead man's dagger. He was about to pick out another when Urkii's hands came down to rip out the coat out of the pile. The pickings fell to the side with a clatter. Bern's grip tightened on the dagger as he turned to stare at Urkii. The big man paid him no mind. In two long stride, he moved past the brute straight to Einsleigh's side.

Urkii kneeled, then carefully put his arm beneath the woman's armpit. The palm of his hand burrowed through the snow until it was in place to support the woman's blood caked head. Gently, he propped her up with his free hand spreading the coat beneath her. Erkii dropped to help, Torgy too, together stretching the fur as his brother lowered Einsleigh's torso onto it. Once on there, Urkii carefully lifted her legs the swaddled her slender body with well practiced motions. Pink foam dribbled out of her mouth.

"Mertle, go to Mertle," said Erkii, lifting the dying woman into his arms. *If anyone can help, it's Mertle.* A year ago something in the woods got him – an animal he hadn't known – it dropped on him out of the air and latched onto his leg. Jaws bigger than any bear and much wider at the end of a bulging neck with four arms like those of a man – Urkii cut it deep and it fled – but It chewed through the flesh, scraped up the bone. He washed the wound, treated with boiled cloth, but the stench still came and it wouldn't wash off. Death was at the door, but the witch said no. She cut out the rot and filled the abscess with boiling sludge made of plants and things he had never seen. If they could get Einsleigh to her there was no doubt in his mind she would live. They just had to make it before her last breath.

"You'll just fuck up your back and she'll die anyway." Bern twirled the repurposed spear head that Gesleg used to slaughter goats and clean his nails.

Bastard, he readied himself, hoping that if need be he could put down the dying woman and draw before the brute got to her. By his side, he could feel the tension grow in his brother. Torgy seemed uneasy too, and the boy just watched from behind his bright red brows, eyes jumping perplexed between the two deserters.

Torgy was first to act, getting to his companion before anyone else had the chance. "Get your arse up."

Bern looked him down from under a raised brow, then slowly propped himself up. He walked towards Erkii, no urgency in his movement as he looked on without expression. His hand moved to hover over Einsleigh's chest, in its fingers sitting the little bronze ring.

"For the wedding, little lover." His scarred lips curled as he slid the ring onto Erkii's pinky. "Live long."

3

"A little fat piggy hopped across the snow,
But the fat little piggy didn't really know.
She didn't stop to look, she didn't wipe, oh no.
Ice went crack, and the piggy drowned bellow."
          – Nurhdvalian rhyme.

Each step a crunch, they made their way through the woods. It was difficult to walk. The large contraptions of hardened leather and twine that the locals tied to their feet were unnatural, threatening to hook the ground at any moment and send him face first into the crusted powder. The Nurhdvalians had no issues, the wide and high walk that the shoes called for being a part of their nature, but not so for Urkii and he. Even with the months of practice, they still struggled to keep their pace; though, as awkward as walking with the contraptions was, it was near impossible without them.

They've been trained to walk in line, everyone stepping in the footsteps of the one in front, the last in line dragging a harness of branches to sweep away any tracks. If anything were left, Vulf would nip the back of their neck with a long leather strap leaving a welt the colour of gooseberries and the shape of a cock. All of them had one at a varying stage of fading. It was a topic of frequent jest, and in a strange way, that built camaraderie. They had something in common – they all had been *fucked by Vulf*.

The man trained them as if they were dogs, punishing mistakes with what he thought appropriate amount of pain. Even Jonathen, the farmer's boy who was just returning from his first raid, had his hide thrashed that day – it was for going off to piss while marching. There was fear, there was hate – there were many times when Erkii wished to do exactly what the sorcerer did – but there was also respect. He was no shackler. Each strike of the strap and each fist to the gut were there to keep the pack safe. It had worked, and now after his death, the five of them walked in ways that would ensure they and their would survive.

Torgy walked first and Bern at the hind pulling the harness. They had barely spoken since leaving the site of the carnage but, between the rhythm of the march and the distance between them, the hostility brought on by the fight seemed to have eased. Jonathen strolled before the brute, his hand all but glued to his new sword. Every dozen steps the boy would draw the blade and caress its edge with his half nailed thumb, seemingly making sure the scabbard hadn't blunted the blade. A child with a new toy, he made no pretence of anything other, and it put Bern into a rather good mood. Whenever the blade was drawn, he would give sound advice, such as *careful not to cut your prick*. After each quip, the boy would try to be more subtle in his joy, but no matter how hard he tried, Bern would find something to tease him about. Not that he needed to look hard, as whenever Jonathen wasn't playing with the blade, he was fondling the blouse that sat scrunched inside his pocket.

Blouse will buy us a castle, Torgy had said. Though, Torgy had said a lot of things. The rogue liked to tell stories. He seemed to have one for every occasion. And while Erkii hoped this one was true, promises of riches seemed about as likely as those of any of them living a happy, prosperous life. It seemed to be something that Jonathen hadn't learned yet. There was a spring to the boy's step as if he were returning from some farm girl's home, one moment smiling for her kisses, the next moment grimacing, hand on hilt, staring down the girl's brothers. *Still a boy – sixteen, maybe seventeen.*

It was no rarity for someone this young to take on a brigand's life – maybe more common than for someone old enough to know better – but most who did were orphans and urchins. It was a life only those dirt poor with no kin to leech off and no land to inherit would take on, and even they were rarely happy and willing. Jonathen was. *I'm a robber,* is what he said having wandered into their hideout on an autumn evening, *I've come to join*. It amused Einsleigh greatly so she decided to keep him and now here he marched.

Erkii and Urkii walked in the middle. The body stretched between his arms was short and wiry, but it weighed enough to drive each of his steps deeper than they otherwise would have. Every couple yards one of his snowshoes would get caught, leaving him tugging as Einsleigh life continued to drool away. She was cold and limp, suspended breaths weaving between missed heart beats, gargles carrying foam out her mouth each time her lips parted. It was the song of the dying.

Whenever Urkii heard the wretched sound, he would turn in his stride to wipe off the spittle with his sleeve. There was no more anger in him, the spatters of blood crusting his face being all that remained of it. *He's back in Sur Khat, caring for a dying calf. Ukii,* he used to call him, back when they would sleep bundled beneath their mothers heart. *Where is Ukii?* He would search only to find him in the barn, huddled beside a sickly beast on a stormy night, keeping it company to whatever end. That same boy still walked before him despite all that they've been through, ready to nurse yet another creature to health. He hoped that was the end that the kind woman was destined.

It was half a day's walk between the road and encampment, three streams they all called something different – Fox's Tail, Silver Snake, Golden Slip – not that it mattered. *The big one, the middle one, small one,* were names good enough for Erkii.

Besides Gesleg having pissed in it last summer, there was nothing remarkable about the little one – water frozen over rocks covered in a dusting of snow. It was a flat bit of white to walk over. The middle was where the spirits left a cruel little token, a sign he had thought, head of a trout poking through the pale grey surface. *Got caught in the freeze*, Torgy explained it, *the cold came so quick it had no time to swim to deeper waters so it froze.* The scaly body was near entirely preserved in the ice – all except for its head. Whatever scavenger found it had stripped the flesh right down leaving but a bit of bone sticking out of the surface, white amongst white. Tweak was the one to spot it, two months back when they crossed, wheezing out a duster's giggle as he cleared the snow off of the slight bump it had formed. Back then it still had some flesh on it. Ever since, each time they crossed, one of them would check whether it was still there. Today, it crunched under Jonathen's boot. *Fish head stream*, that could be its name.

The big one was as he had named it – a river all but in what locals called it. It was also the deepest, and while winter would armour its surface with a thick shell of ice, even its coldest breaths weren't enough to reach the pebbles at the bottom. Year round, water would flow briskly until coming down a fall to crash into the river he had remembered but couldn't say, Stigr. As winter gave way to spring, the water got closer and closer to the thinning ice making each crossing more unsettling than the last. Torgy had already begun to cross with Bern lifting the harness and following close behind.

Snow stuck to their boots, each step clearing a wide print in the ice. Dark water rushed below. It seemed to give Jonathen a pause. He glanced uncertain between the ice and the two men walking ahead then again before making his mind up to take a cautious step. The ice held without a creak, and his next step was far more certain. Snowshoes keeping them steady on the treacherous surface, the three of them made it to the middle before realising that Urkii and Erkii were still at the bank.

"What's happening?" asked Torgy in a voice stripped of its usual melody.

"She dead?" Bern raised his scar split brow in case the question was mistaken for concern.

"Bastard. Ice break and we will death."

"Well, the three of you," mumbled Jonathen, a snicker from Bern giving him confidence to speak louder, "we will be on the other side."

"Farm boy's right," said Bern with a smirk, "but if you need some reassurance, here you fucking go." Before Torgy had a chance to stop him, Bern jumped. Then again and again, springing off bent knees and landing with a thump. He then grabbed onto the boy.

"Go on, jump," he pulled on Jonathen's patchy wrapping, "jump I said!" The boy did. The two of them bounced up and down, the ice beneath them creaked and bent, but it didn't break.

"There you go, girls." He stuck the landing and pushed past Torgy who stood with a loose thumbs twitching towards the fingers. Jonathen walked right behind.

While it put the brute's sanity to question, Bern's stunt was enough to convince them of the strength of the ice. Urkii took the first step, then a few more. Even with his massive weight, the ice sheet barely shifted – the slightest of humps forming between the banks. Erkii stepped on after.

He could feel under his feet as water brushed the grey surface from beneath – some great beast having its belly tickled. Looking at the others' prints, he could see it too, torrents rushing past quick enough to sweep them away never to be seen again. Death was close. It should have been terrifying, but as it was, framed with white trees, the smooth frosted grey was rather enchanting. Any fear that should have been there, any worries and aches, seemed to fade as he walked across leaving nothing but calm space within him. It was an opening for something else to enter.

Warm, pulsating, alive, it webbed out from a point within him. Strange, unlike anything other he had felt before, it was a sensation he tried to explain by one of Einsleigh's bone pushing into him and numbing his flesh. He ignored it, focusing his mind on walking instead, hoping that the sensation would fade. It only grew.

Erkii's bones began to throb, vibrating as if they were the strings of a fiddle. Pressure built within, filling him as if he were the bladder of a goat being blown full in the game played at Sylthian weddings. It had to stop or like the bladder he would burst. *No more,* he pleaded to no avail. Beneath his scalp crawled ants, they were boring their way through his skull to make a nest inside. Hundreds and thousands pushing in and squirming around in a mass. *No more, please.* There was an opening, a cork keeping it closed, he could feel it. All he had to do was push it open.

The little bronze band turned hot as a piece of ember.

Erkii's bones splintered into countless shards and the world went black. His existence became a deafening ring of a temple bell as a spasm of contradicting currents whirled through the air before him.

What was little more than seconds felt like an eternity of being suspended in darkness as if he were swimming inside a flooded burial chamber. Through a crack, the world forced its way back through. He was standing, arms still attached, bones seemingly unbroken supporting both him and Einsleigh. He looked to his finger expecting to see a charred stump where the ring felt so hot but the finger remained. Everything was there, except for Urkii. Where Urkii had stood was a hole.

*

An oval opening had formed in the ice, hundred shards floating in the grey water which swallowed his brother. Einsleigh slipped out of his grip as he fell to his knees.

"Urkii! Urkii!" His arms were reaching into the grey, fingers turning numb as they grasped in the freezing current in search of anything to grab onto. There was nothing. No arms, no hair, no fur, his brother had been taken by the spirits. *Where are you, brother?* He pulled in a deep breath and dropped his head in. It felt like a stave cracked over his skull. He tried opening his eyes but the eyelids refused.

They wouldn't open in the icy current. *Come back! Please!* There was something in his palm, slipping between his stiffening fingers. He clenched steering the water flow around his knuckles instead. Someone pulled him out by the collar.

"There, idiot!" Pulsing in and out of focus, Bern stood over him pointing a blurring finger somewhere down the river. A spot in the ice was moving. Someone was already running along the bank towards it. Legs swinging wildly as not to trip in the clunky snowshoes, the figure moved quick with arms gripping an axe. By the time he could make out it was Torgy, its iron head was already carving into the ice.

Water trickled beneath his fur wrapping bringing a chill that cut deep to the bone. Jitters overtook him as he began to stumble towards Torgy. *Please, La'Uth, our father. Don't let your lamb perish so cruelly.* His surroundings were morphing around him, stretching and contracting with each passing moment. Suddenly he was on his knees, chips of ice grazing his face as Torgy dug into the grey. It was moving. There was a wild thing beneath the ice, a spiny beast with two sets of bulging eyes which swung frantically within their sockets. It was pushing upwards in bursts trying to break free. He started striking the ice with his hands, yew stave swinging from one side to the other as something swam up to the beast. A thing long and pale, it circled around it, running a fleshy hand over the monster's sharp edges. The beast's eyes began to slow their crazed glances. Each push against the ice was weaker than the last as the beast settled. His brother was dying.

Erkii caught the stave's end and began to stab at the ice in futility.

"Fuck me, move out of the way," barked Bern, once more pulling him firmly by the collar, "how is he meant to break through with you on top?" He threw Erkii back on his arse then started swinging an axe alongside Torgy. The ice splintered into a web of cracks, adding a new one each time a metal head kissed its now still surface. "Go on, you fat fuck. Go on!"

"Come on!" Torgy was swinging even more frantically than before, axe head splattering water.

Ukii.

Bern and Torgy fell back as the ice beneath their feet lifted, a fang shaped stretch from bank to middle lifted over Urkii's back. The frozen sheet broke under its own weight and the man collapsed onto a newly formed shelf. Sprawled arms and heaving chest kept him anchored to the ice while his legs were made to dance at the mercy of the current.

"Fuck." Bern got up, draining water out of his boot. "Snares been empty all winter and the bastard's still too fat to cross a stream."

Water picked up by Urkii's wrappings was pouring out any opening it could find. Its flow followed his outline, trickling in streams which seemed to merge somewhere beneath him and funnel down the slope that his weight bent into the ice. It was escaping back into the current, stealing with its touch the warm ebony of Urkii's skin. Body in jitters, teeth coming open and shut in uncontrolled clacket, his brother had been left a greying blue husk.

"Bad luck, you big bastard." Unlike Bern, Torgy managed to maintain his footing without taking a dip. "We need to get your clothes off or you'll freeze before we're anywhere near home. Look at your brother," he said, nodding towards Erkii, "one little dunk and the water already fucked his head."

It was true. The world was beating along with his heart, wrapping about the entirety of his being then expanding, spilling through the surrounding air. *Fucking shit.* A heaving heap of sharp spines shivered before him, shrinking and smoothing with every breath. It was Urkii. A hound laid nearby, clumps of fur growing between weeping sores. It was heaving, tail slowly grazing the ground. He met its eye for a moment before they averted to the side. The mouth of a pit came gaping out of the white. There was something within – he could sense it – but nought that he could see. The hounds head snapped towards the river bank. A twitching knot laid in its snow. Hundreds of fibres wove over and under in a clueless tangle, a cluster of worms tipped out of a jar.

The world pulled back in and they were gone.

He looked at the ring wrapped about the base of his little finger. The heat that scorched his skin subsided. It no longer burned. It seemed a regular ring once more – one worth so little that even a grave robbing brigand gave it away in jest – yet, it wasn't. A hint of warmth remained, coming out in tiny pulses that tickled right down to the bone. He could feel it in his fingers, he could feel it in his neck and cheeks – tingling. He felt it just like he did the burning but moments passed. There was no doubt in his mind that the ring was enchanted.

He remembered the Al-Fazhi shackler and his brace, an extravagant chunk of gold and rubies that a mage had forced power into. Whenever his question was being answered, he rubbed it as if it were a kitten. Apparently he could feel it purr back. One day, he bought fruit loaf at the bazaar, *delicacy from his home that no foreigner could ever match*, or so he said. He left that loaf in a saddle bag while tending to his duties. While he was gone, Ghunii stole it. Starved, they all reached out for a piece but the wild eyed tribesman swallowed it whole – he even picked the crumbs from the dirt.

The shackler returned not long after. Having found his bag empty, he cursed and tugged them into a line. *Did you eat the loaf? Did you eat the loaf?* He asked them one by one, each time rubbing the brace. *No,* they answered one after the other. Then he reached Ghunii. He too said, *no,* with a face accustomed to deceit. The Al-Fazhi cut him down before the lie finished trickling off his lip. There were three more to question but he had no need. He already knew, or rather, the brace did. It told him. There was power within it, and yet, whatever power was trapped inside its thick walls of gold, he wouldn't dare compare it to the magic within the little bronze band.

The tingle in his cheek suddenly turned to pain which he could no longer ignore. He lifted his hand to feel it – to make sure it was still there. His hand was struck by Bern's palm.

"Finally," he barked. "We need to move. Get up."

Slowly, he worked his way to a stand slipping off the ring as he did. Its warmth remained – or maybe it was that of his hand squeezing it tightly. Either way, it terrified him. He dropped it to the bottom of his deepest pocket. Urkii, propped up by Torgy, was already standing on the riverbank. In the light of the dipping sun he stood naked and grey. The clacket of his teeth could be heard from where Erkii stood.

"Come on," said Torgy. The skinny rogue tried moving but the much bigger Urkii wouldn't budge. "What are you, frozen?"

Urkii's lips parted. "Ww...ooo..." His jittering jaw chewed the words up into indistinguishable chunks.

"What?"

Urkii pulled in a lungful of air and held it, trying to calm the jitter before speaking again. "Woo... maaan", he moved his arm, pulling Torgy helplessly with it. His fingers twitched in the direction of Einsleigh's body. "We... not... leave."

"Belthar," Torgy looked to the sky as he called on the god. Getting no response, he looked to the far more present Bern.

The brute shrugged as he dipped his bare foot into the snow. "I ain't getting back on that ice – not for a fuckin' corpse."

Erkii agreed – as much as he liked the woman, Einsleigh was as good as dead. Urkii did not. He dragged his feet up the river bank and once land couldn't get him any closer to the body, he dropped prone and began crawling. Each movement was paired with a heave as his arms and legs worked in unison to move the large body across the frozen surface. Inch by inch his shivers grew, but he pushed on until his hand landed on a boot. Einsleigh twitched. He pulled her in, then moved his body back, pulled her in, then the body back. And again. And again, but slower. His muscles were ceasing, movements turning to those of a slug – all but his breathing which only grew more rapid. Then he stopped moving all together.

No. Erkii dove right onto the ice. He wriggled like an eel drugged on red sugar. Before long, he was holding onto his brother's shivering foot. He could hear a clatter of teeth as he pulled, all his strength placed into the motion in an attempt to get the big man onto land. But there was no give. Urkii's hand was clasped about Einsleigh's shin anchoring both to the ice.

"Come on, let go!"

Urkii moved but did not let go, instead he was shifting the woman's body towards him. Erkii ignored it and continued pulling, but Urkii had dug in and all that Erkii could do was move himself about the ice.

"Let go!"

The big man kicked back and Erkii lost his grip. *I don't want to lose you.*

"T... ttake," Urkii jittered as he heaved the woman into Erkii's reach.

I can't move him, there wasn't enough strength in his body to. There never was. All he could do was what was asked.

He grabbed onto Einsleigh's foot just as Urkii's big hand loosened and fell onto the furs in which she was wrapped. The mass of his brother's arm pinned the coat to the ice causing it to unravel as Erkii dragged the little woman across the river.

La'Uth, he pleaded, *don't let him die. Please, please, don't.* Crawling backwards, he watched over the top of Einsleigh's body as the shaking in Urkii's great mass began to slow. By the time he reached the river bank, all of his motion stopped. The rattling had stopped too. His brother was little more than a heap of flesh and bone.

No, no no no, no! He sprung, leaving Einsleigh where she lay, and ran to Urkii's side. *Don't be dead.* The ice creaked as he leapt forward. *Should not have come here. Should have stayed on the wagon.* He fell at his brother's side just as he calmly rolled onto the furs. The big man sat up as if nothing had happened, deep brown eyes looking at the running Erkii in confusion.

"Brother, are you okay?" Urkii asked as if it were he who had just fallen into a frozen river. Wordless, he watched his brother wrap up then move ashore to lift Einsleigh into his arms.

4

"Before you shake hands, always ask – anyone
love him? If someone do, make it double 'cause
one day you'll have to kill them too." – Spoken
between killers of little importance.

Hazel specked with green, that was their colour. Not
long ago he saw them open for the first time – so much
smaller back then, so much wetter. Now, they wouldn't
close. He tried over and over, pulling down on the eyelids
with his grubby fingers, but they would pull back up as
soon as he let go. He was a big boy, far bigger than most
boys of eight years would be. In his arms he felt so.

"Is he okay?", asked Joran. He's been asking for a
while now. The tears which rolled down the smooth
crevices of the boy's face were soaked up by his father's
sleeve.

Bear didn't know how to answer. There was something
turning in the pit of his stomach, a clump of maggots
spawned amongst rot. They were crawling up his throat.
Words so simple, *he's dead, my baby is dead.* He knew
them, but he couldn't say them. Once he had, they would
become true. Joran knew already of course, he wasn't daft –
not the sharpest but definitely not daft. The boy wasn't

asking because he didn't know but out of hope that he was wrong. Bear would have to crush that hope soon enough. For now though, he just wanted to hold his little Sassa, keep him safe until Mor would carry his soul into her eternal bosom.

Sassa's limp body was being tossed in his arms by the sleigh's motion. Gorgie has kept the shaggy mare at a gallop for the past hour, pushing both her and the sleigh to speeds neither was in shape to handle. The gaps that time forced between the timbers were widening more so than usual, and it was beginning to seem like this would be the day that the sleigh would finally give out. The question was whether the mare would collapse before that. Strings of gooey spittle dribbled over her rusted teeth and from behind collar and harness poured sweat. In her winter coat it lathered, dropping down her flank in waves of white foam. Yet, she wouldn't stop. It wasn't Gorgie or his reign that kept her moving – all he did was curse under breath since they escaped the madness. It was fear. The mare was terrified, determined at all cost to escape whatever all of this shit was.

Fucking magic, fucking mage. That's what that Sparrow was – he was sure. Treacherous bastards the lot of them – skiving in their high towers and marble citadels, indulging in power that should not belong to man, power they had stolen from the gods. And the gods don't look kindly on those who steal. They're cursed, and when they leave their hiding the curse follows them like a sickness. Bringers of misfortune wherever they go. *It's his fucking fault. His fault.* With all his heart, he wanted to believe that. Yet, it wasn't the mage who shot that wretched arrow.

There was little more than finger's length of shaft left – the arrow had sunken deep into Sassa's chest. It pointed to his heart which meant he would have died quick. It was small solace to know that. Yoona was staring. There were new wrinkles on his face, a decade gained in an hour. Ellinor and Mary were still tangled about him. Despite the mounds of fur they've been wrapped in, the three trembled like lambs squeezed fresh out the womb. None of them had spoken since the robbery, just whimpered.

Yoona's eyes kept jumping between the arrow's nock and a plank in the sleigh's side, his lips parting and closing. It took them a few tries before they opened wide enough to let words pass.

"I think," he murmured with a voice barely audible over the scraping of sleigh on snow, "I think I saw him before."

There was a ringing in Bear's ear and it drowned nearly all of what Yoona had said, but he understood. His eyes stopped caressing the green specks and moved to the narrow bridge of the man's hooked nose. "Again."

Yoona tried returning Bear's gaze but whatever he saw changed his mind, instead he spoke at the planks. "One of them, with a bow – I think I saw him before. There was a redhead... I know his face. Hard one to forget." He spoke under breath, words chasing each other out his mouth. "A bloated toddler with a hairy lip, I saw him with another who looked like that but older – in Haran. They were looking for a few strong to plow and sow on their land. It was good pay too. I was thinking to take them up –"

"Did you work for those bastards?" Bear cut in. Joran was clutching onto his arm, silent, just like he used to clutch onto a shaggy rags not so long ago.

Yoona met Bear's gaze. "No. They weren't the type I'd work for. One moment they were talking, then suddenly the old one is beating the young one like he was some stringy piece of rump he had to make tender. Thought he was going to kill him." Yoona's eyes bounced off the side board to the body in Bear's arms before dropping again. "Vollundr split them with his dogs, threatened to set the monsters loose on them if they didn't leave his village that very moment."

"You know who they were?"

"No. Haven't seen them before, nor have I seen them since." He was telling him true.

"You'd know, Gorgie, wouldn't ya?" He looked to the driver whose head was twitching in all directions. "Gorgie," he spoke louder. "Gorgie." The driver twitched once more. "Gorgie!"

Gorgies body shook in a motion starting at his feet and ending at the neck. He looked left then right then to his mare. Seeing her state brought him awake. "Wooah Brenda, wooah. Easy," he soothed the beast, pulling back on the reins. Brenda resisted. "Easy!" he tried to soothe her but the mare paid him no mind, she just ploughed on through the pressed snow, prints dragging into narrow trenches. Gorgie pulled even harder, bracing himself into the footrest, wrapping the leather round his elbow. "Easy!" The strain of the straps pointed her face to the sky. Both eyes open to their brink and marked in a web of red, her mouth hung open and dribbled foam like some grotesque fountain. No longer able to see, Brenda began to slow.

Her legs were shaking, splashing frothed up sweat into the snow. Once she came to a stop they buckled, dropping her to ground. Gorgie jumped off the seat and clumsily dragged himself to the mare's side. His coat was off in an instant, then thrown over the heaving mare's back. Tenderly, as if looking to a sickly child, he began dabbing the clumping hairs dry. "There you go, there you go," he said to her, and "fuck me", he said to himself. His usual rosy colour was gone, replaced by pale grey of a corpse.

"Gorgie, you hear anything we said?"

"No," he said, carefully wiping the mare's mouth with his sleeve. Brenda's muscles twitched with little control as she tried to lift herself.

"Tell him." Bear tossed his head from one man to the other, shaking loose a greasy strand of hair.

"I saw one of them before, red hair, smooth, fat face with a bit of hair on the lip."

Gorgie's eyes remained on Brenda. "Easy," he let the vowels linger as he gently wiped the mare's neck. He spoke to Yoona without as much as a glance. "You're not giving me much here. How did you come to know him?"

"Haran, him and old one looking for people to plough fields. Then the old one started beating the young one and Vollundr chased them off."

Gorgie lifted on the mare's underside trying to assist in her struggle. "Got land but short on hands to work it... short temper. Wearing green and red checker?" He looked at Yoona, who nodded. "Guhdlval clan – near all red of hair with a shapeless face."

"They the ones who robbed us?" asked Bear.

Gorgie was now patting down the mare's other flank. "Don't think so. I gave 'em a good look – none the others were red haired, unless it was too dirty to tell." The driver seemed far more concerned with the mare than finding out who Sassa's killer was.

"Could have been more in the trench," he said. His arms were beginning to turn numb beneath the boy's weight.

"Aye, could have," huffed the driver, beginning to wipe the horse's belly. "Maybe the Guhdlvals fell on hard times, moved to the other side of the Solemn Forest and started robbing travelling farmers instead of taxing their lands. I bloody doubt it. Proud lot they are, clinging onto their noble past like piglets to a nipple – you even suggest they're thieving and I bet they'll kick your teeth in. Besides, these are the king's lands and it would take an awful lot of stupid to try robbing right under his nose. We were jumped by scum spawned of city gutter – is what it is."

There was reason in Gorgie's words but there was also a glaring fault, *the king's not here no more*. That was the truth. For whatever reasons, the young troll's grasp no longer reached as far as it used to. Villages and towns too small to bring in good coin were left untended, roads even more so – it would have been a lucky day for any to get a Marshal's attention. Even then, that attention would be divided at best – not that there was any use for it now. What was needed now was blood, and if any were to be taken, it would by his hand. "Take me to them."

The driver paused his tender patting of the mare's side. "You're not listening, are you. What do you want to see them for? It wasn't them who tried robbing us. Them who tried robbing us have been put through a meat grinder and those still alive are probably running till they reach Dharollian dirt. The Guhdlval are proud, very proud, proud to a point where it borders stupidity. If you stroll up to their keep even thinking to call one of theirs thief, you will hang until your breath runs out and it won't be by the neck."

Bear stood up, the boy's feet swinging with the motion. They gave him a soft kick on one side, while on the other Sassa's head dangled. It rested over his forearm, upside down, lifeless eyes stuck open. "If there's a chance they know who did this, I will risk it."

Gorgie turned away from his horse ready to retort but seeing what he saw changed his mind promptly. The maggots that stirred inside Bear's gut had settled to the bottom leaving behind emptiness.

*

Potatoes, that's why he left his home that day, to barter preserved eel for potatoes. The sack lay undisturbed between the sleigh's benches. With Sassa's corpse in his arms, it seemed such a trivial thing to be thinking about. But was it? Sassa wouldn't feel hunger ever again, but Joran and Miska still had bellies that need filling – be it today or the day after – once they could eat again.

"Grab the sack," he told Joran. The boy seemed to jump within his skin and gave his father a questioning look. *I know.* There was a redness in his son's eyes, redness and pain that swollen eyelids tried to obscure. There was nothing Bear could do to fix that. For a brief moment, the two looked at each other before Joran bent down for the sack. He worked it over the sleigh's siding and then over his shoulder, weight of the bag near sending him into a spin but his footing held.One step after the other, he began treading home.

"I will be ready tomorrow," said Bear.

"Aye, but who said I will be?" the driver murmured, then clicked his tongue to send the horse along. The sleigh turned before setting back on its own tracks. The sun had begun to set. Bear followed his boy.

They walked down the cleared path which ran through the opening between Esther family's two great homes. If his arms were at a stretch, he could touch both their outer walls, run his finger along their darkening logs. He used to find comfort in them. They were product of human labour – their labour – that stood so steady and certain. It was a reminder of what they could do working together. Now, it felt as if the walls were watching him walk in shame, judging in silence and grieving their boy. They would have kept him safe. There was loud giggling ahead.

Joran and Bear emerged out into Kalrka's centre square. Two boys, one a Gerlfeird and one an Esther, were dashing across with little white boulders tucked between their arms. They moved past the well, blissfully unaware as they cut across Joarn's path then ducked between the houses to continue stacking their wall of snow – a barricade to stop whatever monster was set on razing Karlka that day. *Sassa should have been with them today – building walls, playing monsters.* He should have left him here to play instead of dragging him along for reasons he no longer remembered.

A face peeked out a window, the ever watchful Ursula Esther. Wrinkled like a foot left too long in a warm bath, brandishing a nose that resembled a big toe, she sat there dawn to dusk – sometimes longer – making sure that everyone and everything was as it was meant to – ordinary and uneventful. What she saw today wasn't. Her aged face quickly vanished from behind the glass. The door to her house began to rattle but he paid it no mind.

Father and son walked down the alley which would bring them home, but as soon as he saw it, his feet began to drag then stuck to the ground. His eyes followed Joran as he turned into the narrow path that snaked up to their home. It wasn't the biggest but it was theirs, each tree felled and dragged, stripped and carved by their hand or their neighbours'. You could try do it all alone around here but even the heartiest of protests couldn't keep the folk of Kalrka from helping. Whether you were swinging an axe or striking a chisel, there was someone else ready to pick up another to swing or strike beside you – usually one of the Herlfeirds. With their help, Bear and his family had a roof over their heads before the leaves would even consider falling. That was nine winters ago. Since then, the little house spent every day doing what it was meant to, keeping them warm and safe within its walls. Today, he was frightened to step beneath its roof.

Joran was already at the top of the little steps, knocking on the door. It was a heavy thing, few inches thick, and the boy had to knock with his entire fist to be heard. Not long after, it moved out of the way to make space for Miska. A loose dress of faded blue draped down her body with a sash tying it in at the waist. Seeing her boy at the door, she leaned forth to wrap her arms about his. Joran didn't return the embrace. He just broke down. Miska pulled back, blue eyes looking him over then over his shoulder. She looked past him, past the steps and the little path, and into the alley's shadows where Bear stood holding her youngest.

Miska's face shattered into angular shards, lips opening to a chilling shriek, "Aaaahh!" In a blink, she lurched under Joran's arm and straight at Bear – a banshee descending on her prey. Before he could take a step back, she was on him. Her hands crashed at speed into his sternum, digging in as they wrapped about Sassa's body. The wind left Bear's lungs and he fell to the ground as she tore Sassa out of his grip. By the time he could breathe, there was a crowd standing at his back.

"Poor man. His little boy is dead – I saw it out my window," said Ursula Esther. It seemed as if the whole village, old and young alike, had been roused and came to find the cause of the commotion. The alley filled with a hum, muffled chatter loud enough to hear but just too quiet to understand. They were talking about him yet not a single word was for him to hear.

Miska was gone, taken Sassa away, but it wasn't a mystery as to where – the door was still swinging in its hinges. He could hear her pain coming out of the house, no longer a shriek but a wail that rose up and down in waves. They were the cries of a wounded beast struggling to claw its way out of a spiked pit. Having taken a few steps closer, he could see it too. Past the open doorway, Joran hanging off her neck and Sassa limp in her bosom – his family was a clump of bodies swaying slowly back and forth, back and forth. He wanted to make it better with all his heart, give all he had, give the gods his life to put the drum back into Sassa's heart. He didn't deserve it. They didn't deserve it.

He took a step down the snaking path as someone's hand fell on his shoulder.

"Friend," said a warm voice, a composed voice, "come with me. Give her time to grieve or in her grief she might kill you." Grey and hunched, it was Eadmunt. His bony hands rose into the air, waving the crowd away like some pesky insect. "Get about your business – nothing more to see." The provost moved quickly to the doorway, pulling the timbers into the frame before the onlookers had a chance for even the slightest peek. Then, like one does the dog's cuff, he grabbed Bear by the shoulder and pulled him straight through the dispersing crowd.

He was surrounded by wallowing eyes, pity from those who could never understand. One of the little builders was there. "Someone died in there!" he heard the boy say in excitement.

Eadmunt led him through the alleys, taking sharp turns and long paces until they reached his house. A white cow with three black patches stood at its side, walled in by a circle of stone that she could easily step over. She never did. With her head down, she tugged away at some frozen strand of grass hiding in the snow. Logs protruded out of a foundation of stacked stone, their grain seeming as aged as the man who owned it, if not more, coloured a deep hue that was nearing black. It was the first Herlfeird home, built by Eadmunt's father when there was nought here but a clearing amongst the trees. There were taller buildings in Karlka, there were bigger ones too, but none seemed to stand quite as proud.

The provost stretched his crooked body then pushed the door open.

Before them was a stretch of floor covered near entirely with furs. At least a dozen rabbits, a few deer, boars and bears, one or two hides he couldn't recognise – a large table sat amongst them with two benches running down its side. Like most things in Karlka, it was built far sturdier than a table and benches would ever need to be. At the table's head was a chair with arms and elaborate carvings chiseled into its timber – a near identical one sat before an iron stove. Its grate gave no hint of flame nor heat, the house itself little warmer than the outdoors. Even so, Eadmunt pulled him towards that stove.

"Sit, sit," said Eadmunt putting Bear in the chair. Once he was seated, the provost opened the grate and picked up a fire iron. The arms of the chair had been shaped into wolves. "Sorry about the cold," he murmured into the open stove, jiggling the iron within its inners. "I thought it best for Miska to have some time without you." Eadmunt picked up a handful of wood shavings and placed them carefully over the embers. His thin, spider veined cheeks puffed out as he blew a little flame into life. "Don't want her killing you is all."

Bear remained silent. The provost spoke in jest, yet there was truth to his words. His wife had bad temper and a heavy hand, even with matters that were benign. There was no telling what she'd do when the matter was the death of her child.

Eadmunt placed a splintered log inside the stove, watching as the flames tried to grasp it. "There, that'll be going soon enough." Satisfied, he sat back onto one of the mysterious hides, fingers gently combing its thick fur. It was a peculiar thing, shaggy on the back and near entirely bare on the limbs which were covered in adjoining clusters of hard growths. Bear tried imaging the beast which would have carried it on its back but to little success. He stared and stared and nothing.

"Troll," said the old man having caught him looking. "Must have been forty years back when the poor sod stumbled into the village. Strong noses they have – he could smell the fermenting fish and salted meats in our cellars. Thought they would make for a good picking. He spent the next three weeks sneaking in at night, breaking into one after the other. We thought it was a bear at first or brigands or someone's kids getting up to mischief. A few of us decided we would hide and see with our own eyes. And we did. He came just like he had every other night, hunched down and looking carefully over both shoulders, opening Kvatchs' cellar so slow and quiet – smart, very smart trolls are. They also eat children... or at least someone said. Never seen it happen, but we couldn't take that chance. So, the next night we waited and as he went down into the cellar, we locked the door right behind him." The provost moved to the stove placing a second log by the side of the other then sat back seeming finished with his story.

They sat there, wordless, watching the flames. There was warmth pouring out of the stove now, washing over to engulf him. He shivered. When outside, the cold was a reality he had gotten used to, but now the warmth was prying it out of his flesh and bone straight through the skin.

"What happened to the troll?"

The provost took a moment to stare into the flames before speaking. "We left him there for five days. He spent most of them knocking, throwing his body against that cellar door, but we had barred it and weighed the whole thing down with a pile of rocks. We gave it till the banging had stopped before we opened it. Nine days without water – he laid sprawled out in the middle with arms still swinging through the air above. He tried to stand when the light hit him, walk towards it. There was hope in him – I could see it in his big black eyes as he tried crawling out that cellar. And then I killed him. He looked at me, you know — *why,* he was asking. And I didn't have an answer. I told myself then that it was the only way to keep my people safe, but really, it was just the easiest." The old man began to sob, tears making their beds within the crevices of his face. There was no shame to it, no efforts to disguise or hide the hurt in his heart like a younger man would. Bear began to sob too.

Without turning from the flames, the old man softly asked, "What happened to your son?"

He told him everything – about the wizard, about the bandits and the Guhdlval, and about the arrow that took Sassa's life. They murdered his boy, tore him away with no mercy and nothing would ever be as it was. Eadmunt listened silently, tears flowing free as his eyes watched the flames.

"What will you do now?" he asked with measure, face inching closer to the glow.

"I'm going to kill them."

*

He left Eadmunt's home well after dark, mind bordering peace. It wasn't until he had said that he realised what he had to do, but now that he had, the purpose was enough to keep him from falling apart.

One foot at a time, he made it to his doorstep. There were a dozen baskets by its side – wicker trimmed with branches – inside them loaves, hard cakes, and dried fish brought down by the Karlkan families. He thought of knocking, but decided not to. Instead, he sat between the baskets and slowly drifted into a chilly slumber.

5

"These gods of yours... all your life is spent praying to them, yet all they do is watch and wait till the day when they can put you in a jar!" – frothing preacher in a city square.

A hundred tiny fingers scratched at the underside of his wings – air pushed against their feathered surface. It was a beautiful sensation, one he had tried to imagine since he was a child. At times, he even thought he did. It seemed laughable now to even think to compare the reality of flight to being a burden atop a galloping horse or the flailing free fall before meeting the surface of a swimming hole. This was an experience unlike anything other. He was cutting through the air, carving a path with motions large and proud, and motions so subtle that they would be invisible to an observer. Every inch, every feather, muscle and tendon was designed for this. Easier, more natural than breathing, it was free. It was effortless. Yet, even flight couldn't sweep away the fears he had discovered in the hours passed.

Chimes, footsteps, limbs flailing behind the curtain, the terror brought on by their collapse on his entirety. All that remained. He was fortunate that his death came unexpected – if they had been waiting, he had no doubt there would have been no chimes or footsteps but an all engulfing grasp about his entirety. As it was, he had time enough to find another vessel that could anchor him to this world. It's not that he was afraid of dying – of turning to nothing. That seemed comforting, even soothing, and he would have welcomed the prospect. But that's not what death is. Death is the cutting of the anchor, leaving you free for plucking.

There was a rustle in the snow, something small and far away – he knew exactly where. With a minute adjustment to the wing's curve, he turned sideways, gaining speed as he turned between the trees. It was there, scuttling desperately to return to the safety of its layer – too late. He folded the wings going into a dive. The earth came at him quick, threatening to break bones and leave him for dead – the slightest mistiming would assure that. However, his timing was perfect. He opened his wings two yards from ground, giving enough time to stop as his talons sank about the critter's spine.

As far as vessels went, this one was a most fortunate one.

He landed on a looming branch with the mouse still moving in his grasp – futile attempts at escape. The curved beak was sharp, a brilliant tool for tearing through the little hide, for making an opening through which he could grasp onto flesh. The critter moved more frantically as he pulled the flesh through the pecked out hole like pulling the strings of a marionette. Warmth coated the inside of his beak and slid down his gullet to fill up his belly with nourishment. It satisfied every last bit of him down to the tip of the last feather. It was a feeling no food had ever brought him before. *Raw field mouse – who knew?* It took a while for the moving to stop – near as long as it took him to feed – yet in some way, that added to the pleasure. With the tastiest flesh picked out, he was ready to focus on what needed doing.

*

Shivers contained within their gullets, they stood as still as any man could, exactly where he had instructed. They were vigilant in their watch, three of his best. He would put them to good use soon enough, as despite the primal pleasure it had brought him, this vessel was not fit for his purpose. For now though, he would savour the simplicity of this tiny stretch of his existence.

6

"Friend is a brother as long as it suits, ask him for laces but knot your own boots." – Sylthian proverb.

"There is nothing I can do for her. I'm sorry, boy." Mertle's voice was a croak that cut right through the smoke that drifted beneath the rafters. Every so often, her wrinkled hand would drop strange leaves and needles into the embers of a modest fire in the hut's centre releasing puffs of smoke to melt into the cloud above. A cauldron the size of a helmet – which at one point it may have been – hung over the fire, bubbling at the brim with a boil of leaves. It was so very warm.

"What about this?" said Erkii, lifting a handful of leaves out of a jar – one of about dozen that sat within the clutter on Mertle's bench. "Make thing you made me and put it on woman head."

Mertle sighed, her nose moving side to side in displeasure. "This is not how it works. You people think that all you need to do is breathe and for your heart to throb. That's not where the soul is hiding."

He stared back blankly. This caused another sigh to slip out from between her narrow lips, the upper of which supported a moustache not unlike that of a boy on the verge of passing his rites.

"It lives here." She lifted two knuckles to his forehead and knocked. "Right in there, a little off centre – up the front and closer to the left than right. It's a little, cosy home for a person's *person* to live, and unluckily, her's was shattered by an axe. It's best we not prolong it – let her pass now."

The light outside was all but gone, leaving the little fire and a candle to light the hut alone. Shadows played on the walls – a chasing game that they all seemed close to winning. The darkness obscured Mertle movement as she grabbed something from the bench. *Knife*.

Half steps that barely left the ground, she moved quick towards Einsleigh's cot. *She's going to kill her!* Mertle was already an arm away from the woman who had taken them in. Somehow, Urkii had forced himself between them.

"No," his brother said in a voice that rolled through the air like the tide. A wall, he stood before Mertle, the sorcerer's coat draping down his shoulders. The low ceiling bent him crooked to stare down at the crown of her thinned hair.

"Move out of the way, stupid boy. Shoo, shoo!" she waved her hands as if the giant man before her was little more than a pesky goat.

"No." Urkii remained a wall.

Mertle sighed while taking a step back. Her eyes looked into Urkii's. "I want to give her mercy. She is suffering and there is nothing else that can be done. There will be no pain – just a little blood."

The woman was certain but she was wrong, she must have been. But it still gave Urkii pause. He could tell his brother was thinking hard about what she had said – his face always scrunched and shifted in the same way when he thought deeply.

"You can't help," Erkii spoke. "Who can help?"

It took Mertle a moment to understand what he was saying. "No one," she burst out, "absolutely no one." Frustration began to give her voice an edge. "You might find a healer who would keep her heart throbbing through the suffering – I spit on em." And she did on the ground. "I spit on anyone who would prolong this torture, imprisoned between the worlds."

Torture? That's the last thing he wanted for the kind woman, and she was kind. A year ago she made him and Urkii men again. Others would have kept them their property – two strong bodies to fight in the pits or double as cattle – but she had freed them. There was no weight of gold or jewels that could pay the debt they owed her. *But she is in pain, suffering* – the old woman seemed certain of that. He looked to Urkii whose face betrayed a conflict within – something he's gotten used to seeing. He knew. Deep inside, they both knew that what Mertle had said was true. The kind woman did not deserve to suffer, but it wasn't Mertle's gift to give.

"I will do it," he said, reaching for the knife in Mertle's wrinkled hand.

Mertle eyed him up for a moment then handed over the stubby bit of black stone. "Cut here," she drew lines with her finger at the top of the woman's neck, right beneath the edge of her slacked jaw.

He took a step past Urkii and kneeled by the cot. There were no protests, just two dark eyes following his wrist as he put the blade to the side of the kind woman's throat. Her mouth still dribbled foamed spittle and her breaths remained too shallow to see. There was something else too, laid in the same space as she was. It had antlers and fur and laid in a curl just an inch from his hand, close enough that he could feel its laboured breath brushing against him. *Just like in the river.*

It was the ring. Putting it on had changed the world, turned it into something else, made him see things. That's why he buried it between the roots of a tree, so that they would go away. The effort seemed futile now – the antlered doe before him was proof of that. She was like the hounds and monsters from before, except much closer, much more real. He brought his head forth for a better look, as he did, its head lifted and turned to face him. Their eyes met.

The doe gasped, "Don't kill me," its voice eerily familiar. It was the voice of the kind woman. A hallucination, it must have been. Yet it seemed so real – real enough to send his hand into jitters causing him to near drop the knife.

I can't kill… her. Quickly, he pulled the edge from the doe's throat. With it gone, she seemed to relax, laying down her head onto curled up chicken legs.

"Urgh, pass it to me, boy," he heard Mertle say, her long fingers wrapping around the back end of the knife's handle. He lifted the blade upward trying to get it out of her grip but the woman wouldn't let go. She held on tight, crooked spine stretching straight as her bare, bony feet began leaving the ground. When she relented he near put the blade through the thatching.

"Stupid! What do you think you're doing?" her voice cut through the smoke.

"Who you spit on?"

"Do not test me, boy," Mertle's hunch resembled that of a snake preparing to lunge. There was clear threat in her, one that would have been comical for someone of the old woman's statute were it not for the utter confidence backing it. Even his brother whose waist sat level with Mertle's scalp seemed to tense in his stance. It should have been a warning, but it was a warning he chose not to heed.

"Who make she live. Who?" He asked calm and still, a reflection of the respect that the frail figure deserved.

The old woman eased ever so slightly as she pulled back to look him over as if a puzzle had been etched all over his front. "You stood there a very long time. What did you see?"

"What did I see?"

"Yes, yes, what did you see, what did you see. Don't play stupid with me, boy."

I don't know what I saw. He wasn't even sure if he really did. *But the wise woman might know, maybe she can help me.*

"I saw deer. It had horns and legs of chicken."

Hearing that, Urkii grinned. He thought it a joke, and a deep chuckle rolled through gaps in his teeth. The chuckle rang lonely within the hut. No one seemed to share his amusement and his expression turned to that of confusion as his eyes struggled to find a place to rest. Mertle didn't share his problem, eyes locked on Erkii from under her hunch. Silently, her eyes drilled into Erkii's as if trying to get through to whatever was within, to read his mind and find out whether the words he spoke were true. *I am no liar,* he let the protest ring through his skull in case she could hear it.

"Did it talk? Did it say anything to you?"

"'Don't kill me,' she said." *She did, she really did.* He looked to the cot where the creature laid a moment before, but there was nothing to be found.

Mertle sighed, her shoulders dropping into an even deeper hunch as she murmured, "Then that's the lady's wish." Purposefully, she waddled to her bench, plucking dried leaves off of twisting vine then placing them into an empty bowl, them moved to the cauldron. Carefully not to let any leaves wash out, she skimmed the bowl across the bubbling surface to cover the leaves. She stirred the brew around with a wooden mortar, pressing the leaves into the walls of the bowl in twisting motions until, satisfied, she moved past Erkii to the head of the bunk. The pungent steam rising from the bowl cleared his nostrils.

"Stupid girl," Mertle mumbled.

Fingers unbothered by the heat, she soaked a cloth in the steaming bowl and began wiping away at the cluster of blood and hair stuck to Einsleigh's head. The warm liquid began melting the clumps into scarlet dribble, most of which she caught with the cloth before they could reach the furs. Every now and then, as dictated by her method, she would soak the cloth again, wringing it back into the brew which steadily progressed from pink to scarlet.

"Pass me that," she waved her hand in Erkii's direction, "the knife."

Erkii made no move prompting what must have been a hundredth sigh from the old woman.

"I won't kill her, stupid boy – I promise. Now, give me the knife so I can clear out the corrupted flesh." She reached back, twirling her wrinkled fingers in anticipation.

Reluctantly, he placed the blade in the woman's hand and moved in closer. *If she tries to, I can stop her,* he told himself, knowing very well he probably couldn't even if he was holding Mertle by the wrist. At least here, all but perched on her shoulder, he could pretend. But what if she did it anyway? What was he to do to a woman who had saved his life if she killed another who had done the same? His stomach turned as he realised that he was powerless. Thankfully, Mertle seemed to have given up on ending Einsleigh's suffering.

The stone blade was far sharper than any sword or dagger he had ever seen, little more than a tap of the edge and the skin would part like a flower in bloom. He learned that when it was his leg that was being cut up. First, when the monster got him, and the second when he got himself, or rather a travelling merchant did – though not on purpose – as his poor parry sent the man's sabre down a rail into his own leg. Overnight, the cut turned into a festering crevice. It was a wound far bigger than Einsleigh's, yet, Einsleigh's seemed to take far longer for Mertle to treat. Each cut was slow and deliberate removing but a tiny morsel of flesh at a time. It was like watching the nobles of Rhyz at their grand tables, shaving cuts of stallion with their gilded cutleries, and if anything was certain, it's that they would be here for a while yet.

There was a candle sitting atop Mertle's bench, by the time she was done its wick was near drowning. She took a step back, heel digging into Erkii's foot, and when she felt it, she shifted her weight to dig in further until he winced. Hearing it, she bounced forth, wrinkles merging in a satisfied smirk before she moved to the bench. There, she reached right to the bottom of the largest jar pulling out a handful of leaves that she dropped inside the mortar at the bench's centre. With well practiced movements, she turned them into paste.

The wound was now a neat opening, a little hole walled with shades of red and pink and an edge of white that was Einsleigh's skull. Mertle began to scoop the paste into the opening one tiny smudge at a time, patting each into a smooth surface before adding another. Layer after layer, she filled up the opening until the white of bone could no longer be seen.

"Give me that," she pointed at the array of jars and utensils cluttering the bench. Getting no response from Erkii, she clarified, "the candle, pass me the candle." He did, placing it between her impatient fingers. Once it was there, she tipped it. Wax oozed out the hollowed shaft putting out the flame and pooling right over the wound then spilling out over her skin and into her hair. Mertle watched carefully as it dried, and once she deemed that enough time had passed, she gave it a prod. Satisfied, she gave one more forceful. There was no give.

"Perfect," she said, standing and turning towards the two men. "Now, she needs rest – for whatever it's worth. You can go... go, go!" She flailed her hands at Urkii until he was out the door. Erkii tried to follow, but just as his brother turned to him in confusion, a frail arm barred his way. "Not you –you are going to stay."

The brothers looked at one another neither sure what to say. Mertle was first.

"Goodbye now," she said and shut the door.

*

The fire crackled merrily as it chewed through herbs and timber. He sat before it, right where Mertle put him while forcing a clay mug into his hand. The pungent steam rising from the brew within made his eyes water. Mertle was unbothered, sat across the flames with a mug of her own, she began to sip. Her eyes were on him yet seemed out of focus, looking to memories somewhere in the depths of her mind. It made him uneasy. He wanted to hear words but couldn't bring himself to be the first to speak. He joined her in sipping instead. By the time the bitter warmth trickled into his belly, her eyes returned focus.

"It's tea, if you were wondering," she said, her nostrils whiffing the steam.

"I wasn't."

Mertle smiled, baring gums that wrapped about a handful of worn down, discoloured teeth. "Most of them out there would not have drank it – not unless they were dying. Knowing is frightening for them, and I know things they couldn't even dream up. Yet you," she said, mouth disappearing behind the cup's lip. It returned with the smile missing. "You know things even I could never learn. So tell me, what do you see?"

What do I see? He didn't know how to answer that without putting himself in a spot for ridicule. Surely, what he was seeing *was* ridiculous. And yet, Mertle seemed serious in her questions, serious enough to have kept him in her home far longer than anyone else would have other than on the death bed. "I see people. I see animal... monster. They in," he said, showing with his hand – folding one into the other so that she could understand, "they one... like cake."

"'Like cake', " she repeated. He thought it mockery but the witch showed no hint of a smile as she mulled over his words. "That's what he said it could look like. Is everyone a monster – everyone you see?"

"No. Sometime. At river – yes, monster. Not all." Mertle didn't respond He wasn't making sense. Most times he would have blamed that on this strange tongue that they spoke, but this, he was certain he couldn't explain in the tongue of his own.

Eerie silence backdropped the night without as much as a hoot or crunch stirring the air into action. It wasn't so unusual of course, with Mertle's home being far removed from the main camp, but even then, at least a hint of laughter or conversation would make its way down into the marshes. The silence left space for his head to fill with monsters, though these shapeless things were ones he was certainly imagining.

"I didn't believe that farmer's boy when he spoke of the sorcerer," said Mertle, coming out of thought, "thought the sodded lot of you decided to fight it out, and that's all that got back. Yet, hearing you speak makes me think there was truth to it. Something inside must open for one to see what you see, and a sorcerer's power could be just the thing to do that. You better be telling me true."

"I am true," he said meekly, mind mulling over her words. *Open,* she said, *something opened inside.* That thought did not bring him joy. He was imaging a door into his soul flailing loose in its hinges for monsters to crawl in – monsters he saw in those he loved. What cruel life will that be with all around him turned to beasts? Ugly, deformed creatures – not real – he didn't want it, none of it.

"I want closed. You make closed," he pleaded with the witch.

"Closed? Boy, you have been blessed! How can you not see?" Her brow tightened in a moment's agitation. "Unless… you don't know what you're seeing."

He twisted his head in answer she didn't wait for.

"They're souls! You're seeing their souls!" Frustration was pushing her voice louder. "The very essence that the gods forged us with, you can see! Thousands upon thousands would kill for it – I would kill for it."

He looked to the cot where the kind woman was resting. "Deer is Einsleigh?"

"Forget Einsleigh – the stupid girl – she's a coward who wants to cling onto a useless body. Her wish has been granted. Focus on you now!" The old woman leaned in from her spot, her chin nearly brushing the flames. "There is a power that is beyond what most can even dream, and you're standing right on its edge. You need to let–" She was interrupted by four taps on the door.

"Go away or I will turn you into a toad!" she croaked.

"You're welcome to, as long as you open the fucking door," called a voice muffled by the slabs of timber. Mertle's face softened in the firelight. She waved Erkii towards the door which he opened to the sight of Torgy. For whatever reason – though there were many rumours – of all the exiles living in their little settlement, Torgy she seemed to tolerate.

There was tension to him as he stood there at the door, one he seemed to carry since the sorcerer turned their companions into smears. They all did. But unlike Bern and Jonathen, he hadn't traded his in for a cup of piss.

"Urkii said you were busy," he said, tilting his head sideways to where the big man sat, "but this can't wait." The rogue slipped past Erkii.

"Don't you know it's dangerous to disturb a witch?" asked Mertle with a sly smile.

"Is my face that bad? I do apologise," said Torgy with a bow, the jest lacking his usual lustre.

The answer seemed to appease the witch. "Close the door," she said to Erkii, "it's letting the cold in, and unlike your brother, I'm not interested in freezing to death. Now, what do you want?"

Erkii looked to his brother slumped against the wall. Breath a rhythmic whistle, he slept unbothered by the cold. He closed the door quietly.

"You need to tell them that Eins is going to make it. They're grasping for power – the lot of them – and as soon as she dies there will be fighting. I can already feel it."

Mertle smiled sweetly. "Do not worry, Torgmund – this is your lucky day. Thanks to Erkii, she is going to live."

Whatever Torgy expected, this wasn't it. Taken aback, he glanced towards the cot, then between Erkii and Mertle. "Good. That's great! Great news!" he exclaimed, overcome with joy.

Mertle looked him over. "It is good news. Go and share it with the others... both of you," she said, waving the two of them away. "Out, out and good night."

He near tripped over Urkii as they stepped out the door. The big man had fallen asleep and he had to give him a hardy shake to bring him to. He had been dreaming – it could be seen on the look in his face as he returned to reality – in a way, Erkii was somewhere else too. I need to learn, that's what she said. And now she's sending me away. Wise women were not to be trusted, he was always told – if there was anything that this visit has taught him, it's the truth these words held.

"And boy," Erkii heard her yell from behind. The three of them turned but it was he she was looking at. "I want you here tomorrow – I need some roots and you will do my digging."

"Yes," he said, before pulling Urkii to his feet and following in Torgy's step.

*

A path beaten by their own feet wove between buried trees and shrubbery back towards the camp. Though they had walked that way before, they moved slow with eyes a step ahead of their feet. By day it would have been a short walk but the night had masked the burrows, roots, and ditches which now perched in wait to catch a stray foot. He could feel the strain build as his eyes searched for over footprints left on the way up which were certain to be safe. After far longer than it ought have been, the first of mounds appeared by his side.

These were little shacks of sticks and mud, snowed over in the winter passed. They sprung up like mushrooms from a buried spore as the year went on – half of them had certainly appeared after he and Urkii had settled last spring. That was unusual, or so he was told. It wasn't a life many would choose, and yet, many had reasoned themselves into it in the year gone by. Some explained it as bad harvest or lack of work, and others a neighbour's dispute or unfair judgement, but when it came down to the truth, that was a difficult thing to know for sure. Not that dishonesty was uncommon amongst them – everyone has stories they'd be wise not to share. As it was, whatever their reasons, men and women – many with children – had chosen to live in the middle of the woods in a cluster of tiny shacks. Tonight, these shacks stood empty.

As on most a night, the settlement had gathered about a great flame ever burning beneath the old tree. Brigands, husbands and wives and children and relatives aged beyond use sat tightly together, sucking up heat in a hopeless bid to thaw their bones. It was a moment's respite, and though they had little, they shared all that they had – scraps and roots and stories. To many, it bore semblance of a great hall, the homes of chieftains and provosts where families would convene to feast and drink and pass time on a cold, winter's night. It was an ode to happy memories, and bar being short a few walls, it was a faithful one. There was warmth here, companionship, and care that stood proud and stubborn in the face of the world that had wronged them.

Like in any great hall, every moment was filled with stories real and made up or – as it usually were – a mixture of the two. Silence wasn't welcome. It let minds wander back to the sounds of the present, to the rumbling bellies, persistent coughs, and wheezing breaths. Many were repeated. He must have heard old Vas recount the story of how he had hidden the strap of a commander from his youth on eight separate counts, and that's just over the year that him and Urkii have been here to hear it. They were up to seven on how he saved a shield wall from collapsing. The first time that the stories were told was a thrill – despite them not understanding much – and the one after just as good. The following retellings were carried by the old man's enthusiasm alone, but they did their job just fine. He and Urkii would sit back and suck them up in silence – unlike the others. Those on their twentieth, thirtieth, fortieth retelling would groan, and share muffled whispers, yet all remained sat by the flames. Despite the complaints, that was what they needed.

Torgy told stories too, tales of a rogue moving from gutter to gutter, army and mercenary work in between. Like for Vas' tales, there was little silence for Torgy's – though for a reason entirely different than when Vas spoke – nearly all were laughing. The rogue had a way of treading the line between the real and not so that even the dullest of morning shits would turn into a story that would have both children and parents alike choking on spittle. But tonight, it wasn't Vas nor Torgy telling a story – it was Jonathen. All eyes on him, his boyish voice was backdropped by a silence so deep one could think he was talking to himself.

"– he said, 'you will never take my money when I'm alive' and bam," he exclaimed, firelight dancing over crusting gorges cut into his cheeks – a little blood still seeped. "The wizard pointed a finger and, suddenly, he was on fire. We couldn't even raise our bows before Gesleg melted right where he stood. Einsleigh was still fighting the fat guard, dodging like a cat – nothing could touch her. She was about to cut him down, but the wizard saw it. He turned his hand towards her and just closed it, and her sword just disappeared. He was laughing, the most disgusting laugh I've ever heard as the fat bastard dropped his axe right on her head."

Two girls leaned in, their mouths somewhere between a droop and a grin as their little blonde heads worked their way through the story. Torgy dropped into a squat behind them and gave their sides a little poke. Engrossed in the story, they just swatted their father away without the usual giggle. The girl's lack of attention didn't seem to be a bother – it was far made up for by Elna as she planted a long kiss on his scruffy jaw and pulled him into an embrace. With her arms tangled beneath his, they sat listening through the gap between their daughters' heads. It was a moment which Torgy enjoyed briefly, before worries began to scrunch his brow and set his eyes adrift.

"With a crack – like a tree stump being chopped – Einsleigh fell to the ground and started twisting in pain then the wizard looked at Twick and –"

"What about my Vulf?!" a woman cut in yelling from across the fire. "Tell them what you said!"

Jonathen's jaw seemed to lock, the wounds to his face suddenly clear. Her mousy hair flew wild about her deceptively soft face, but there was no deception in her eyes, just madness. Doubtlessly, she clawed up the boy when she saw him carrying Vulf's sword and, judging by her barred teeth, she seemed ready to do some more. A child looking for help, Jonathen quickly turned to Bern who had just finished looking over the tree's crown.

"He charged, remember?" said Bern calmly. "Tell your aunty Margret how he charged."

"He charged," Jonathen repeated the words stiffly, eyes wide open as he stared at the woman. She seemed to relax which gave him enough courage to continue with the tale. "He charged like a monster from the stories, howling a cry that made my blood chill. The guard swung at him, too stupid to realise that there was no use – he was fighting a werewolf with peasant steel. The axe bounced off of Vulf's hide as he tore the fat bastards arm off."

"How'd he die then?" she asked from across the flame causing Jonathen to clench up once more.

He glanced to the tree before exclaiming, "Magic! Steel could never hurt him and the wizard knew it. He heard the howl and saw that it was a real werewolf standing over him and he was scared. But there were still tricks, scary tricks, at his disposal. And waving his hand in the air, he made a sword of pure, dark evil." There were huffs of excitement around the fire – and not just from the two girls. "He sliced at Vulf but only hit the air. Then Vulf was behind him, striking. We thought he would put him down, but the wizard turned and made a shield just as black as the sword and he blocked the strike then cut Vulf on the arm. But that wasn't enough to stop a real werewolf – he managed to grab the wizard's sword arm, and his arm grabbed his foot right from the cart –"

"And then Torgy said, 'shoot now, kill them'," Bern's words cut right through Jonathen's tale putting him to silence. "The wizard was good as dead." There were murmurs, some dismissive and some disbelieving, but all tense as eyes turned to Torgy.

His face was tense, cheek trembling as the teeth behind them grated against each other. "You're a liar."

"Liar?" Bern rose to his feet, scarred features scrunched in anger. It was anger he believed real.

"Settle down," old Vas tried to calm them only to be drowned out by the upheave, "settle–"

"Tell 'em, Jon. Tell 'em the truth," barked Bern.

The boy took only a quick look between the two rogues before his mind was made up. "He's telling the truth – Torgy told us to shoot." That was all that Margret needed.

The she wolf pounced through the space between those seated and the fire. Spit rolled down her face, dribbling as she stepped through the tangle of limbs in her way. Her eyes were locked. Torgy pulled his girls in and turned to drag them about, his back a shield from the crazed Margret. His body braced for the attack, but it never came. As she leapt past, old Vas raised his foot. With her ankle caught, the she wolf's pounce turned to free fall which she broke with her hands – one hit the ground while the other grasped embers.

"Aaagh!" She wrenched her hand out of the flames falling back onto her hind. Her foot swiftly tapped the ground as she began rocking. Women and men straightened in their seats and children stood on their toes to get a look –

it was entertainment like that of a city theatre but with actors of greater fame and far lesser wealth.

"Put that in the snow, girl – it will feel better." Old Vas got to his feet, lifted the writhing woman beneath the armpits and dropped her by a snowbank. "There. Now, you," he said, turning to Urkii and he. "Tell what happened and tell it true. What was the order–"

"What the fuck are you asking them for?!" cut in Bern. "It's like listening to a trick crow speaking human tongue." Erkii could hear his brother's jaw crackle.

"They may speak a stranger's tongue like a 'trick crow' but that don't mean they have the brains of one. Now shut your gob before I smack it, Bern." The old soldier seemed ready to do just that. "What was the order?"

All happened so fast. One moment they were holding then the next they were loosing arrow after arrow into the mayhem. If Torgy ordered them to, he didn't remember, but he knew what he wanted to say. "No order – we shoot. No fight. Everyone die." Bern's eyes were fixed on him, unblinking, lips pressed into a narrow line.

"That's a lie!" Jonathen yelled. "They fought valiantly – like warriors from stories! We all fought like warriors from stories. I even shot one of the guards! Got him right through the spine!" The attention he held but minutes ago had vanished, along with it his confidence. He now seemed a child asking to be noticed.

"Well done laddie, you shot a man in the back," said Vas without as much as a glance towards him. "Maybe if you did so sooner, we wouldn't have lost four of our own."

"Three," spoke up Torgy, "Einsleigh is still breathing."

"Hah! At least the witch knows her stuff. Thank the gods." Vas turned towards the tree searching for Bern but the brute was no longer there. He looked to Jonathen who was left glancing nervously from side to side, open mouthed, looking even younger than before. If Vas had words to share, he tossed them aside with a shake of the head before moving onto an issue more important. "So, the wizard – that's all he had?" He pointed to Urkii whose back was adorned with the sorcerer's coat. "A pelt?"

"There was a little gold – should be enough to feed our lot for the next few weeks," replied Torgy.

"*For the next few weeks*", Vas chuckled, "I'd like to see the size of that purse. You can show me when we go spend it at the market. Anything beside gold?"

"No. Nothing else," said Torgy, "the sleigh rode on with all his coffers."

"I see."

*

He had buried the ring while pissing outside Mertle's but now it rested atop the fur before his eyes. He gave it a prod with his finger expecting *something*. Nothing happened. He pushed it through the furs a few more times as Urkii snored, curled up within an opposing pile of furs – it rose and fell at a steady pace. *It almost killed him*, he was so sure of that at the time – the ring near drowned his Urkii – but the more he moved it about, the less likely that seemed. The ring was insignificant as it looked. He put it on – nothing. He took it off. He put it on. He took it off, and soon, his eyes fell shut.

His sleep was a set for the most vivid of nightmares. A thing of a hundred arms and legs moved across the earth, its limbs working in twisted harmony, pulling and pushing as naturally as the shimmer of leaves in a summer's gale. Its long, winding body was of flesh and bone, outlines of ribs and humps of its vertebrae etching and shaping pale skin that stretched taut over its entirety. It had a mole – a tiny mole that he spotted despite the expanse of the thing's skin – and it made Erkii's spine tingle. It was the skin of a man.

There was a large satchel attached around its mid, coils of twine twisting round and round between the limbs. The white skin was thicker beneath the wrappings, hard callouses forming mounds which the twine grooved and in places fused with.

Its front end stood erect, partly robed in shapeless cloth. A hood shrouded the thing's face and sleeves enveloped its two arms. But the sleeves were far too short. They came up to the thing's elbows, leaving two long, lanky arms protruding out of the openings with hands that seemed to have been crushed and stretched to resemble branches of a willow. Each knuckle moved with absolute freedom, working like joints of a contortionist wriggling on a circus stage as they ran down the things back in chase of *something* that desperately tried to escape.

It was a little speck of silver-white fur – a hare or a rabbit trying to make a dash for the surrounding mist. Each time it got near the edge of the thing's back, the twig like fingers wrapped around it and carefully put it back inside the satchel. Then the creature would try to escape again. Over and over it tried, and each time, one of the freakish limbs would put it back more panicked than before. It was a desperate struggle for survival and a game that the thing of many limbs seemed to take pleasure in.

Erkii could feel his body, the dampness of furs that surrounded him. He was watching, frozen within his sweat soaked lair, a helpless spectator to a game he wished to never be part of. *Please go, please go,* he pleaded with the world. Anyone or anything that could take this nightmare away was welcome. But here, there was only one thing listening.

The creature of many limbs stopped and turned towards him. Its head twisted in question.

7

*"What's better my dear boy, to make a definite
example of one or a moderate one of many?" –
Edwed of Swasia as spoken to his son Alfred.*

It was definitely loose, wobbling back and forth inside
the failing grip of his swollen gum. He pushed on it with his
tongue until a twang of pain made him stop. Then he'd do it
again, each touch moving it a little further. His mother
would have tried to stop him, tell him it would fall out if he
didn't, but she was fifteen years too late. *It will fall out no
matter what I do,* he told her – but mostly himself – and
continued pushing the pointy tooth into his cheek.

He was back on the sleigh. Miska sat opposite looking
at him with what seemed reluctant acceptance. It was she
who knocked his tooth loose, with an aimless kick after
having found him asleep at the doorstep. That was what he
awoke to – pain, blood pooling under tongue, and a second
kick that fell on his shoulder. There was a bruise there now
and a few more on his forearms and ribs. Looking opposite,
he could see the purpled hand pressed into her wrist but he
wasn't certain Miska did. If so, she paid the bruise no mind.
Neither mentioned the harm they caused the other – that
would be best forgotten and could easily be with the pain

that they shared. Their eyes kept drifting to the seat where Sassa's breath ceased. *Gorgie must have scrubbed it,* as the blood which seeped out Sassa's wraps and down his lap was but a vague stain hiding in the grain. The driver had barely spoken to them since the morning, choosing to murmur under breath and jerking his head left to right as he steered the mare. He seemed unusually sober.

Miska swallowed a yawn. She spent the night pulling barbed arrows and shreds of flesh out of Sassa's body, washing the caked blood off of his supple skin, combing the knots out of his lanky hair, living a mother's nightmare. With care she had wrapped him in clean cloth and, after beating the man who was meant to prevent that, she buried him – they did it together at sunrise, breaking a shovel and chipping another by the hazelnut their boy used to climb. It was a lethargic moment, one whose pain they ought to have embraced in memory. But the soil had no time to settle before she wanted revenge.

Flailing skin, tearing flesh, crushing bone, and burning while they still screamed was all that she spoke of when she did. The killers and their families were one and the same – they were responsible – and she wanted them screaming before they stopped breathing. She was capable of it – having seen her fight, he knew it to be true. She was a soldier like he was, fought in the same lines he did, at times holding the shield which kept his flank. If he were to ever tell it true, he would say that she thrived in the soldier's life far more than he ever did. The battlefield brought the same comfort to her as a blanket or a thatched roof overhead. At heart, she was a killer. That made the two of them.

"Ts," Eadmunt's tongue smacked at the end of a breath causing Miska to flinch. The old man sat where the sorcerer did but two days back, rubbing some warmth into his hand.

His hunch was deep enough for his elbows to rest comfortably on his knees which was how he had spent most of the journey. Bear hadn't asked him to come – the gods know Miska hadn't either – yet the old man was the first sat on the sleigh. *I'm coming with you,* was all he said when the two of them stepped on Gorgie's sleigh. They had no reason to argue and, for Bear in the least, he was welcome. "Ts."

"Will you stop that?" barked Miska.

Eadmunt eyelids fluttered. "What happened?" Seeming disoriented, he turned to Miska.

"Shit," Gorgie cussed under breath. He pulled back on the reins bringing the sleigh to a stop.

Miska was at half mind to give Eadmunt a yelling and with the sleigh stopped once more she seemed ready to yell at Gorgie too. Undecided on which one to start with, she settled on a groan instead. Bear wanted to groan with her.

The journey to Guhdlval Keep turned out to be much harder than expected. Way stones and markings that would have led them there in summer were buried beneath the snow. Even Gorgie, who supposedly knew the woods better than any beast or man, had to stop periodically to make sure they were headed the right way, at times even backtracking to take another route. It was meant to be a two day trip there and back – that was what he had said – but they were still in the woods as light began to vanish.

Supper was sparse and night was spent cramped on the sleigh's floor. Miska had packed more thorough but what she brought she chose not to share, and for the night, she laid herself across a bench instead. She wouldn't come near him.

They emerged out of the woods near noon the next day, a change so sudden it seemed like coming awake. One moment they were surrounded by thickets of trees, the next flat plains of white stretched on either side, empty and desolate but for a few distant mounds of snow. These were farm lands – if they were anything like home, they must have been – the soil of the south was rich and blessed with fertility. Yet, there were no men, no women, no children, nor a single abode in which they could be living. The only hint of inhabitants was a stream of smoke rising from between hills a good hour away.

"Where are they, Gorgie?" he asked.

"There," said the driver pointing to the smoke, "could've guessed that yourself, couldn't ya."

"I mean farmers," he explained, choosing to ignore the quip, "where are the farmers – the ones working the land. Why is there no one living here?"

The driver shrugged. "Probably ran away to somewhere better," he murmured without as much as a turn.

Wouldn't be here were it not for the gold. Bear had to dig beneath the floorboards to pay him for the trip – money squirrelled for all the other days one wishes will never come. He looked at Miska whose hands had been stuck in a clench since the morning.

"You 'right?" he asked but only got a brief glance in reply before she turned to the wagon floor where her gear lay. She wasn't alright – not by a long shot. But he didn't expect her to be, not until there was justice or, as she'd prefer, vengeance.

"It was a curse," said Eadmunt, straightening his body into a lesser hunch. The driver gave him a glance over the shoulder, and Miska spat at the sleigh's floor.

Eadmunt looked up from where the spit landed, eyes meeting her's. "You don't believe in curses?" There was a smile on his face, a small hint of goodwill that never seemed to leave. That may have been what Miska disliked the most about him.

"My mother believed in curses and faeries from stories," she said while unravelling the furs that warmed her torso. "Father knew better. Superstitions is all they are and ever will be."

Eadmunt's head came to a tilt. "Do you know what superstition makes you do?" he asked softly. Miska carried on stripping. She expected the old man to finish his thought, taking a moment's silence to realise that he wanted an answer.

"Makes you stupid," she replied with a bite before dropping her furs carelessly onto the sleigh's floor. The rigid shapes of muscle and breast contoured the loose linen tunic into a harsh landscape as she reached down for her boiled leather.

"Aye – it makes you bleed a goat in the moonlight before you cook it or stops you knocking a fourth time on a neighbour's door. That's superstition. But you know what it will never make you do? It will never make you tie all you got to your back and leave your home to winds and devils. No matter how strongly they may believe, folk don't do that. They will sprinkle salt at the door, burn lavender in their hearth, but they will never uproot their whole lives on a whim. It wasn't superstition, it was fear. Those who lived here were scared for their lives – the lives of those they held dear – and so, they ran." He paused, eyes glued to a sticky clump of fur on the back of their driver's wraps. "What do you think Gorgie? Ever seen anything like that?"

"Aye, I have," he replied, eyes still fixed on the smoke. "But I hope to be wrong."

The snow mounds grew larger as they got closer, irregular in shape and size with arms and legs stretching outward. Crumbled walls and collapsed thatching under a blanket of snow, they were homes. "Why?"

"Thought the two of you would know – but I guess soldiers don't tend to look much at the village after you're done murdering its sons and raping its daughters."

"Say that again," said Miska, rising abruptly. The leather breastplate hung half laced off her shoulders. The threat of the woman standing behind him was enough to turn Gorgie on his little bench, but he didn't back down.

"Why would I say it again?" he barked. "You heard me – you heard me plenty. So, if that's all it takes, you better kill me quick, because if gods see, I promise you won't be seeing your boy in the life after."

Bear looked to his wife and tugged on her wrist. *Sit down.* She gave him a quick look before tearing her hand out of his grip. Tense and wide-eyed she perched down on the bench. The man's words cut him too – they did as much as they did her – but no matter his words, the greying, red faced coward was still here, taking them through this eery place, if only out of greed.

"A war band's been through here," Gorgie carried on, "cleared the whole place out."

Eadmunt shook his head, somehow still maintaining his usual measure. "No. If they were chased off by a war band, we would have heard of it. Someone would have come to Karlka or a place nearby. This was slower, driving them off one by one." The crooked provost was right. A war band would have left drifters in its wake and many would be seeking refuge in nearby steads. Karlka was far enough removed to feel safe but close enough to get to in winter time – if there were any folk displaced, they would have been long living among them. But Gorgie remained of a different mind.

"It's war, Eadmunt. The Sylthian bastards shoving their slimy hands where they don't belong – that's all they talk of south of the border. Maybe that's one of them, come with a bunch of those pompous twats to cause havoc in our father land."

"Yoona said they've been looking for men to work their fields," said Bear. "Their lands must have been empty for a while."

"… because of the curse."

"Fuck your curse, Eadmunt. Fuck it," said Miska. There was frustration in her voice, though not as much as before – most of it seemed to have been spent on the driver. It was an order for Eadmunt to speak different, but unlike Bear or the boys would have, the old man took it as an invitation to dig in.

"The curse is older than this. It's older than whatever happened here, and it's been driving people away from here for years. It's madness passed on from father to son that keeps good folk away from these lands. The Guhdlvals are the curse that's been keeping people away from these lands as long as I can remember." Eadmunt lowered back into his usual hunch.

It all made sense to Bear – frankly, having seen magic but two days ago, he would have accepted a mystical curse too. Miska didn't.

"So where are the Guhdlvals?" she continued. "Drove themselves away too?"

"Probably over there," Eadmunt nodded up ahead to where the smoke trails ran lines from behind the hills, "sat inside their hall, waiting for winter to pass."

As it turned into a gap between the hills, the road took on a slight incline. They were getting closer to the smoke. Bear could smell it now – they were burning pine like back home – but there was something odd to it, a strange little note that lingered inside t his nose and just refused to leave. *Maybe they're burning cedar, or getting rid of the needles,* but if they were doing either, he would have known it in an instant. Yet, the scent seemed familiar still. He smelled it before – a sweetness with a hint of earth. *It can't be.* The smell was accumulating in his nostrils then slithering through his sinuses and into his mouth, building up as they got closer until the back of his throat was coated in ooze that began to trickle down into his gut. His stomach clenched in protest.

Miska's agitation turned to alert, like that of a dog sensing danger to its owner. *She smells it.* Gorgie adjusted his arse on his bench and Eadmunt straightening to a point where his hunch all but disappeared. *They smell it too.*

"Bodies. They're burning bodies," he said, seeming only to confirm what the others already knew of the sweet and sickening stench.

Gorgie was twisting about in his seat. "It bloody smells like it."

"People die – may be a funeral pyre," said Eadmunt. Despite his words, he was seeming unnerved.

The stench overwhelmed all else, but even the rankest of odours eventually fades into the background. Soon, Bear's nose began to tolerate it, leaving his mind to pick on something other – a bird call, an unusual one. It ran high as a tip-of-the-tongue whistle while maintaining a certain depth as it bounced between the hills. Sassa used to make a noise like it when he was little, pursing his lips like he saw others do, then screaming at the most piercing pitch. For a week it seemed it was all he did, torturing their ears until he was put to bed. Miska would kick him outside. Joran would kick him. But the little bugger kept going. Then one day, the boy got bored and never did it again.

The call stopped.

As the sleigh wove between the hills, another call came but different. This one was louder, deeper, irregular. *Foxes,* there was an uncanny resemblance to their shriek. He wanted to believe so, but the screams echoing through the hills carried an unmistakable note of humanity that was only ever brought out by most excruciating pain.

"Fuck this, we're turning back." The man's mind seemed made up as he tugged on the mare's reins bending her neck in half.

"No, keep going!" barked Miska as the sleigh's turn nearly tossed her off her seat.

"Are you deaf you stupid cunt?!" Gorgie's words came in a burst. "They're being killed down there and I sure as shit don't plan to join them!" His words carried over to the mare who began snorting and tossing her mane.

"We're finding the bastards who killed my boy!" Miska leapt forward and grabbed the reins, tugging counter to Gorgie. The two of them pulled the mare into a halt.

"You can do it on your fucking own then! Get off the sleigh!" said Gorgie, one arm flailing from the hip as the other tried to wrestle the reins away from Miska.

"How about I throw you off, you black livered bastard?!"

"Miska, sit down, please," Eadmunt tried to ease them. "We can always come back, but whatever's going on down there is none of our business."

"Sit, Misiu, sit!" He could see her embers stir before he finished saying the last word.

"Shut your fucking mouth!" she ordered. "We wouldn't be here if you didn't let Sassa–" a piercing whistle cut her off.

"Halt at the honour of your king!" The words came from a nearby hilltop from where a blue clad figure stared them down. A straight sword hung by his side, a plain tool forged en-masse that Bear recognised too well, issued at least a decade back when the king still had a standing army in his employ. On the man's chest stood proudly a silver stag. He had worn it, so had Miska, and seeing the way in which the man carried himself, he suspected his words to be true. Since her sword remained in the sleigh's den, Miska must have agreed too.

The soldier half walked, half slid down the hill's gradient dusting the air with loose powder. Once down, he approached the sleigh with efficient motion, walking in precise steps that betrayed no fear of who or how many they were. Up close his face revealed to be well kept, shaven no more than a day back and sheared so that not a single salted black hair could reach his brow. There was a certain youth to the way he looked and the way he moved – he could have easily mistaken him for a man of thirty was it not for the stag. It was a common thing for the embroidery to unravel with time, especially when there was blood to scrub off – Bear's stag would lose a few threads each year. The soldier's one had lost two legs and an antler.

"State your business," said the man staring expectantly at Georgie and Miska, both of whom still held the reins. As vocal as they were but minutes before, neither seemed ready to respond.

With measured calm, the provost looked to the soldier. "Our business is ours to keep, friend," he spoke.

The soldier leaned past Miska's flank to inspect the old man in kind. Pale, grey eyes darted between points of interest before settling on the old man's eyes. "That may have been true a few days ago. It may even be true a few miles back. Unfortunately, on this day and on this road... and looking at you – with the armour, and the steel, and *these eyes*," he said spiralling Miska's face with his fingers, "*eyes* that tell me you're here to use it. At this very moment, knowing your business becomes my honour bound duty. So, tell me, what do you want with the Guhdlval?"

"Oh, we're just passing through," said Gorgie putting on a voice that was a little too chirpy.

"Passing through to where?" asked the soldier, turning to the driver. "Ulager? Seinevla? Or are you on your way to admire the great keep in Radventyl?" Gorgie had an answer ready.

"We were–"

"Let me save your breath," he interrupted leaving Gorgie to take on a red hue. "Whichever it is, this is a detour – it is always a detour. No one travels here unless they're Guhdlval or have business with the Guhdlval, and I need to know which one it is. Now."

Judging by the stern look on his face, the soldier wasn't looking for another lie. Before Gorgie could come up with one, Bear told him the truth, "They killed my son."

The soldier inspected him with a similar glance that he did Eadmunt. "I see." Without seeking permission, he grasped the timber siding and pulled himself onto the driver's bench beside Gorgie. "I think you will find your grievance resolved. Go ahead," he said, giving him permission with a controlled flick of the hand. The driver did as he was told.

Another scream sounded ahead – higher, more desperate. This time, he could even make out the words. "No! No! Don't do it! Don't do it! Don't do it! No! Noo! Aaargh! Noo –" the words melted into a wail. It stretched and stretched then suddenly ceased.

"Carry on," said the soldier, nonchalant to the noise as his head turned from hilltop to hilltop. Whatever could be up there seemed much more a worry to him than the screams. The Karlkans did not share his calm.

"What's going on there?" asked Bear, ready to stick the soldier with the hunter's blade on his belt. The thought left him as soon as the man turned.

"Nothing to worry about – unless you've been committing treason that is," said the soldier. "If you have, I'd be quick to put that knife in my back – right between the shoulder blades – and run that horse until it dies spitting foam or gets you to Dharollian dirt."

Bear had no time to follow the soldier's advice. The next bend brought them out of the hills to a low, stone wall with a squared arch at its centre. Behind its loosely hanging gate lay the courtyard of Guhdlval Keep. The smoke, the stench, the screams had their explanation within. His mouth filled with vomit as the scene began etching itself into his mind. Not even war had prepared him for this.

A pile of bodies laid to the side, the skin of each a mess of bubbles and boils that formed as the fat beneath rendered in heat. They stared into the skies with discoloured eyes, some cloudy and others black, as their mouths carried on screaming in silence. Atop their heads, all that remained were a few patches of copper red coated sparsely in soot. *The Guhdlvals*. The little he heard of them was enough to seed distaste in his mind – one of them killed his son. Yet, that's not what he wished them. No matter their sins, they didn't deserve *that*. No one deserved that.

There was another one, a man judging by the stretch of emptied skin remaining at his groin. He was hanging limp over a flame, skin cracking and charred to black flakes. Ropes tied to each wrist stretched him wide between two posts, beneath was a fire pit, logs kicked into dishevel. Looking at his misshapen toes he knew exactly how that came to be. The only part of his that the flames didn't seem to have reached was the face, though that amounted to very little. In pain, he had bitten off a chunk of his lip which now hung loose to reveal yellowed teeth hiding behind. While not by fire, it had been disfigured by anguish.

Men in blue held the ropes that bound him. Their lips bore a scowl and eyes were fixed on the surrounding hills. Seeing their comrade heading the sleigh, they extended arms in salute – all but for a youth who seemed fixated on the corpse, a sight that he couldn't look away from.

He doesn't want to but he has to, there was something to the boy's eyes that had Bear convinced of that. *What's he going to say. No? A soldier does what he's told.* That's what soldiers did. That was what he had done many times before.

"Drop!" the youth ordered. The men did and the corpse fell to ground. The boy spat, leaving a glob of yellowing phlegm that slowly dribbled through the gap in the dead man's mangled lip.

"Stop anywhere to the side," said the soldier, hopping off the bench as Gorgie brought the sleigh to a halt. If there was time for a stabbing and escape, it had long passed. The only choice left was to do as told and hope they'll come out the other end as many as they came.

"Go inside and see the captain."

Gorgie cleared his throat. "Someone has to look after Brenda, she's had an awfully long day. I can stay behind and look to her."

The soldier gave the mare a brief glance before turning to the plump driver. "Don't worry yourself with that, friend. I will unhitch her myself and make her feed and care my personal duty."

The driver quietly slumped into himself.

Is this it? Between the pile of bodies and the pyre, hope was a difficult thing to find. *They're king's men*, they keep the law and order. Those were the only thoughts that kept him from running as fast as he could. *I wonder what it's like to burn alive,* he thought as they crossed the snow lipped doorstep.

*

At their finest these halls must have been a thing of extravagant display, but on this day, Guhdlval Keep lay in dire disrepair. It seemed as if each of their steps was traversing over crumbled mortar or splintered board that sprouted out of moth eaten rugs like mushrooms out of a forest floor. Chairs and tables have been piled beneath the stone walls, timbers torn away to feed fires. Judging by the amount missing, it wasn't only the soldiers who had done so. These were the tables for guests, men at arms, and unimportant relatives that would have filled these halls during feasts of decades passed. Now, they were reduced to seating dust and rats. The only table to remain standing was the lord's

Raised upon a platform, it was a grand slab likely too heavy to be moved. The centuries spent in service had left their mark within its grain turning it to near complete black. Two dozen men could have sat along its length, yet there were but eight great chairs to be placed there, all on the same side with their backs to the wall. It was where the lord would have sat with those he decided to honour that day, watching the proceedings from a vantage. Today, there were no lords sat there, only a fat ruffian in blue silk adorned with the king's stag.

Left cheek pitted with grotesque scarring of a wound left to fester, she was leaning into a sheet of parchment as low as the iron beneath the overcoat would allow. Her brows were furrowed with intensity as she laboriously scraped letters into the treated hide.

"I thought there were no more peasants on these lands," she said in a voice far more pleasant than he expected, composed, looking them down from behind the table. "Where are you from?"

"Kalrka, my lady," replied Eadmunt, the flattery causing her face to flash the vaguest hint of a smile.

"Refresh my memory," she said twirling towards them with loose fingers. "Where is this Kalrka?"

"Solemn Forest, my lady."

The woman's face contorted, remaining so as she spoke. "*Solemn Forest*. That will have to do for now – won't it." She scratched something on a new piece of parchment before looking back to them. "And who are you?"

"I am Eadmunt, the provost of Kalrka, my lady."

"All of you," she rephrased once more, lifting her quill.

"These are my people – Bear, Miska… and Gorgie."

She mouthed each name as she scraped them onto the page. Done, she sat back in the lord's chair and looked them over once more. "Very well. I would ask why you came here but, as you may well know, the Guhdlval are no more. They have been trialed for the crime of treason, and having been found guilty, they have been executed but for their last born herald who will be sent into the world within the day. Therefore, as the matter stands, any debts they may have owed to you, any debts you may have owed to them, are nullified in the eyes of the king."

Any debts... "They killed my son," he burst out.

The woman paid the raised tone no mind. "Did you not enter these halls through the courtyard? There is little more that can be done in this matter. However," she said, something of a caring smile forming on her lips, "I will add your sons murder to the record of their crimes. Consider your matter resolved." The smile disappeared as she began flipping through a stack of hides to her side. Finding what she needed near the bottom, she began writing once more.

He looked to Miska who stood to his side – there was a change. Her brow had smoothed, eyes moved slower, and even her mouth seemed to droop. *She's happy with this,* the burnings and the record – it seemed to appease her. It did not appease him. Seeing the bodies in the courtyard brought on sobriety in his grief, and what he saw in that sobriety wasn't justice. He wanted it to be so, but those who lived here had nothing to do with Sassa's death. He wished they did because – all that had happened here would make sense – but it wasn't so. Worse yet, he no longer knew if the Guhdlval had anything to do with it at all. He didn't see them, didn't recognise them. It was only Yoona who had, and Yoona was an idiot.

"There was more – in the forest."

"In the forest?" The captain looked at him over the tail of her quill. "Which forest are you speaking of?"

"They killed my son in the Solemn Forest," he said.

The woman straightened in her seat. "Solemn Forest is awfully far from here – especially in winter. Why would the Guhdlval go all the way down there to kill your son? Did you owe them money?"

"No," Gorgie cut in, "they were bandits, vermin from a gutter them that tried to rob us. But one had red hair so *he* thinks it was Guhdlval. I told him as you said, *Guhdlval are too far, it don't make sense for them to rob us,* but he don't listen. Please, lady, forget him and have us go home."

The captain looked Georgie up and down, contemplating his words. When she spoke again, she spoke slowly. "There is a thick line between robbery and murder. Most brigands, as little as we may think of them, are clever enough to avoid the latter. Kill one, all others come armed. So, why did they kill your son?"

"They stopped us to rob us and then a fight broke ou–"

"You mean," Gorgie huffed over him, "you put a fuckin' axe in one of them without thinking there may be more, archers hiding in the trees!"

"I did it to keep you all safe!"

"No, you did it 'cause you're thick as a fuckin' wall of shit! They were gonna go – that other arsehole paid them off with a big bag of gold but you just had to start swinging that fuckin' axe!"

The mention of gold pulled the woman up right. Weighing each word they blurted, she pushed herself into the backrest of the grand chair. He should have stopped there, *but that fuckin' bastard…* "You would be dead without me, coward!"

"I would be back home without you! Warm and safe, and not in the middle of fuckin'–"

"It was the wizard you fat old fool – he started it all!"

"My arse 'it was the wizard'! He was payin' the bastards to fuck off – he was dealing with it! But you just had to jump in and make a mess of it. And you know what? If you hadn't, your boy would still be breathing!"

He wanted to strangle him, make the life stop at his throat and never move through it again.

"What was the wizard's name?" said a quiet voice from somewhere behind. Neither paid it any mind.

"I will break you," he growled at the driver, "every single one of your bones, I'm going to break it, and everyone who knows you will be glad, you greedy fucker! Even your wife might come back from the dead and thank me for it." In his anger, he meant every word.

"What was the wizard's name?"

"I take you through the woods on snowed up paths you wouldn't find in a thousand years and you... you fuckin' weasel!" The driver squared up his shoulders and pulled back at the elbow. But Bear was quicker.

He sprung and turned off his right foot in a single motion. It was coming high from the left – the way he moved, the old fuck may as well have told him that yesterday. He was ready to duck it, bring a fist under the ribs, all his weight following through with the shoulder smacking the man's chin as he'd bring him to the ground. Then it'd be done. *Stupid fucker,* he thought of the man who never had to lift a fist in his life. But he wasn't the only one seeing the intentions clear. Eadmunt stepped between them, his hunched, skinny body rooting itself to the ground. Forearms stretched outwards, he braced for impact. Bear tried to stop, but his motion was already decided. He crashed into the crooked provost sending him into an awkward fall.

"Ugh," Eadmunt grunted as his feeble form hit the ground. The sound was a dunk in a cold bucket.

"Are you–" he was cut off by a whistle identical to the one in the hills. In the confines of the hall it rang far louder.

"Quit this nonsense," the soldier closed the distance, standing dominant between them. Their ears still hummed from his whistle. "The wizard. Did he have a name?"

Gorgie, whose fists remained clenched, already had a reply, "Swallow."

"Swallow?" the soldier paused, examining the old man whose face had turned redder than it ever had from drink alone. "Are you sure about that?"

"Yes, it was a stupid bird–"

"Sparrow, it was Sparrow," said Bear from the knee. He was right by Eadmunt whose hind seemed stuck to the stone floor. Each attempt to prop and rise on his legs ended in a fold and a grunt over which he had no choice.

"What happened to him? Where did he go after you got back?" For a moment he misheard –mistook the words as concern for the old man crumbled on the floor – but the soldier had no interest in that. He was standing over them with eyes locked on Bear – motionless and unblinking.

"He didn't get back. They had archers hiding in the woods. When the fight broke out, they came out of hiding and started shooting. The wizard took a few in the back, and when the sleigh moved, he fell. He's dead."

"What about the body. Did you see what happened to the body?"

Bear managed to get Eadmunt to sit, yet that alone seemed a questionable position for him. The old man's body was in a twist, purposefully trying to keep its weight on the right side, flinching at even the slightest touch to the left hip.

The soldier knelt, looking at Bear from across the provost's body as if the old man wasn't even there. "Did you see what happened to the body?"

"We left it there."

"Where is *there?*"

"It's in the woods," said Gorgie, glancing between the captain and the soldier then back to the captain, "about half way between Karlka and Drwhal's Clearing. I can show you." Though his eyes were on her, the captain gave no reply, looking to the soldier instead.

The soldier turned to Eadmunt. "Can you move?"

Eadmunt gave an unconvincing nod.

"Very well. Now," he said springing to his feet, walking an arch through the hall until he came to a stop besides the scarred woman. "You're going to show me where *there* is."

"I'm not letting any one of them back on my sleigh! They can walk and freeze for all I care," said Gorgie.

The man's face was that of a fantasy young girls shared round the flames, yet in this instance, the sudden edge that it took on made the driver count the scuffs on his boots. "You're going to do as you're told. Captain Yaghl," he turned abruptly, voice softer but equally decisive, "I'm taking five men. Make allowances, finish the papers, and send a bird to the capital on our progress. Add a line as to our pursuit of the foreign agent."

"Yes, Marshal Ser," she replied with a stiff dignity as one would their father, before pulling a blank sheet of parchment from a stack and, as instructed, beginning to scribe as the Marshal looked over the papers from her side.

"And don't forget the heralds," he said, stood with his hands holding the table's edge. "The account must be spread and the consequence of treason against our land and against our king must be understood." His voice was tense, hands squeezing tight. "We will take one with us."

8

"Mamma, do dead people scream?" – a child
mourning her father.

The soul taker stared, four beady eyes twinkling in the light of the flames. Its long, needle like legs pierced the earth as its spiralling digits molested the smoke. Mucus dribbled down its chin but it didn't come from a mouth – the soul taker didn't have one. Instead, like honey through a rag, the liquid seeped through a stretch of skin below its eyes. Even after three decades, it was still unnerving to see. It was the reason he pissed his bed every night from birth until near seventeen – 'til his first night inside the Citadel.

You are not seeing them, he was told all those winters ago, young, staring doe eyed at a scholar in decadent drapery. *You cannot see them. But do not misunderstand. They are there as certain as that chair you're sitting on or the table before you. You just cannot see them true. No man can. But as each of us glimpses beyond the curtain, we see all that we are capable of seeing – monsters made of the familiar rearranged.* The words had brought some clarity, but it wasn't they who kept his sheets dry.

Dreams stopped the moment he crossed the ornate arches, leaving him peace whilst between the Citadel's marble walls. At first, he thought it was the feathered bed or the lush blankets that weighed him down at night – maybe the velvet draperies that hung the walls – but he learned soon enough that it wasn't extravagant wealth that kept his nights peaceful. It was the brazier in the corner of each bed chamber, spouting cedar smoke laced with the tree's soft needles and the leaves of a snowberry. It drifted beneath the high ceilings, servants dropping handfuls of greenery by the hour just like his men did now. The surrounding flames spouted the sour smoke in hopes of keeping the monsters at bay, but as his soul entered yet another vessel, he hoped desperately that this time they would succeed. The smoke wouldn't keep him safe forever.

There were four bodies off to the side, each a failed attempt, each with a soul that was left detached and wandering among the flames. It wasn't that his men were incompetent – far from it. But they were inexperienced. They haven't studied the arts like he had nor have they experienced spotty guidance of mountain hermits, wise women or savage druids. All they had to follow were words and images he could deposit inside their minds. With that alone, even the most talented apprentices would be expected to cycle through a hundred subjects before nearing success. They had to manage with five.

The first one was bled too quick – there wasn't enough fluid for the heart to move the life around, and so, it gave up on a futile job. The second, a boy barely bordering adulthood, was a far better attempt. His spirit would make slow spirals inside its misty home seeming ready to surrender and detach, but when he tried to displace it, its spark returned and collapsed the entire vessel in a thunderous implosion. Lightning chained inside near striking both of them out of existence. Sparrow got out in time to see the boy's final twitches. It was his fault – he wasn't gentle enough in coaxing the boy into whatever after life he had been promised. If he were a little more careful, the others could have lived, and he *did* regret their deaths. He never intended for them, but this wasn't the time to mourn. The next two attempts were a complete failure, so much so, that he expected to spend another day drifting the currents in search of peasants unfortunate enough to pick today to wander these woods. But as he watched blood trickle down the thigh of a bard whose pathetic attempts at serenades couldn't make the lousiest of fantasies come true, a space formed. It was a clearance into which slithered.

Cold, so very cold, that was the first sensation to greet him. The coat had been warming him for so long, he couldn't remember the last time he felt it so. He didn't like it one bit. Any other day, he would have just reached out and leeched the heat from beneath the snow, from beneath the soil. But the vessel wouldn't let him. It was resisting and all the feelers that he spent decades to acquire were grasping at its shapeless walls just to hold on. It was dark too, either because there was nothing to be seen or that there was nothing to see with. His tongue wasn't moving either and ears refused to pick anything up. All that moved were his fingers – *they must have... or did they?* There was no way to know for certain.

"Breathing," said a voice as if through a wall. Cold and measured, he knew it.

"No instructions," said another, difficult to discern from the first.

"Dead?"

It was as if he was eavesdropping through a gap beneath the door. But he could hear. The body was beginning to offer the reins to its new owner.

"It worked. Well done," he said, voice the precise monotone he commanded since childhood. It passed through the air like a lord through an unwashed crowd – clear and decisive. He was ready to assume authority.

"Again?"

"Listen to me," he asserted tensing the tendons in his arm that should pull his fingers shut. "Listen!" No answer. He felt the urge to punish, lock them in a cold cell for two nights as if the fault was theirs. It wasn't, and he knew it. *They can't hear me because there is nothing to be heard.*

"See it?"

He felt pressure in his palm. Using all there was to spare, he pulled the same tendons he did before. His fingers came shut, grasping a crackled, cold oblong.

"His foot!"

The oblong tried to escape his grip but he wouldn't let go. He could feel the back dragging against the snow, the skin, bare, grated by the frozen crystals of the crumbling top layer. The muscles began to ache. He tensed them, pulling the shoulder blades together.

"Sparrow."

A marble slate loosening to that final hammer tap, the body surrendered. Limbs, digits, even the tongue, once again he could sense them. They were numb, clumsy, and foreign. It had only been a few days since he had them – they should have been familiar – yet, controlling them was awkward and indirect. Hearing alone resembled in feel the handling of a horse with spurs and bridle, as if he were a rider of his own senses. It was the same with pumping of the heart, with movement of his diaphragm – he was holding a hundred reins as if trying to rob the Emperor's stables. It was so easy in the body he was born into. It was easier to be an owl. Drifting the southern currents in search of prey, sense picking up the tiniest of movement, connectedness to the world and the hunt – the dive, sinking talons, grating of bone. Flesh he tore away so fresh warm and runny, it tasted better than the finest of meals to grace the Emperor's table. In a way, he was still the owl, but how could he? The owl lay discarded on the ground. He could see it there – he could see.

Still and unblinking, three faces stared down from above. Each differed in features like a boar from a pig, yet in his mind they were one and the same – he never had the need to make a distinction between them. They were three appendages of one beast, three prongs of a single tool. He trained them to be so, and so they became. No views, no opinions, they were purposed to observe, collect, inform, and if needed, to act as directed without hesitation. He was the master and they were his hounds. Yet, unlike a hound, they had no names – neither real nor pseudonyms given whilst in his service. They had no need. They were extensions of his will, and forever would the months of their forging haunt him with guilt. The tools he used... they were tools made necessary by the context of their time and the time to dwell on their use wasn't now.

With utter focus, he forced the body to sit. The frozen ground burnt his anus. He looked down to see breasts sat atop layers of ribboned folds. They were breasts of a man whose body suffered decades of neglect. He couldn't bear looking at them.

There was blood pooled in a slush beneath his thighs, seeped out of wounds now closed with needle and thread. Draining was needed for the ritual just like the scorching circle around them. The flames began turning to embers making way to more smoke. Hundred wisps merged to a column overhead to obscure the sky, making the stars above seem like children hiding behind a twirling grey tapestry. It wouldn't be long before last of the berry leaves would burn and the smoke would be just that of cedar and the soul taker would be free to collect his due – five souls ripe for plucking. He could feel their despair, the panicked flutter as they scrambled about the circle, clueless in their detachment. Their screams would fill the void as they struggle against the soul taker grasp. They will find no hope. Despite his deepest wishes, that wasn't his concern – it couldn't be. His concerns were not for the few but for the many for whose sake they gave up their lives. *May your keepers be kind.*

Rising through the branches and high above crowns, having served its purpose, the smoke was no more than a beacon guiding curious peasants to their position. Whether armed or not, that was irrelevant. Peasants meant attention. Enough attention, and someone of importance was bound to look into it. The last thing he needed was one of Nurhdvalian marshals meddling in his affairs. The king had signed, many nobility too, but it wasn't them who held the loyalty of men with pointy sticks. They had to move.

There was already a cloak over his shoulders and a set of clothes on his lap. He worked the fingers over the trousers trying to part their waist. The thumbs weren't bending right – they weren't arching. Instead, they uselessly twiddled the loose strands sticking off the fabric. It took several frustrating attempts to open up the trousers far enough for a leg to fit through. *Almost there,* he thought, encouraging himself to put on *a pair of fucking trousers.* He bent forward while folding the left leg out of the way. As he moved the trousers forth, the fingers released and the trousers dropped into a heap. The three men looked on without a hint of expression. He despised everything about that moment.

With all his will, he moved for the trousers again, getting a foot in, then a whole leg. Coarse strands, loose weave, poor stitching, they were the clothes of a man who couldn't afford better – likely, possessions of the man who occupied the body before him. He shuddered, struggling to manoeuvre his other foot into the trouser, just as hounds began howling in the distance.

*

"Hel... me," he mouthed with a tongue carved of wood. The three picked him up, working the opening of a greasy tunic over his head. He felt shame at his own helplessness, but as the glare of countless torches began to halo in gaps between the trees, the shame turned to reluctant gratitude.

He could hear voices now, words nearing clarity, but too many sounding at once to make out any single word. He had seen many villages turn to a mob. *But at this time?* It was cold, and it was dark, and that made it an even bigger concern than it otherwise would have. There was little needed to excuse a riot in daytime boredom, but on a cold night, it takes reasons dear to drive an entire village into the woods. It would have been foolish to think that these reasons had nothing to do with what they had done.

One of the three lifted him from underarm. They were running. He tried moving each leg to match the pace but, despite his utter focus, his legs lagged far behind. The fire was before them. He had to jump but the legs would not – all that moved him was the man underarm.

"Urgh," he yelped as his foot grazed the embers. Snow gave some relief as his feet sunk into it, then they sunk further. He was dragging, footprints turning to trenches in his futile efforts to keep up. His men left none. They were floating on the snow, pouncing in long strides leaving little more than a dent, all except the man beneath his arm. They were falling behind, inches stretching to yards. Then the two ahead split their paths, disappearing in the trees.

"Aaaaaaaa!" a woman shrieked as the other voices crashed together in a distressed rabble. The hounds barked as if rabid. *They're at the site.*

Sparrow turned the head jaggedly towards the circle. He could see women and men as they flinched and twitched, circling the site in confusion trying to make sense of it all. The purpose would have been clear – in their imaginations at least – though many would refuse to believe it. They would lock it away somewhere deep inside their heads only to speak of it in hushed voices once their children were put to sleep. They would be tales of derangement and murder that the youngsters would regret eavesdropping on through the gap beneath the door.

Before the site could vanish amongst the trees, he spotted a dog at the edge of the embers. The dog spotted him too. It barked, wagged its tail, then jumped over the glowing ring. Shaggy brown thing, it pounced through the snow with its tongue hanging out the side of its mouth as its belly dragged in the white dusting. Two others were close behind but all he could make out of them were fangs coated in mucus and sticking out sharp out of purple gums.

"Look! The dogs got somethin'!"

"It must be the fuckers who did this! Let's go! Get 'em!"

The mob needed no encouragement. Men and women jumped over the fire's remnants and began violently shuffling through the snow. Each step sent a dusting of snow in the air, shovelling a path for those who weren't as desperate to catch the culprits. Despite the fury driving their handicapped run, they were far behind and getting further with each stride. Even the man burdened by Sparrow's new expanse of flesh was making better pace than any one of the peasants.

The unwashed serfs can't see us, he thought. Their eyes were wandering from flank to flank, and with the poorly wrapped torches being their only source of light, he doubted they could even see the trees ahead. But the hounds could. And the hounds were closing in.

Each leap brought the gaping jaws closer. The likelihood of an escape was diminishing with each over encumbered step of his man. *Where are they?* He would have reached them if needed, but even his pathetic attempt at running took so much focus that there were no feelers he could spare for even the simplest message. *They must be scouting, the bastards!* They had to come back and deal with *this*.

He could hear the snow crumpling beneath paws.

There was no one coming back, no one to the side, only grey trees in front, and a mob and teeth behind. His heart was pounding. He hadn't noticed it before – he thought it a distant background noise – but now that he has, it was disconcerting. It was a fault, an opening in his psyche that allowed a cold, constricting fear to begin creeping in.

Come back! He wanted them back. He wanted them back right now. He needed them. The hounds' frenzy – he could hear it in their snarling and see it in their eyes. They were so close and any moment they would leap. He had to try connecting, and so, he let go. The body went limp – the eyes, dark. He immediately tried to latch back on, but he was a child again, getting cocky while riding his father's gelding. There was nothing else to be done but fall as the dead weight of his body pulled them both to the ground.

His eyes opened to a mass of fur and teeth flying towards them.

"Argh!" A muscular jaw snapped shut on the back of his man's thigh. He braced himself for the same, wrapping arms around his neck as the other black furred beast leapt straight towards his neck. A streak of phlegm trailed out its mouth. His eyes closed anticipating the pain, a reflex he no longer seemed to have a choice over.

Thump. The collision blew the air out his chest and knocked him prone. His arms failed to keep his neck safe. It was a stupid way to go and so soon after returning to this world. The beast's paws were digging into his chest, and soon, its teeth would dig into his throat. His eyelids clenched tight.

The soul taker is watching, he knew that for sure. The creature was ready to take him, catch him before he would have even a slither of a chance to escape. But there was no bite. *Why isn't he biting?*

His ears heard growling, felt the weight, but there was little else. He opened his eyes to see the shaggy brown dog lunge off of his chest towards the snarling black beast. The two met, fangs scraping mouth and nostrils, then pounced back to snarling at the other from a bow. Then another pounce. The black dog was bigger, much bigger – with weight alone, he was pushing the brown dog enough for his hind legs to scrape Sparrows neck. Blood began to drip from its muzzle, but the shaggy thing didn't relent. The two lunged again – more blood. The brown dog yelped. They stayed locked, black dog's jaws sunken into the brown's flank. It bit back but got only fur. It tried again, a sluggish effort that missed once more. In a single motion, the black dog lifted it off the ground and tossed it to the side. It fell by a woman's feet.

The peasants had caught up, murder in their minds painted clear on their faces.

"Fucker killed my dog!" yelled a ruffian pointing to Sparrow's man. He turned to see the other dog laid open by his feet. A steaming pile of purple worms lay in the snow beside it, escaping its underside through a gash running its entire length. His man stood poised over its mass, bloodied knife at the ready. The remaining hound took one glance over the scene before scuttling to the safety of its owner's hind.

The peasants began to circle – his man couldn't allow that. He dashed quicker than the woman could react, spearing the blade under her ribcage. Her toes made spirals in the snow as he pulled the blade out. This was enough to put doubt into the unwashed mass. He pounced back to Sparrow's side.

The peasants were still advancing on the flanks. He lunged, seeming to lose balance and dropping to ground – it would have been an awkward fumble if there wasn't an axe flying over his head. The moment it cleared where his head had been, he was balanced once more. A scythe came from his flank, but its blade was already too far to be of any danger. He took its stave on the ribs, locked it down with his arm. A surprised moan left the peasant's rotting mouth as his own scythe slipped his grip and slid into his bowels. The man was back at Sparrow's side.

"Demon," came a gasp.

There was doubt creeping into their beady eyes. A few of them stood near the back began slipping away into the night, following the treaded paths back to their bog. Each one that left seemed to weaken the mob's resolve, giving yet another reason to escape the man none of them could out skill. *They will run,* and for a moment he truly believed that. It was a moment that promptly vanished.

"What are you doing?!" boomed a voice as if it had echoed through the depths of a cavern. A grisly man grabbed the ear of a youth trying to slip away, pulling him back so forcefully it seemed he was going to tear it off. "Rush the bastard! Go, go!" Looming more than two heads over all others, he began to beat and kick the mob as if spurring a skittish horse. All it took was for a few to charge – the rest followed. They screamed out of rage. They screamed out of terror.

The peasants came from three sides – all together, all at once. Sparrow's man gave him a glance, then braced for impact. One by one, they would have been feeding the forest's vermin for the next week, but all his man managed was to lose his blade in a fleshy belly. There were bodies all about, they were everywhere – no light and no air. A hundred hands grasped blindly determined to tear, rip, and kill. There was no holding them off. A hoe cracked down. His man slumped to the ground.

"Kill him!" someone screeched as a dozen feet began to stomp. "For Bronie! For Kuarl!"

The smaller bones of the man's hands and feet were crunching beneath the strikes. An axe dropped and came back dripping.

Once the corpse had no more satisfaction to give, the mob left it like flies lifting off of dried up shit. A pitchfork was sunken in his chest all the way to the crossbar – a dirt smeared farmer was trying to get it loose. The suction of flesh wouldn't let go and his man's torso rose with each tug. A youth just as filthy gave his head a kick. The others stared down at Sparrow still laid on the ground. *They're going to kill me and I won't be coming back.* His crotch was wet and cold – he had pissed himself. When, he didn't quite know. They were looking him over, staring down, though not in anger. Their eyes had little fire left in them – the way they looked at him, it was as if they were looking at a skirt of rotten venison from which maggots were beginning to spawn.

"Why did the gods spare *you*?"

*

"Where is Bronie, you fat bastard?!" a small man spat the words down at him. The light cast by the torches played with the features of his pitted face, elongating, casting features no man should have.

"She's back there, with the others, Guunt," replied a ruffian, nonchalant, with the black dog stuck to the inside of his thigh. "She's dead."

"Shhaaa! Don't speak like that," a woman scalded. "You're always saying the worst things. For once, be hopeful, Sander."

"Hopeful?" he snickered. "You saw that back there – you saw it all. That monster cut the four of them to pieces and all that survived was Knute. Fucking Knute gets to live and Alr and Bronie and Kuarl and Stina die. If I knew it was just him left, would have stayed home and Sof wouldn't have been spilled open right fucking here."

"We don't know that they're dead," said the woman returning far meeker.

"Of course they're fucking dead! Now stop that stupid talk." The black beast growled from between his legs. "What's that, Tof?"

The shaggy brown dog limped leaving a moist red trail in his hind. Each step was a slow and pained effort that brought him closer and closer until he was close enough to lay his head in Sparrow's lap.

"Huh. Stupid mutt, thought he could jump Tof. Should put him down right now," said Sander, half raising his axe in intent.

"He was defending his master," rumbled the giant. "Put that axe down before I break it." Sander turned round with fists clenched but having to strain his neck to meet the man's gaze changed his mind. He turned back to count the hairs atop his dog's head. The giant moved past him reaching for Sparrow's hand. "No one should have to go through that, Knute. Stand now."

They think I'm him, or at least the dog thought so, sprawled out over his lap and twitching its tail. A minute ago, he was sure he would be beaten to death just as his man was. Now, someone was taking pity on him.

He grabbed the man's wrist and the man his. It seemed all made of tendons and veins, packed tight together around an unusually thick bone that ran far longer than his – so did the man's torso and all his limbs. He truly was a giant, or more likely, half. Bones, eyes, skin – they all pointed to that. It took little to no effort on his part to bring Knute's spoiled body to its feet – a lot less than it took for Sparrow to keep it standing. He managed. He held his footing as urine ran down the side of his leg.

With Sparrow up, the giant turned to the mutt. "Come here, puppy." He scooped up the brown dog with a single hand. It winced, letting out a squeak as it was lifted in the cradle that was the man's hand. Held tight and still, the dog seemed content in the giant's grip, but it also paid him no mind – the dogs eyes were stuck on Sparrow.

Must have been his dog. The way it stared, and more so the way it charged a far bigger beast, he had no doubt that the shaggy brown thing belonged to this Knute – the man it thought him to be. It wouldn't have risked its life if it weren't so, and that is no small ask even for a creature so simple. There were many well documented methods of inducing obedience and loyalty that the scholars recorded, and likely, many more they chose not to. Fear, love, reward – the study of each spanned volumes authored by fools and magisters alike and each was credited with some of the most valiant and horrendous deeds done by man. Yet, they were also capricious, unpredictable, and dangerously reliant on the subject's decisions. For his men, like the one minced into the snow but a foot away, he used methods far different. He hoped that after all this he would never have to use them again. Looking at his man, he felt a pang of loss, but it was the mourning of a carpenter having lost a prized hammer. The regret, the sadness, and the self-loathing, it already took place a decade ago when he shaped the man and made him his. There was more to be felt for the dog.

The mob turned back to wherever they called home beginning a journey that, though of same distance, would feel so much longer and so much colder. Anger carried them here for a purpose most would see as righteous – it kept them warm, it moved their legs, and thought their thoughts. But once the deed was done, as it always does and always did, anger left them cold, tired, and alone in cleaning up the mess it left in their loins. They walked in silence, eyes on the woods, feet dragging in reluctant steps. None of them wanted to deal with what lay ahead – not that it mattered.

A woman's foot was first to step into the circle of embers. Death laid here, corpses of loved ones taken so suddenly, bled in a ritual that must have seemed so strange, discarded and piled up like manure. They paused looking at them from a distance, each with toes behind an imagined line so that proximity wouldn't burden them with responsibility. Some even refused to look – *family,* he figured – their eyes stuck to the snow but inches away, delaying the inevitable for as long as they could. The small man was the first to look.

"Bronie!" he exclaimed, as tears began to flow down the cracks in his face. In streams, they dripped onto his rough-spun tunic. He fell atop a pale calf that stuck out from the tangle of bodies, squeezing it into himself as if that could bring the woman back to life. A few others followed behind him, though they did so without a word.

Some occupied themselves with stupidity, stripping bits of cloth to wrap those who needed them the least – fulfilment of burial rites. Other's simply looked on, resigning themselves to silence. None of them paid him any mind – it was as if he didn't exist. Whatever attention he held while sprawled on the ground, faded quickly. *I could run and they wouldn't even realise.* Even if they did, he doubted anyone would follow. It struck him as odd – the lack of concern for the fat man. Was he not one of them? He had been taken from their village like anyone in the pile, yet no one seemed to care. The giant seemed to – briefly – but his concern wasn't that of someone who liked or even respected Knute, it was that of a man honour bound to help those in need. The only creature to acknowledge him was the wounded dog in the giant's hand – he wouldn't stop staring.

"We must move. Farewells can be given once we're back between our walls, with our families," said the giant looking about for anyone who thought otherwise. But there was no challenge. The peasants were ready. Having wrapped the bodies to preserve some of the dignity, they all wanted to leave this place – even the weeping Guunt. He stood straight with back bare to the night's air, his tunic covering the girl laid stiff between his arms. Slowly, they began to walk. Sparrow followed.

I will recover in their midst and move on as soon as I can. Slipping away in a body he had little control over would bring death and, more than likely, one caused by something stupid like exposure from twisting an ankle on a hidden root. With the little attention that Knute seemed to draw, there was no reason to risk that – a far more reasonable course of action was to simply hide in plain sight until he no longer had to. For now, walking without falling to ground was concern enough.

A shiver took over a peasant's shoulders. Before she could rub it out, it spread to the shoulders of another... then another until they all marched shivering in the cold. The sun was beginning to rise behind the trees, the sky overhead brightening with every passing moment. They were bound to see it soon as the trees loosened. Yet, even as they broke the tree line, the sun remained hidden, haloing the silhouette of a giant porcupine.

It was a mound of rubbled rocks covered in a fluffing of snow. A thousand tree trunks carved to a point protruded out of it, vertically for the most part with a few slim ones pointing out like spears over the ledge of a shield wall. *How crude*, and it was that, yet he couldn't help but admire the effort to construct a barricade so formidable. The entrance was a difficult thing to find, enough so that even on the third visit one would need to retrace the peasants' steps to find the thick wooden gate. By its side stood four ragged men.

"Morning to you! Been walking the woods for good health?" jested the greyest of them. The sight of bodies and bloodied faces promptly turned his jovial demeanour. "I'm sorry, Sigrid. We just need supplies and we'll be gone. We have gold."

The giant looked him down as if weighing in his head a difficult choice. The men before him began shifting in their boots, hunger clear in their hollowed faces. "Make the square your home, Vas, but nothing else," he finally answered. The boom of his voice was recognised on the other side of the gate and it was promptly unbarred. A sigh of relief seemed to escape the old Vas.

The barricade surrounded a settlement of tightly packed huts built so close that, shoulder to shoulder, two grown men would struggle to march through. There were no doors to be seen at first, no windows, no gaps – just rows of wood and poorly mortared stone with tight thatching for cover. Any opening in the house facade, however insignificant, faced to the centre of the village. At every corner, there were hemp bound barricades of sharpened stakes ready to be lifted and block any potential intruders in a maze of bottlenecks and dead alleys. He has seen it before, and rather often whilst in fortified imperial cities. The barricades at the mouth of each alley, the hidden windows and doorways, the tight corridors – they were common with the empire – but seeing the same approach taken by peasants of a village that an usurping warlord wouldn't even defecate in seemed bizarre. It was a peasant fortress.

One or two at a time, the peasants were swallowed up by the homes. Doors promptly shut behind them. The mob was dispersing.

"Mommy!" a girl burst out of a door as it opened, tackling the blood soaked skirts of a spectrally thin woman. The two promptly disappeared to the sound of slamming timber.

A muffled moo escaped through the mortar of a nearby home as Sander went inside. His black dog barked twice before yelping into silence in the middle of what would have been the third. Another cow mooed.

By the time they reached the centre of the cluster, it was him and the giant. The giant was looking down at him. His foot was on the first step of a home far taller and wider than the rest as his eyes asked the most obvious of questions – *why are you still here?* The true answer – that he didn't know where to go – would have been far inadequate for someone who lived there. For the first time in a decade, he didn't know what the right answer was. They stood and stared in a silence that was becoming increasingly more uncomfortable, eyes in contact until, finally, the giant broke it. He looked down at the dog in his hand, face relaxing as if in understanding.

"Do not worry. I will make him bindings. He will be good – his wounds are not deathly," he said, gently lifting the shaggy dog. It seemed there was more he wanted to say, but the words seemed to have gotten stuck somewhere between his mind and tongue. It took significant contemplation before he could say, "you come in too. My home will be better for you than the back of some shit piled barn."

9

"There is far less danger to an idiot who understands how little he knows than a wise man certain he knows anything at all," – Magister Septinelius, after being stripped of all merits.

Before the thing could speak, he felt a pull on the shoulder... then another. First soft, the next much harder – hard enough to pull him out of the nightmare – he awoke in sweats, ready for the thing's twig like fingers to snatch him and put him inside its satchel. But the thing was gone, in its place was Torgy lit up by the flickering flame of a lantern.

"We need it back." Torgy's other hand was clutching onto his shoulder, gripping tightly as if he were a rung atop a tall ladder. Eyes fixed on his, the rogue looked at him as if expecting something, expecting him to remember. He didn't, and noticing that, Torgy clarified, "the blouse. We need the wizard's blouse. Stupid, so stupid – I shouldn't have done that. Should have held onto it myself... *why* the fuck did I care what he thought?! Bastards are working together now – they want it all."

"Why you here? What happen?" *Blouse*. Roused so suddenly, he wasn't sure if the man was real or not... and the monster. *Why is he here?*

"Balthar's cock," Torgy cussed, "I'm here because I trust you, Erkii. You're strong and you're honest, and I need someone strong and honest to help me look after the people – our people." Erkii sat up in his bunk, yet Torgy's hand remained on his shoulder. "We need to take the blouse. It's a treasure of kind we will never find again, and without it, we will all be stuck hiding in this fucking swamp. Bern's gonna steal it – I can feel it – and the boy is working with him."

He looked across to where Urkii laid for sleep but the mound was far too small for him to still be laid among the furs. *Urkii?* He may have gone for a piss or a walk to help him sleep – both were a likely thing for the big man to do – yet, he worried. Something wasn't right. *It was a dream,* he told himself, but the dream didn't seem to be fading – the fear of the thing remained, and deep down, it felt as if the thing remained too. From a hiding, it was watching. "You see Urkii?"

"Urkii?" Torgy scrunched his brow. "No. He must be shitting in the woods. We need to go – now." He wanted to check on his brother, but the urgency in Torgy's voice was enough for Erkii to put his worry aside. *He's fine.* If anyone could look after himself, it was his brother.

He moved the mound of furs aside letting the cool air bite into his damp skin. One of them had a hole for his head with a few more attached to it with hempen cord – like for most here, his daytime wraps doubled as a setting for sleep. In the lantern's flicker, he searched the floor for the belt that would keep the furs about him. It was by Torgy's nodding foot. As soon as it was on, the rogue put out his lantern and ducked for the entrance.

On their knees, they pushed through the fold between the heavy hides that kept the chill out of the mud hut and crawled through the short tunnel of packed snow built around its entrance. White bear cubs being birthed, they emerged onto the beaten path on all fours. He was going to stand but Torgy kept him down with his hand, a finger of the other pressed to his lips gesturing for silence. He felt as if he was tending Sylthian sewers once again, crawling sticky in their filth. Somehow this felt worse. They were plotting, *playing shacklers' games*. The busy work of spoiled gluttons who paint their faces white as the Gharan sands. His father spat at their treachery and taught his sons to do the same, yet Erkii still followed the rogue down a single thread of the trodden web.

They snuck between the buried huts that littered their little part of the forest. Jonathen's mound would have sat at the foot of the same hill that theirs did, that is, if he were able to build it. As it was, his efforts were so pathetic that the first Autumn storm blew it down and left him drenched. In the morning, they found him naked by the great fire, shivering as he tried to soak up heat from its embers. The brigands took pity on him and housed him in a hut vacated by a boar who refused to be stuck or rather the dirty wound that the beast left. It was bad luck to sleep under the roof of deceased whose blood you didn't share. *You'll be haunted, boy,* Vas told him. The boy shrugged him off – and maybe rightly so – Torgy and he were the first thing to come.

The rogue went hands first into the dig out that served as the entrance. Half way in he paused, feet unmoving for a moment before disappearing. Erkii followed. *Tight, Urkii would be stuck,* he thought of the big man trying to squeeze through as his hand touched sludge. It was melted snow on its way to freezing again. It reeked of piss. He suddenly understood why Torgy stopped half way through. Arms length ahead the dig out turned upwards into the hut. He could feel the sludge soaking through to his knees as he wiggled himself inside next to Torgy. The rogue didn't seem to notice – in the dimly lit home, his face was that of a child caught stealing from the apple basket.

"What'd I tell you, boy?" Bern's raspy voice cut through the silence of the night. "He'll come to kill you in the night 'cause of that fuckin' shirt. Greedy bastard he is, he'd rather kill you than have to share his precious gold." The brute was squatting across a small pile of glowing embers, and to his side was a stack of furs. Jonathen was sat on it, straight as a spring's sprout, the whites of his eyes on clear display in the dim light. Something shimmered in Bern's hand.

Torgy took a crouched step towards him.

"Careful now," hissed Bern. "The boy is a screamer. Will wake the whole camp up before you can make it anywhere near. You want them all in here voting like some pompous twats on what we'll do with this?" He shook his hand letting out shimmering folds of the precious blouse.

Jonathen was mumbling under breath, "He com to kih you. He 'l co to kihl you." His words were those of a toddler learning his first tongue, yet even so, their meaning was easy to comprehend.

"That's right boy. He'll come to kill you – just as I told you."

"He did. You were right."

"Now, quiet boy," Bern hissed, flicking the back of Jonathen's hand with an open palm. His strike stopped the mumbling.

"We're not here to kil–"

"The words of every killer caught in the act," Bern cut in.

Torgy moved his eyes from the boy to the brute. His face squeezed and turned before he hissed, "What the fuck was that at the fire?! How am I supposed to trust you after that?!" Torgy's hiss neared a shout but Bern calmly spoke over him, composed as before.

"You were going to kill the boy, take the treasure, and run off with your pet Gharans." Torgy was louder – not that it mattered – the only person who needed to hear him was Jonathen, and the red haired boy was hanging onto the brute's every word.

"We not kill! Take cloth," said Erkii, his booming voice putting them to silence. It didn't last long.

"Take cloth" Bern's mouth twisted in a mockery. "Idiot. You're not taking anything. Now get crawling! Back through the piss!" His raspy voice rang loud in the small hut. Hands raised high, he forced the last two fingers of his hand against the thumb, striking them to the slick sound of the shackler's click. It was the sound a displeased master made to send slaves away to their hovel.

Erkii's body tensed, shrinking in on itself in a pathetic, defensive motion. There was no choice, no decision to be made behind what his body did. It was instinct. *Beating, another beating.* His mind was that of a slave again, small and helpless, accepting of the punishment he *deserved*. The master was fair. He had to do better. The piss soaked snow squelched through the gaps between his fingers.

"I bet your girls wouldn't run like that, would they?" Bern's voice carried over his shoulder as he emerged out into the woods.

"Threatening my girls, Bern?" Torgy's voice was drowning behind Erkii's own breath.

"Don't know anything about–" A loud crack was followed by Torgy's wince. "Keep your hands away from that boot! I'll spear you through the eyeball 'f you try that again!

A sound of limbs scraping through snow, then Torgy emerged out the entrance. The night was coming to an end and the sky's hue began to brighten into that of a clear, spring day. Torgy's nose was broken.

"Why did you leave me?" asked Torgy, snorting up blood that was trailing down to his chin. There was an accusation in his voice for which Urkii had no answer for. "They can't see me like this."

"Who?"

"No one can see me like this! We're going to the witch. Go!" Torgy's voice broke like that of an adolescent as he abruptly took off. His feet moved erratically, half walking, half running, leaving Erkii to keep up as he made his way between the litter of huts.

They moved over the frozen marshes – the little good that the winter brought. With the longer days bringing a promise warmth, it wouldn't be long before they would again be a pit of near impassible treachery. As it was, their only worry was tripping over buried bushels as someone else had done in the hours passed – there were impressions of a man left along the way, each followed with short trenches kicked into the snow from frustration. Whoever it was, failed to notice the withering tracks left yesterday that Torgy and he made, choosing instead to force his own way to the witch's hut. *Urkii*.

*

By the time they reached Mertle's hut, the sun was wide awake. It was shining through the gaps in the swamp's looser growth, blinding them as they climbed up hill to the moulding door. Sweet, pungent smoke poured out the tiny gaps between wall and rafter of Mertle's hut. Its hazy windows were softly aglow. Torgy knocked.

"Go on! Mertle's voice come muffled through the gaps between the door's slabs. "Let them in, boy! Don't know what your mother told you, but that spoon won't fly away!"

The hut's walls shook as heavy footsteps came in closer to the door. It opened to the sight of Urkii bending down as not to put a hole in thatching with his head.

"Brother," he spoke in their tongue then turned to the other man, "Friend Torgy." Erkii leaned in to embrace him but Urkii was already walking away and all he managed was a pat on his turned back.

"Urkii," Torgy nodded, a thick drop of blood detaching from his nose. "Mertle."

"I saw– *ruhgh*!" the witches words came from somewhere near the fire, chased by a coughing fit.

"You saw what?"

"*Rugh ugh!* The blood dripping on my door you imbecile," she was sitting by the fire wrapped in so many furs and blankets that she seemed little more than a laundry pile. All that could be seen of her was face and hands which moved in short, controlled motions, whittling obscure shapes out of knotty timber.

"I... wha–"

"Don't make me come over there, *boy*!" she waved the little knife that sat between her finger and thumb at Torgy.

130

"This one's already been keeping me up all night with his stomping – so bleeding big and heavy it's like I'm keeping livestock in here. My floor's going to sink in is what's going to happen. *I need to feed her,* he remembers in the middle of the night – like she's going somewhere. Now wipe the bloody thing up, Torgy… and yes, yes! I will fix it up soon." Everything said, Mertle continued to whittle.

Torgy stood there for a moment twiddling about, looking for something on Mertle's bench. Not having found it, he dropped to his knees and began to wipe the floor with his sleeve. With the little light coming from either flames and windows, it was difficult to tell whether he cleaned the splatter or rubbed it farther and further into the wood's grain. Mertle didn't seem concerned – putting Torgy on his knees was enough to bring her out of the mound of furs and blankets.

"It's the break of dawn," she mumbled as she walked, each step paired with a creek of wood or bones, "middle of winter, everyone sleeping in peace and, somehow, you get your nose broken in two – hold still!" Gripping Torgy's hair with the left, she pinched his nose with the right, tugging and twisting it with a crackle. Her head moved from side to side, observing from all angles as Torgy's face contorted in pain.

"Ahh–"

"Shush! I've known toddlers tougher than you. There!" She took a step back from her handiwork, ripped two nettle leaves out of a dried bunch that laid on her table, then rolled them between finger and thumb into little balls. "Put these up there and let them sit – it will stop the swelling. Now, tell me what happened."

As told, Torgy pushed the little dried up leaves up his nostrils, flinching as he did. "Bern." Mertle's mouth curved to a wolfish smile.

"So, it's finally happened – the dog finally bit you." Her voice was laced with satisfaction, that of a mother whose child experienced exactly what they were told. "Oh, I still remember you two stumbling in all those years ago, you in that stupid cloak and he stuck to your hind, smirking as if it was the king who was on the run from you. That gait you walked with – you were two mean cockerels tossed into a new roost. Only the roost already had cockerels in it, and they were much bigger and meaner than you. So you learned to accept that, and as hard as that was, it turned out well for you – you found a hen and fathered two precious, little chicks with golden locks. But you forgot how to be that mean cockerel. Bern did not."

"I still remember," he said with bits of green hanging out of his nose.

"Oh Torgy," she sighed, smile faded. "I hope you do. I really, really do, because the next time he puts your tail in a curl, you might not make it back here."

The rogue opened his mouth as if to say something but closed it soon after. He turned to the door, walking in a stutter of short steps and two awkwardly long. They put him too close to the door so that his body stopped it from opening. He struck it with an elbow before moving himself about and out.

"Yes, go on. See your children," said Mertle as Torgy moved into daylight. The door shut shaking the frame. "He won't make it," she mumbled as soon as it did.

Urkii was by Einsleigh's cot. Though sat on the floor, the big man still towered over the narrow bed frame and the woman laid atop. He held a spoon, his eyes seeming fixed to its tip as he moved it carefully through the air towards the woman's mouth. Tenderly, he would push her lip down with the bottom of the spoon before slowly drooling pale sludge into her mouth. He was feeding her the oat soup they've come to know so well through this northern winter, and though it would have never been either of their choice of a meal – if they were ever given a choice – its frequent shortage made him grow quite fond of it.

"She's sleeping, dear brother. But I think she will be okay," said Urkii in the warm comfort of their native tongue. "Look! She's swallowing." And she really did, throat contracting then relaxing, moving the food down to her stomach. Yet, besides that and laboured breathing, Einsleigh gave no sign of life. The spoon circled the bowl, scraping up the oat gruel into a heaped spoonful. Erkii's stomach rumbled. He hasn't eaten since the morning of their excursion, and now that there was food before him, he could think of nothing else but his own hunger.

"How long have you been here?" he asked, mostly to force his mind to think of something else. *Maybe I could have a bowl?*

"A while, brother," Urkii answered, putting the spoon to Einsleigh's mouth. "It was dark and cold still when I came here. I was a little worried about the witch – that she would be angered by someone waking her at this time of the night. She is a powerful woman," he said, flicking his chin towards Mertle, "and I was scared of knocking. But she opened the door before I had the chance to."

"Strange. Why wasn't she sleeping?" he asked.

"I have been wondering that since the moment I came here. Quite honestly, I think it is worry that keeps her up – or even fear. Remember how they talk of her – that she has amazing powers?"

"I remember – they really do talk a lot. They're scared that she will turn them into frogs or send down frost wights to take their children in the night. Do you believe it?"

"I believe they believe it, and if they do, there must be reasons. They say she can see the future too. Maybe that is what scares her?"

He glanced towards Mertle, his eye immediately meeting hers. She looked as if every word of their language was clear to her. *She can't understand* – very few here, if any, would have been able to. And doubtlessly, if she spoke their tongue, they would have known a year ago, because what would have been the purpose of keeping it secret? *Maybe she can use her powers to understand.* "I would rather it wasn't so," he replied before flicking his wrist towards the bowl. "Any more of that?"

"That pot over there," Urkii dipped his head sideways. There, an iron pot sat at the fire's edge with the boil of oats at its bottom growing a skin. *She wouldn't min–*

"No," said Mertle sharply before he even had a chance to reach for the warm sludge. "You need to be hungry."

"Why?" he asked, indignant. There were hempen sacks all around, propped against the hut walls – doubtlessly one or two or maybe even three were filled with the precious grain that she now refused him a handful of. *Selfish hag.*

"You must be hungry," she said sternly.

"Yes!" he returned louder than intended. "I lot hungry! Many day no food!" He wasn't angry to start with, but now, being denied even the slightest drop of food – food that was already there – and by someone who he considered a friend, it was beginning to heat his head. *She can't stop me,* he told himself, reaching for the pot.

Ou! He flinched as something hit his knuckles. It bounced high and landed on the floor – the little piece of wood which Mertle was whittling.

"Do not touch it!"

"Why?" He rubbed his knuckles, feeling the scraped skin covering them.

"Because you need to be hungry for you to learn. Your entire being must be open to the world, and hunger is going to help with that. I told you I will teach you, boy, and I will do just that – as long as you follow my instructions."

He searched her face for signs of a joke. There were none he could see. He may find himself a fool soon enough, but in that moment, he was convinced the witch meant well.

"Learn?" he asked, finding a little calm amidst the rumbling.

*

His stomach was twisting like a chicken about to have its neck wrung. A constant discomfort he couldn't put to the back of his mind. And he tried. In a few more days he knew he would be used to it – the feeling fading away, coming back only if he made the mistake of thinking about it – but in the first few days, it was near impossible to stow that feeling away. So, starving and shivering, he sat in the snow staring across the frozen bog outside Mertle's home.

The witch would walk down every now and then, asking whether he felt something, or saw, or heard voices. Each time he answered *no* and each time she went back inside, screeching *clear your head*. He could feel the warm air rush past each time she slammed the door before it quickly melted in with the cold. He wanted to leave, go check on Torgy, have a meal, crawl back into their hut and sleep, yet for whatever reason, he didn't.

The ring was still in the folds of his wraps, stowed away right where he stuffed it. He was sure that the little bronze thing was what broke the ice that day, sending his brother into the freezing currents. But it may also have been Urkii's own weight. *The ice was too thick,* he kept telling himself though with a lot less conviction than he did last night. He was terrified to touch it at first, laying it on the furs as if it was to come to life and tear off his nostrils. It did not, and when he put it on, there was no sign of it being anything more than a bronze trinket. He flipped it around in his pocket, looking over the desolate landscape as his body screamed to be nourished.

He found it fascinating at first – back when they arrived – the white, the cold. Urkii and he would lay there for hours without clothes, bare skin to the snow, feeling it warm and turn to water under their backs. They watched it fall from the sky, hundreds and thousands of flakes slowly gathering, coming together to turn the entire world white. It was like watching a desert form before their eyes. Now, that desert had become the ordinary old he no longer cared for or thought of.

A dusting of snow shot up in the air as a hare pounced over a distant mound. Its legs moved in a flurry as it fled something beneath the snow. *Come out, thing, come on out and show yourself* – whatever it was had to show itself soon. It didn't. It was either too tired to chase or too busy chewing through a hare that wasn't as quick as its friend.

Mertle's door opened.

"Here. Eat it and go," she placed a bowl of boiled oats in his lap, the gruel long thickened to a wobbly, crusted solid.

"No stay?" he asked. "Learn."

"*Learn*… I see you out here fiddling about like a child told to scale a trout – twisting, turning, looking for *anything* to take your attention. I told you to clear your head." Mertle sighed. "Forget it, we will try again tomorrow." The woman turned and began to walk.

"Urkii here?"

"You could say that," she said without a pause, stepping indoors.

He stood in time with a fox, copper snout emerging out of the hidden burrow. Two hares were trapped in its teeth – one caught by the rear paw and other dangling by its neck. But a moment ago they were still moving, happy and content with their own existence, then something much more powerful came for a visit, something they could not foresee. Now, both were dead, but the fox would live. *Such is life,* his father would have said, and yet, it made him sad.

With its head weighed down, the fox carried his catch over the rise, disappearing into the swamp. The world returned to stillness as Erkii followed Mertle inside. Urkii was still sat by the cot, leaning forward. It was as if he was inspecting a stain or a hole punched in the hemp upholstery, trying to figure out how to mend it. Yet, he was also eerily still.

Brother? He stepped forth just as the big man folded. Bulky limbs stopped giving support and Urkii sprawled out on the side of the cot. His back rose slow and steady as a roaring snore stretched through the silent hut. Next to him laid the doe, and upon seeing him, she perked up with excitement.

"Erkii! Are you looking at me?! Thank the gods! Thank the gods you're here, Erkii! They can't hear me, you know? Not even the witch! I tried so much to get them to hear me, but they just can't seem to." The doe turned her snout in disappointment before jolting up in excitement. "How is everyone?! The others? Oh for the gods, you need to bring me back!"

Mertle let out a long grunt causing the doe's ears to prick up. "If that bloody noise carries on, I swear on all that is sacred... I don't know how, but I will drag that bloody oaf into the snow if he carries on snoring like that. Maybe I will put an ember down his trousers and let him do it himself."

The doe's ears had fallen. "She can't hear me," she mumbled resigned. "Can you, Erkii?"

"Yes, I can hear you," he replied.

"Of course you can hear me, you daft boy. It's your brother I'm talking ab– who are you speaking to?" she tore away mid sentence flicking a wrist towards the cot. "Is it her?"

"I am so glad! Urkii had been so caring, feeding me as if I was his baby – I can't even say thank you. Please, please, please, make sure to do that when he wakes up – but don't wake him," she said laying her chin on his brother's hand, "he needs his sleep."

"Are you talking to her again?" asked Mertle more insistent. He nodded, which caused her mouth to curl.

"Erkii, I need my body back. It is so lonely and cold here. You cannot see, but it's frightening here – I'm scared! There are things out here, watching and lurking, waiting for a chance to eat me. I don't want to be eaten. Help me, Erkii – make the witch bring me back!"

"What did she say?" asked Mertle, leaning in close to hear him speak.

"Scared. Thing want eat her."

"Of course she's scared, that's why she's still here! If she just let go, it would all be over and her soul could move on. Tell her that! Maybe you can change her mind."

He looked to the doe but all he saw was the cot buckling under the weight of Einsleigh and Urkii, though mostly Urkii. *Maybe if I close my eyes and then open...* he squeezed his eyelids shut, keeping them so for a moment. He opened them. The doe didn't return.

"She's not there is she?" Mertle asked a question then answered it herself, "No, of course not. I can tell by those faces you're making. Anything else she say?"

"She say – tell Mertle 'bring me back'."

Mertle turned her head from side to side, "Stupid girl, trying to change what she cannot change – what even I cannot change." For a moment, he thought there was a hint of sympathy in the witch's voice, a brief fault in her nonchalant mask – even her eyes seemed to show care as they hovered still over the cot. She released them with a shake of the head then shifted them to Erkii. With a withered hand, she nudged the bowl he held to his belly. "You better eat that."

*

Though the days have been growing in length, they still gave little time to accomplish anything of substance. By the time he left the witch's hut, the sun was already settling for rest, and Erkii looked forth to doing the same. Urkii chose to stay and keep watch over Einsleigh – much to Mertle's dismay – and so Erkii walked alone. He didn't mind. His feet seemed to step on their own, leaving his head to float.

We made good progress, she told him as he left out the door and he believed her. He saw spirits – Einsleigh's. He could and no one else. It was just the beginning and the expectation for what was to come turned to excitement that welled within his belly and filled it with warmth. The power he released into the ice was still there within him. It wouldn't be long before he could use it, wield it like the sorcerer who so carelessly slay three of the greatest fighters he had ever seen.

A flutter then a thud brought his head back to ground. Besides the beaten track stood two men, bows in hand, one's falling while the other's rising in draw. The fletching touched his cheek. He lined up the arrow, and he released – a flutter and a thud. The arrow sunk into a distant tree trunk, finding company in a dozen arrows already sunk. The two stood nothing alike – one shorter and stockier, the other crowned with a red mane. *Bern, Jonathen,* he made them out in an instant. The recognition forced his heart off beat.

He wanted to fall flat, cover himself in snow, wait till they left. Many a time he did so, hiding from a master's punishment – cowardice that ensured his survival. But the year of freedom, the power he now knew to be within, revived his pride and dropping down in fear was not something that pride would let him do. Though it did allow compromise, and so he steered off the path to circle through the woods behind their backs.

"You have been shooting a long time – I see that," he heard Bern's raspy voice from somewhere behind the white thickets. "Yet, still you aim like someone who hasn't snapped his first string."

Each step made the snow crunch as his feet sank through the top crust. He tried walking slower, dipping the feet with care, yet no matter how slow, the sounds he made seemed to echo. *Your imagination is making it louder,* likely, the tension he felt did the same. Outside his head, no one else would be listening as close as he.

"You must look with both eyes and both ears where you shoot. The arrows will follow."

Their talk will drown out any sound, he convinced himself, loosening a little in his step.

"I won't hit shit without looking down the arrow," said Jonathen, his voice that of an apprentice who forged for a hundredth time a nail not-good-enough.

"Stupid fucker. You won't hit shit this time nor the next thousand. But after that thousand, you'll be drawing and releasing as soon as you hear or see."

The thickets and trees gave him cover from sight, but as he reached the half point in his bypass, they parted. Looking down the clearing he saw both men, locked firm in place as Bern took a draw. The arrow reached his cheek, yet unlike his advice, he didn't release.

"Say, there's a deer," he spoke with the fletching brushing his beard, "and it's making new paths behind us."

What deer? He turned looking for a deer that wasn't there. He realised too late what Bern had meant.

"I hear it. I shoot."

The arrow whistled through the air, lodging itself in a tree to his flank.

"That's a special kind of deer – the Gharan deer. Cowardly thing, makes circles in the bushes when it's scared," Bern showed his crooked teeth. "And look how in its stupidity it stands."

He was right. His body was frozen stiff and trembling. *He will get me* – having hunted with Bern, he knew him to be a great shot and quick stalker. If he ran, he would be dead within a hundred yards.

"Let's see if this little deer can sing us a little song."

The ruffian and the boy were moving closer, and the closer they got, the easier of a target Erkii's body became. But the arrows that the bowmen held remained undrawn. *They're not going to shoot,* at least not yet. And he was bigger.

"What should he sing us about, Jon?"

Twenty yards.

"How about he fucking tells me why he was going to kill me?!"

Fifteen.

"That sounds grand to me."

Ten.

"So, explain to Jon and I. Why do Gharans shove their cocks inside dead boy's a–"

Crrt, he smashed his temple into Bern's mouth.

"*Arbgh,* fwuck!"

Jonathen swung his bow into his side. His ribs bent in. *The bow.* His hand shot out, fingers snatching the bowstring. He yanked. Bern's fingers came loose, releasing the staff. Jonathen's stave fell on his ribs again. This time, he clutched it with his arm and spun. He ran. There was little grace as he moved through the white, the stringed staves bouncing and dangling about him.

"The fuck are you doing?! Fuckin' get the cunt!"

He heard the crunch of steps behind him but he dared not look back. Smothered saplings and shrubs stood all around watching the chase like an onlooking mob closing and parting, reaching out with wooden limbs to tear away at a felon in a procession. He forced his way through the gaps, turning sideways and tearing through the branches. The air behind was a dusting of snow. He turned again meeting resistance – the bow in his right was caught. He let it go, but too late. Nails trenched through his neck as a chilled hand grasped the fold of his collar. A forceful tug and he was falling through the air. His back slammed into something firm hiding below the snow. His lungs emptied. Bern's face stared down from amongst the tree crowns.

"Stupid whore-son!" he exclaimed then sucked blood from his split lip. Mixed with mucus, he spat it into Erkii's eyes. "You need to learn your fuckin' place." He pulled back a boot. Erkii's arm folded in as the first kick flew at his ear.

The world was ringing as the next strike landed on his knuckles with an agonising crunch. He flailed with his other hand trying to catch a hold, to pull one of them down, but they just stepped aside leaving him grasping through air.

"Now, you! Go on! Kick him!" shouted Bern, voice sounding muffled through Erkii's battered ear.

The blood and mucus sat an ooze between his eyelids, forming a pink haze over the world. Through the haze he saw as the ruffian grabbed Jonathen's shoulders and pulled him in front. *Ring,* he suddenly remembered, *ring, ring, ring*. The power it released at the river – he needed it now.

A kick landed on his ribs. It was soft, aimed with uncertainty and causing little pain. He moved his hand inside his pocket, fingers feeling for the bit of bronze.

"Harder."

Jonathen obeyed. The second kick carried far more weight, forcing a crunch he felt all through and down to his toes. *Urgh,* he winced aloud, but the pain couldn't distract from what he had to do, not now... he found it, right over the stitching the ring hid. His finger worked itself into it. It was abuzz as if hornets had built a nest within.

"Harder!"

His eyelids were near stuck, but he knew where the last kick came from. With all that was left, he sprung into a sit. All the passion he could muster, the fear and loathing, he focused on the two men standing behind the pink haze. *Die you washed out spawn!* The hornets grew wild within the bronze – *now* – but they had no intention to leave. *Now, now, now!* For a brief splinter of time, he sensed exactly what hid within – amusement.

"Down, bitch!" The toe of Bern's boot met his temple and turned the pink world to black.

*

The thing's legs were folded beneath its body forming a grotesque mass of limbs. Its eyes shimmered from beneath the hood – pale blue crystalline formations stuck on him without motion. They were watching with the fixation and focus of a house cat tracking a stray mouse. Yet, unlike a cat, the thing didn't seem intent on pouncing. There was a contemplative calm to the way it looked at him. There was curiosity too.

After an eternity of staring, in a grating monotone that belonged to nothing and to all, it spoke. "A little curiosity you are."

IO

*"My lord. My king. My friend. I weep at the
thought of what must be done, and yet, my
advice remains the same. We must show
strength."* – Marshall Obert, during a private
audience with his king.

Bear watched closely as the old provost walked about
the clearing. Each step began confident, determined to
deceive, to convince them – and likely Eadmunt himself –
that the fall caused him no ill. But as soon as his toes
touched the ground and weight rested on his leg, the
deception faltered. The provost was maimed.

If I can only get him a healer, he told himself, yet he
knew very well that even the wisest of crones would have
nought to offer for someone Eadmunt's age. It was his fault.
The provost will never walk proper again, pain dragging
down each and every step until the day he dies. Cruelly so,
the remainder of the old man's life still promised more
fulfilment than that of the lanky, red headed boy – the boy
they turned into a herald.

Whimpering under breath, the boy limped meekly
about the clearing. His legs were bowed, spread as not to
agitate the wound spanning his groin – a wound that

already had come open to further soil his rags. Pacing without aim seemed something of a rest for him, a distraction from the memories of his clan being burnt alive. In the least, it seemed to stop his wails much better than threats. Of course, threats were the first thing the soldiers tried when his incessant wails became a nuisance, raking the boy's ribs with knuckles for good measure. But the threats made no difference for what was there left to threaten the boy with?

Galt he was called – or at least that's what Bear could make out before his words turned to incoherent mumbles. He would never be the same, and that was the intent – a permanent reminder of the consequences of treason for those whose mind it might cross. The last who would ever hold their name, stripped of land, kin, and manhood, he was made a living scarecrow.

A very special punishment that is, he could hear his captain Hujrlva's rasp clear as if he were sat with them at the fire. *Met one myself. Fuckin' terrifying. You can see it in their eyes, you can even fuckin' smell it if you got close enough – the madness. They just float around staring ahead and out their mouth comes this fuckin' dribble – my father was this and he did that, and his land was razed – all that shit. And in that fuckin' moment you were glad that it wasn't you who pissed in the king's oatmeal. Me, I'm just fuckin' glad our Young Troll don't have it in him.*

They had left the keep late, and though harnessed to a fresh horse, the sled had gone little more than a dozen miles before the night caught them. The commander was intent to travel through the night, ordering one of his men – Kettil – to sit by Gorgie with a lantern to light their way. He was met with disappointment. By the time the lantern ran out of oil, Gorgie had already lost the path twice. Reluctantly, the commander put them to a stop in a small clearing and told his soldiers to dig for ground – despite the size needed to fit them all, they were near done.

Hands, shields, and the single shovel brought along made quick work of the snow which was piled about the edges to build a wall at their backs. A shelter from wind, but for a little boy this would have been a dream fortress, one that they would expand with caves and tunnels until the whole thing collapsed overhead to bury them in a white cloud. Laughter would have rolled between doorsteps until some grumpy old prick chased them off with a cane. Having watched them work, soldiers didn't seem that different from little boys themselves as they dumped snow behind each other's collars or letting the shovel catch another's arse on the backswing. They tugged and pushed, laughing off bruises, and hurling played out insults as they worked. And somehow, that work was still done quick enough.

With the pit finished, they brought forth timber and kindling packed in hurry onto the sled. Fire steel sparked smoke and glow out of a handful tinder, and about it, a fire was quickly built.

The soldiers sat on a side of their own, their conversation beginning in a hush but promptly turning to shouting. They told stories of fights lucky and not, plunder and women, stories he had heard many times before in a life he no longer lived. *That was me,* thought Bear, a soldier with stories and comrades of his own to laugh through the evenings with. One of them killed a midget with his back swing whilst unaware that the little man flanked him by the river – his name was Jahn. Another, Astir, he wed a Gharan slave that he had purchased then freed and together they made babies the colour of caramel. Also there was Sujr – he cut the balls of the red headed boy who stood banging his forehead against the nearby pine.

The Karlkans had a side to themselves, opposite to the soldiers. Gorgie was the dividing line, sitting as far from Bear as he could which meant being flanked by the young Sujr, and Eadmunt. The commander – Marshal Obert as they so found out – sat in a place of his own, neither with his men nor with his guests. Every now and then, he would turn his head and chime in the soldiers conversation with obscene jest and banter that they always accepted with a chorus of laughter – some, they even returned. They'd make quips about his mother and manhood that most officers Bear had known would have punished with lashes. Obert returned full grins before turning back to whatever thoughts consumed him. Sometimes, he turned to talk to them too, the Karlkans.

Whoever he spoke to, whether soldier or farmer, he looked in the eye, nodding as his trimmed face contorted and lit in response to every word. Eadmunt's hip was a thing he asked about rather often, mostly when the provost tried to move or stand, or seemed as if he would struggle to – he even seemed to wince in time with the old man. He spoke to Bear too, asked about Sassa, about how old he was and what he liked.

The memories – treasure them, Obert told Miska and he back on the sled. *Write them down or have someone do it for you, but make sure that they're written.* His voice was warm and words oozing with care, and he wanted to believe both but for reasons unknown could not. In his mind, the voice and the words did not belong on the tongue of a man who had killed and torture three score but few hours passed.

As it were, Bear didn't know what to make of the man, nor did he know what to make of his fascination with the dead wizard. Their departure from Guhdlval Keep was so sudden he wasn't sure they were ever really there. Obert had the sleigh out of the gate within a quarter. He was certain it was the mention of the wizard which put him into such hurry – at least he whilst in the keep. Once they were out, there was no mention of the wizard at all nor a sign that such a wizard ever existed outside his head. It was as if they were sledding to visit distant relatives. The Marshal showed no concern at all, his face and body still and silent. But it wasn't calm, it was control – absolute and complete control over his body and mind. Something hid beneath all that control, and whatever it was, Bear had no trust for it.

Miska on the other hand seemed to have made her mind up before they even left Guhdlval Keep. The scent of rendered human fat and charred skin that remained stuck inside Bear nostrils lifted his wife's spirit to a place where their son's death no longer mattered. She cared not for the wizard nor where they were going. Revenge was taken on those she judged responsible. Her world was square once more and Marshal Obert who made it so was the hero at its centre – a handsome hero, with a clean face and trimmed hair. Bear had spent the day looking at her, hoping to catch her eye, but her eyes seemed to be constantly occupied ogling the man. That alone was beginning to seed a certain distaste for the man. *Jealous* – maybe that's what it was – though if it were so, the Marshal's actions alone would have put him at ease as he seemed far more interested with the flames than his wife.

"My mare – when will I get her back?" asked Gorgie, finally breaking the silence he sat in since they had left the keep. It was a silence only partly of his doing. He had made the mistake of taking one of the soldier's jest to heart, turning red instead of paying it forth. For that, they named him Strawberry, supposedly after a whore one of them knew who blushed just as well as he.

"At the nearest convenience," replied the Marshal, his eyes remaining on the flames.

Gorgie looked down in search for satisfaction in that answer. He found none. "What does that mean?" he asked, agitation beginning to show through in his voice.

The Marshal lifted his eyes from the flame. "It means, that it will be done as soon as it can be done. More than likely, the mare will be safely stabled and waiting for you to return home."

"And when will that be?"

"Soon enough," the Marshal replied sharply, a tone of someone who was finished answering pesky inquiries. It was a dismissal, an order that Gorgie didn't seem to pick up on as he readied yet another question. Whatever it was, he didn't get a chance to ask.

"My dear Strawberry," said Sujr, sat by Gorgie's flank. His voice was made high and nasal, a clear mockery of a city courtier. "I see you have an eye for the captain, but could it be I you consider?"

"Do not listen!" said Jahn, his tone matching that of the young Sujr. "I tell what my heart means to tell, and that is courage you will find in our love." He leaned over the young soldier's lap, stretching out an arm towards Gerogie in an overly-flourished bow.

"Courage being your cock?" asked Astir with a grin. Gorgie leaned his back into the side of the pit looking nervously between the soldiers.

"The only thing Jahn's cock gives is the black peel," said one they called Kettil, "and from what I hear, he bites too – careful Sujr or you might lose the tip."

150

Jahn turned far more serious. "Oy, I've been cured – been given liquid silver by the healer. Good as new it is."

"While you were at it, did ya ask for something to make it bigger?" asked Astir.

"Haven't had a single complaint – plenty big is what they say."

"They say that 'cause you're always paying."

"Best bit of coin a whore will ever make is having her fanny tickled with a pig's nipple. Why'd she ruin that by complainin'?"

"I guess we'll have to see what the new Strawberry says–"

"That's enough," the Marshal cut in, scolding the men with his stare. "Gorgie, our guide, had legitimate concerns that needed to be addressed. It's done."

"Yes Ser," they replied in disheveled synchrony. It was enough to put Gorgie at ease, and though he remained with his back in the snow, his shoulders did seem to drop.

With the fun over, Kettil hopped out of the hole. A creak of timber and he was back with a sack, out of which he pulled what looked to be a handful of leaves. He began tossing them through the air, each one landing in someone's lap. Bear knew what it was before his even landed. *Fuckin sutton*. They called it that thinking they were clever, *sun dried mutton – sutton*. It was followed with a hunk of yesterday's bread.

Chewing through a mouthful of the leathery meat, Jahn spoke eerily quiet, "I do miss the real Strawberry – the colour of her cheeks, her smile, her tits." He followed the mutton with a mouthful of whatever his wineskin held. Astir gave his shoulder a firm pat.

"See her soon enough–"

"Marshal Obert," spoke Eadmunt, his soft, measured voice standing out in the sudden moroseness that the soldiers turned to. "I need an explanation too – if you don't mind?"

The Marshal was chewing through a piece of bread, late to realise that the old provost meant his words as a question. "Go on."

"Why are you here?" The Marshal's chewing stopped as Eadmunt carried on in measure. "Farmers talking of a wizard – most wouldn't even bother sending a gout ridden hound to verify a story like that, but you decide to go down yourself. Why?"

The Marshal's blue eyes scanned the provost carefully. "Sparrow – that's the name your man gave me. Unprompted, without as much as fleeting mention, he said his name was Sparrow. True – it's a name common folk could come up with on a whim – a glance at a picket could give them the idea, and if they assigned it to a particularly small or mischievous child, it would not have gotten my attention in the slightest. But it's not a name they should have tied to a powerful sorcerer – certainly not without being told so first. This leads me to believe that it was indeed Sparrow that they have met."

The soldiers' melancholy turned to silence.

"Ser. Are you sure?" spoke a mellow voice Bear couldn't recall. It came from the soldier sat to the Marshal's right, and it was only now that he realised the man hadn't spoken yet.

Obert looked to him with a moment's pause. Unlike before, it wasn't a look of scold. "I've given it thought, Wyhltrem. There is nothing to be gained from secrecy – not at this time." The Marshal turned to Eadmunt. "We are headed for war, my dear Eadmunt. Sparrow was one of

Emperor Ardian's pets, and if it is true that it was he who crossed our border, in all likelihood, Ardian's army will follow soon, and Karlka will be one of the first settlements to know."

"War?" Eadmunt sat straight, something he avoided since falling to the cobbles of Guhdlval Keep. His jaw twitching as he swallowed a wince. "Marshal, the merchants have been quiet. There hasn't been as much as a word of supplies being requisitioned nor levies raised – and that's coming from as far as Sylthia itself. We would have heard rumours – complaints."

"Provost Eadmunt," said the Marshal firmly. "The Emperor Ardian is a man of utmost cunning – no man as capable of trickery and deceit has ever been birthed. If anyone is capable of moving an army in such secrecy, it is he. The army is there - an army bigger than anything you would have ever seen – and it is marching our way. I am certain of that." The soldiers nodded with his words and Miska along with them. Eadmunt remained unconvinced.

"If I may ask, what proof do you have?"

The Marshal glared at the provost, the old man's doubt seeming to rile his calm. "What proof do I have? Do you mean other than the glaring truth of our kingdom being the very last place free of the Sylthian disease?! Or besides Ardian's spymaster having been killed – thank the gods – behind our border?! Who knows what damage he had done to the already frail unity of our realm. The greedy, Sylthian beast has been resting, but now, it is awake. It is foaming at the mouth at the mere thought of Nurhdval, and we must be ready to greet its crooked jaws with steel." A string of spit came to rest down the length of Obert's stubbly chin. He wiped it away as his breath calmed. "I apologise for losing my calm, provost."

Eadmunt nodded.

The Marshal looked to the old man expectant of an apology of his own. Realising none was coming, he barked, "It's time to sleep. Sujr, bind the boy for us"

Sujr looked, hesitant. "Ser, it's just that–"

"That what?" asked the Marshal, devoid of patience

"Can someone else do it? He looks at me like the witches do when cursing travellers who won't give them coin. There is something in his eye there, and he has it in for me since it was me who –you know – seared his balls."

The Marshal's lips remained tightly sealed. His eyes looked on unblinking. This seemed answer enough for Sujr.

"Yes, ser," he replied, rising up and climbing out of the wide pit. He moved slowly, turning his head from side to side, searching the near surroundings. "Boy! Where are you? Get your arse over here."

"Should be plenty easy to find with that hair of his," said Astir.

Jahn peeked over the lip of the hole. "He's pro'lly butting the back of a tree again like some retarded goat."

Sujr walked hesitant towards the nearest tree, a great, burly thing that must have stood there for near a century. He looked behind it then about.

"He's not here!"

"Look at the ground, idiot. If he went somewhere, there will be prints," said Kettil.

Eadmunt lifted his hand, loosely extending his fingers towards the edge of the clearing. "There, he left a trail between the trees." He spoke in his usual calm, face betraying nought to those unfamiliar, but Bear could see a glimmer in the old man's eye – a hint of satisfaction. The quiet Wyhltrem seemed to notice it too.

"You saw him leave and said nothing," he implored.

"Keeping guard was not my charge – it was yours. Myself, I thought the boy could use a little peace," Eadmunt replied. The glimmer in the provost's eye trickled into one of many trails carved into his face.

The young Sujr abandoned the tree line and stood over the old man. "A little peace?!" he shouted. "Fucker will come back and slit our throats in the night, you stupid, old cunt!"

"Please, sit," said Eadmunt, paying no mind to the insults. "The boy is far more scared of you than you are of him. I doubt it would even cross his mind to turn back."

I'll be fucked if he sits after that. He knew soldiers, and the sudden tightness in the young man's jaw told him he was right.

"Scared of him?" Sujr readied his boot for a kick as Bear rose to his feet.

Little shit. The boot dropped towards the provost's temple at speed, meeting Bear's hands with a dull thud. Sujt's eyes opened wide, mouth followed suit. Bear pulled back with a short, forceful jerk that spun the boy about and sent him flapping his arms like a chicken jumping off a roost. He fell flat on his back. There was a ruckus across the pit.

"Fat fuckin'–!"

Bear braced for an attack. He pivoted on the spot, shifting his weight to the back foot. None came.

"Hold yourself, Jahn," huffed Astir, grabbing Jahn under the armpits as the bald man tried to pounce right onto Bear. "Sujr lost his footing along with his fucking temper."

The other just watched with grins which their lips struggled to contain – all except for Marshal Obert. With a furrowed brow, he let the struggle continue. Astir turned back and forth between Jahn and the Marshal, his grip loosening as he waited for the order that should come at any moment. But the order wasn't coming, and with each moment that passed, Jahn was closer to ripping free.

Sujr kicked back. All his strength, all his weight, but it wasn't enough to loose Bear's clutch. *Little shit.* Bear twisted the foot, flipping the young man like a skewered rat over a stove. Sujr's face sunk into the snow. His arms pushed against the ground to keep him breathing, but each time he caught purchase, Bear tugged him flat once more. Struggling to breathe, Sujr's movements changed from aggressive to frantic.

"He did lose his temper," the Marshal finally spoke with words weighted, "but didn't we all? You can sit, Jahn. And Sujr – if you would unhand him, Bear – this has been quite unnecessary. Our tempers must stay chained until the inevitable day when we can set them loose on the Sylthians."

With the Marshal's thoughts clear, Jahn eased in his struggle and allowed Astir to sit him back by the fire. This was enough for Bear to let go of Sujr's foot.

"Hhhuuuhhh!" the young man gasped, sucking in air. He looked back to Bear, face contorted and eyes wide as he struggled to catch up on lost breaths. He then looked to his comrades for reassurance but seeing them sat gave him nought.

"Sit, Sujr," said Marshal Obert. "Have a rest – tomorrow will be a long day."

*

For the first time in days, Miska laid by his side. Her hair tangled in his beard, catching in its coarseness as her head sought comfort in the flesh of his chest. It was a pleasure so simple – giving another comfort – and it warmed him from within, slowly letting his mind adrift. He could hear the breath leaving her mouth, and he felt the air sneak through the opening in his wrappings. It came to rest amongst the hairs of his chest. His eyelids became gooey and his world began turning to haze.

"Next time, if the old man wants to die, let him die," she whispered.

Something moved in the tree above, shaking a branch and loosening a white dusting. It came down with a rustle, falling on both their faces. His world cleared and eyelids sprung open. Miska didn't even flinch. *Let him die.* His chest began to ache and the warmth was gone. Having Miska's head on his chest seemed little more than supporting a rock. He felt like this before and not just once.

There was a harshness to his wife, one brought about by years spent behind shields and entrenchments. He knew of it before he even asked for her hand – a woman soft and gentle wouldn't choose to swing steel for a living – and for a woman, it was always choice. No woman was honour bound to fight, and so, those who did were there because they wanted to kill. Miska wasn't like that, he had always told himself, but did he ever really believe that? Her hand was heavy with the boys, that of a sergeant training new recruits. *They're kids,* he told her so often, each time seemingly unheard. It felt at times like he and the boys were themselves together in trenches – comrades. And as a comrade, most of the boys' secrets and mischief he kept to himself. *Just kids – his kids.*

He was back on the sleigh with the boys under arm. The wizard's cold, dead eyes staring him down from under the furry hood.

"Let me take them with me." The man motioned to the empty stretch of spruce to his side. "They will die if they stay with you."

"Be quiet, will you."

"They will die – both of them. They will die because of you."

"I can keep 'em safe. They're my boys!"

"They will die if they don't come with me."

"They're not coming with you." He brought the boys into a tight embrace.

"They are going to die, Bear. And you are going to kill them."

His arms began to move. They were his arms, he could feel them – a part of him – but there was no control. He tensed and pulled. The aching strain was there but nothing moved. He was helpless in watching his body do exactly what the sorcerer said it would. Slowly, his arms unraveled. Joran turned away. Sassa turned to him. His eyes were lidless and leaking.

Bear's hands rose upward, and his fingers wrapped about the boy's neck. Supple and soft, it folded under his grip as air hissed past the opening which was being squeezed smaller and smaller. The boy's eyes bulged out of their socket, a cloud of red spread through the white and surrounded the blue.

No… no…

The hiss stopped. Sassa went limp in his grip.

The sorcerer spoke again, "Let me take him with me – he will die if he stays with you."

Joran. He turned on the spot to find the boy no longer there. In his place was a shovel with dirt encrusting its blade. Dirt encrusted his hands. Under his nails, in the marks that webbed them, it would remain forever. Joran had joined Sassa in the ground, and he had put him there.

Bear awoke in sweats. A wolf howled.

II

"Knute, my dear Knute. I can't. You know I love you, and I always will. But it's the kind of love you hold for a little brother, not a husband. I'm so sorry!" – Rhina, as spoken to Knute the day of his disappearance.

Silence hung thick, smothering the village folk in their own thoughts. There was no noise distracting them and so they sought something else – a scuff on the boot, dent in the table – anything that could occupy their minds. But the clay mug remained on its side, rocking as its contents dripped down the gap between oak slabs to strike the stone flooring in slow and measured *tap... tap... tap*. Behind the mug stood Guunt. Face withered by decades of working in the sun, he was the father of a peasant girl they took. She was promising, strong in body and mind – a little too strong. Her mind refused to surrender the body before it reached the tipping point. When they were done, she was left in gore, pale skin painted black, blue, and red. Seeing the girl in daylight made Sparrow question himself, his cause, his own commitments. It was difficult to imagine what it had done to her father.

Maybe knowing the cause would ease his pain? It would have for him – knowing that the girl's sacrifice served to prevent the suffering of many. Yet somehow, he doubted it would serve the father so. The way he viewed things was far different to the way small folk did. Unable to separate their mind from their little lives, their thoughts began with what they have and ended with who they know. That was the extent of their world, and for Guunt, its entirety had been drained through a single slit across the thigh.

Eventually, the farmer sat down, though his body seemed to find no rest with its hind on the wooden bench. He continued to twitch, mumbling as his thumbs worked their way into a knot in the table's timber.

"Play us a song, Knute," peeped a mouse haired girl, smiling a smile as sweet as she could muster. All day, she has been doing her utter best to lift the village folks' spirits, smiling and chirping to bring out joy out of the most minute of things. Green shoots, bovine calves, and children squealing as snow got behind their collars – she would call them out for all to see. Now, she decided that he would be their amusement. "A song is exactly what we need!"

He hadn't spoken a single word to any one of them – a necessary precaution given the little knowledge he had of this Knute. He did have the man's throat, and was he disguising before an alien crowd, he could have used it to great effect. But disguise alone wouldn't work if trying to imitate a man who was known to every single peasant in the smoke stained hall. Doing so believably would have required intimate understanding of how the man used his voice – of his diction, tone, and cadence, of his accents and inflections, and even of his breathing patterns. It was knowledge that took months of observation and study, and several of practice before one could fool even a most seldom acquaintance. Without that, he may as well have been a last minute replacement of the great Cordecius, painted and robed and shoved out onto a stage to be devoured by the expecting crowd. *Leave me be,* and for his sake, he really hoped she would. The girl did not.

"Please, Knute! Please! Don't make us beg." She smiled at him sweetly – at Knute – something he figured to have been rare for the fat bard. Along with the body he had found heartbreak, misery, and the weight of failures recent and old. It wasn't an unusual story, one the man shared with most other bards. Yet, there was something unusual about Knute. Most bards, while equal in failure, hold a place of sympathy amongst their people. Knute did not. Wherever he went, they looked at him from beneath their brows – if they even bothered to look at all. They stepped sideways to avoid him, and if there wasn't a chance whilst in a narrow doorway, they simply turned as if having forgotten something. He couldn't figure out why, but it seemed as if the entire village would have preferred him dead – all but the brown, shaggy thing laid by his feet. How it stunk.

I should leave, go back to sleep on that giant's rug, and a giant he truly may have been – a mix in the least. It was a rarity for sure, though not so much in these regions, and even less so when considering the span of a century. Giants lived in Nurhdval well before men made it their home. They lived split into warring tribes, each claiming ownership of a pile of rocks or a stream or a dirty mound of some sort. They were dishevelled simpletons, and if met in woods or field, they were cut down with ease by the greenest of war-bands. The story was different in mountains and hills. Long legged and hardy, weather and ground made little difference to them as they outpaced even the nimblest of men with ease, hurling boulders and dislodging cliffs as wind and rain wore out their pursuer's resolve. Once the land had done its work, they would descend with thunder on their lips to pulverise the withered remnants of armies once proud. Eventually, Nurhdval's new rulers decided that their men would be far more useful with their spines intact, and so, they left the giants to their mountains and the giants left the men to fields and woods. Be it for food or for fun, the giants still descend from their hills at times, occasionally leaving behind a litter of children unusually tall.

"Yea, go on," said a man haired in wild red, "play us somethin'."

"Fuck me, Rolen," Sander raised his voice in protest. "Really?! Do you really want to put us all through it? I know the bastard nearly died, but–"

"Sander!" the girl exclaimed.

"You know it's true. None of you would be asking was it not for that."

"You really have a way of ruining things," spoke an older woman, grey streaked hair still carrying a burgundy crust from the night before.

"Always," echoed another, eyes drifting between Sander and the young girl. But the girl seemed lost for words.

Seeing that, the ginger man pulled himself out from behind the table. "Go on, play us something," he spoke, walking towards him with something in his hand. It was a lute of crude craft with strings that must have spent twice as long outside the cow than as a part of its innards. But the wood was waxed, the pegs greased, and the ancient strings kept moist. It was ready to be played. The surrounding faces were fixed on him but not in expectation. Mouthes twisting, it seemed more like they were preparing for something unpleasant. *They're waiting to hear the same chords he's played a thousand times,* he presumed – nothing uncommon for small town bards. *But what song would that be?*

Maiden Outfoxed? Most drinking holes would turn to chanting 'maiden and the fox' at a point or another in the night. It was certainly a popular tune through the empire, lively in tempo and melody, but it was never translated – not into the coarse, Nurhdvalian tongue – which was unfortunate as the crude soldier's song would have matched it perfectly. He could have given it a translation – a simple song like that ought have been well within the bard's repertoire. However, even if so, it would have still been a poor choice for this solemn occasion. And what if someone familiar with the song realised? *No, certainly not playing the Maiden.*

Nurhdvalian tune, Nurhdvalian tune... Father's Bones. It would have certainly suited the circumstance these peasants have found themselves in and it would have been known by all too –there wouldn't be a single man, woman, or child living between those desolate hills who hasn't heard it. Yet, he still had his apprehensions, as in its own way, the song was difficult. Any bard able to play it would not be living in a place like this, and he wasn't sure that he could either. His new hands felt as if they were carved of the hardest timber, and though the fingers bent, they bent far too slow. And his voice – could it even hold a note? But he had to play something.

Fingers contorting, he made chord and strummed it. He let it ring as long as the timber would allow, then he twisted the fingers into another. He strummed once more, thumb catching on a string snapping it like a bow string. The sound wasn't pleasant, but besides a groan from Sander, there were no protests. He returned to the first chord. *Words,* ones he had heard before. He started to sing.

> *Good bye my friends passed too soon*
> *The gods have called thee through*
> *To sit amongst them in laughter's roar*
> *To share their fiddle's tunes*

> *So save us a seat by the roaring hearth*
> *Save some ale, pork, and wine*
> *Before long we will be there too*
> *Drunken, merry, fools*

His voice held notes but didn't want to change them, creaking and breaking if he tried to, yet he carried on despite. None seemed to mind, and even Sander who seemed intent on belittling Knute any chance he had listened in silence.

He sang through it twice, mixing up a few words and failing to fully voice the chords. It would have been a passable attempt were he a child, and yet, the peasants stared with mouths split open. *Was it the humour?* That was unlikely. Living in their crude ways, small folk weren't easy to offend. *They're moved – must be.* The simple words must have spoken to their mourning and made friends with it. They were left speechless. The mouse haired girl, the red haired man, and even the giant sat without motion and eyes seeming as lidless as those of a fish. *Something's not right.* The reaction was unwarranted. He made a mistake.

Sander broke the silence was the first to break the silence, "How you learn that?" His voice seeped with self-righteous bitterness that the mouse haired girl didn't seem to notice.

"He's cured!" she exclaimed, beaming. "It's a miracle!"

"Miracle?!" Guunt sprung, thighs hitting the table, jittering mugs and plates. All turned to stare at his worn out face. The attention seemed something the farmer didn't intend but now that he had it, he seemed to fire up. "My daughter," he croaked, "my only, my sweet young thing with a heart too pure – murdered. Alr, Stina, Kuarl, dead alongside her. Peder and Sara gutted. Don't be speaking of miracles to me, Rhina... or you might find yourself needing one."

The girl shrunk into herself.

"Take your peace, man," spoke the one who gave Sparrow the lute. The man's tied up mane of red was beginning to come loose from its bindings, frizzing outwards to frame his chunky face. "Rhina means well – you know that. We all lost friends last night, family we will not see till it's our turn to meet the gods. Peder was a brother to me and more, and tomorrow, I have to dig a hole in frozen ground so that his bones don't make for a fox's play thing. I will be there digging for Bronie too. They're with the gods now, far happier than we." The man's words seemed to find something within Guunt, and though hesitant, he lowered himself onto the bench just as Sander opened his mouth.

"How can we take our peace knowing full well that we've been lied to?"

"What do you speak of?" asked a man sat at his table. Both dark of hair and with faces a square lump, the two were cousins in the least.

Sander struggled to keep his lipless mouth from curling. "Our dear Knute? The retard we have fed and

166

clothed all these years? The one who slept under our roofs while we worked day and night to feed him? A *miracle* she calls it."

"And what?" asked the older woman, working a crumb of dried blood out of her hair. "He decided that today, of all days, is the day to stop his act?"

"Maybe the gods decided that for him," Sander continued. "And who knows who these men were who killed our friends like some pigs – these mad men, these lunatics, these moon worshipping cultists. But why is it that it's only Knute who survived? Was it luck? Or maybe–" he dropped to a feigned whisper "–they were his mad friends."

"You're an idiot."

"Watch your mouth, you old hag–"

A boy jumped to his feet. "That's my mother you're talking to!" No more than sixteen, he stood with legs forced to bend between the bench and the table.

Before Sander could reply, the giant's voice filled the tavern. "Knute, have you been pretending all these years?" The deep boom with which he spoke put the youth back in his seat and all others into silence.

He had no answers. All he could think to say was, "I don't know." For once, that happened to be true.

The hall broke out in angered chatter. His words were no more than a carcass thrown to the vultures, and he began to realise that they were not the words this Knute would have used, if he even used any at all. Knute's vessel was impaired. That would have explained why it has been so challenging to control it, and yet, he had failed to use it in the same way that Knute had. He was about to be found out. Compulsively, he felt his index finger in search of the ring. *Of course it's not there*. He wanted to bring the roof down or spread the hearth's fire – cause any distraction that would allow him to slip away. He hated how reliant he has become on the artefact and the fickle Ngahdetyn lodged within. Yet, even if he had the ring, would the body be wieldy enough for him to let go and use it? Unlikely.

"He doesn't know," Sander's voice rose sharply in a struggle to speak over the increasingly agitated crowd. "Did you all hear that?! He's taking us for fools! For idiots!" His words were met with agreement, and looking around, it could be found on many faces too.

"How selfish – how small you are," Radwha tried to speak but her voice was barely audible over the rabble. Sander didn't even seem to notice.

"Every day he's been taking food from our cellars, sleeping under our roofs – no more." The people nodded and barked in agreement and Sander's measly statue seemed to grow by the second – in his head, it likely matched that of the giant. That delusion was quickly shattered.

"Quiet!" Sigrid roared, his voice swallowing Sander's like some puny morsel. It swallowed all sound – the fire, the wind, the creaking and the crowd – and when he was done, there was only the quiet that he asked for. "Knute. Why were you lying?"

"I…" *Confusion, I will feign confusion.* It was his best option. "I wasn't. I don't know. Things they just… changed. There was fire, and smoke, and blood. And I don't know where I am." He looked around, eyes wide open feigning fear and nerve. The peasants began to murmur, their scrunched faces turning amongst themselves. *They don't know what to think and are looking for someone to tell them.* It was what he hoped for – a sign that he had made a neutral ground that could flip in his favour.

"That is an absolute crock of shit," spoke Sander far louder than he needed to. "He was trying to fool us, to steal and –"

"Maybe he was, maybe he wasn't," the giant smothered the ruffian's words. "I do not know which it is. The truth is between Knute and the gods."

"Then maybe it's the gods he should be talking to!" Sander shouted, staring at the giant's earlobe Sigrid turned to meet his eye. It was a challenge of will, a contest for authority in this measly forum which would help Sander reclaim his face after having been interrupted. But Sander wasn't ready. He thought his standing to be shared by others, but the village folk gave him nought – they just watched with thirst as the spectacle unfolded. The ruffian began to realise that. Each moment that passed sowed doubt in his chunky head until his muddy gaze faltered.

Pale blue of the giant's eyes remained over Sander in contemplation while the ruffian turned to stare at the slithers of froth left drifting at the rind of his mug. In the remaining silence, Radwha finally had a chance to speak.

"All of you who came here with him from Bruunt and Ougreln, you did not know them. Knute and Merla, they were good people – selfless people – the kind who wouldn't leave a babe to the wolves, no matter its ailments. They kept him, raised him through all the fits and screams, and when the day came to name him, Knute didn't even pause before giving the boy his own name. They loved him as one would their child – because he was their child. To them, he was perfect, so much so that on his name day, his father scraped the bottom of the coffer and bought him a lute. Thereafter, we could hear that thing twang any moment that he wasn't tending to the animals, any moment he had he played – and how tender he was with the animals." Radwha smiled in her recollection. "The sound was awful and it carried, but seeing the joy on the boys face, not even Berged – rest his soul – had the heart to stop him. And after a while, I don't know if it was him who got better or us who got used to it, but after a while it started to sound good too. He was a good boy. He would greet you, he would smile, and he would play with the others too. Half the time, you couldn't even tell him from any other boy. Then the fire happened. Their home burnt down with Knute and Merla pinned inside. I, and then my Rhina," she said nodding to the mouse haired girl who now sat uncertain, stripped of the previous joy, "we looked after the boy as much as we could, but he never made it back after that. You may not understand this now – maybe never – but in Sangelk, we look after each other."

She's done it, this Radhwa. I will have to note her name down for an imperial pension. His thought was in jest, yet, the relief he felt was intoxicating enough for him to earnestly consider this notion. Just imagining the peasant finding the small fold of paper, unwrapping it to reveal the unstamped, gold medal. *The face she would make.* She definitely deserved the reward, doing far more than most men on Emperor's payroll ever had. The peasants were calmed, maybe even inclined in his favour, and all he had to do now was seize the moment she had created.

"I don't know," Sparrow mumbled. "I don't remember. But I know you. You have done so much, and all I want to do is pay you back, all of you – if you will let me." He could see their features loosen, faces settling down. *A bucket of slop for the pigs.* The peasants gurgled down every word he offered, all but Sander.

"So we're going to believe him, is that it?" he looked around in search of an ally, eyes stopping on the opposing table. "You happy with this, Guunt?" But the old farmer didn't seem to be listening. Staring at the inners of his empty mug, he rocked it back and forth on the table.

"He's a good boy," he finally said. "Yes, it's strange – fuckin' strange – but that's how the gods work... but maybe some good will come of it." Eyes regaining focus, he stamped the mug on the table. "We need to find the bastards. Two of 'em, they disappeared in the trees before we caught the other one. They'll pay. We'll fuckin' make 'em pay."

His words were met with silence and averted gazes.

"What you lookin' down for? They took our own!"

"Guunt," Radwha spoke up, "they were monsters – fiends from the other world. Didn't you see how quick they was? They have taken their sacrifice and escaped to the other world. No one will ever find them."

"And yet, it's their blood caking your hair. They bleed just like we, and I know who sent them." Whispers rippled between the tables and eyes rose to look at Guunt, all holding the same question behind them.

"Who?" asked Sigrid with caution.

"Who?" Guunt scoffed. "You know it well as me, Sigrid. All of you know it! That fuckin' witch in her swamp is who! It's been bad enough when it was her alone, but she's been gathering them murdering thieves about her. She's been doing magic, putting spells on 'em, turning them to those black devils."

Sigrid's hard, jagged features began to twitch at their edges. "Mertle."

Mertle? He had heard that name before. *But could it really be one and the same?* He remembered the magister's stories as clear as if they were told today, but not for the usual reasons one might have. It wasn't merit that made

Mertle memorable, were it so, she would have melted into the blur shared by all other great sorcerers of centuries passed that the magister droned about for hours at an end. There were very few talented enough to stand out of stretches of that tedious monotone, but Mertle did. That was because she had no talent at all.

Day after day, she attempted the simplest of feats – putting out candles, warming a cup of water, snapping a willow branch – all to no avail. Hopeless she was, completely and utterly hopeless. Unteachable. Nonetheless, she carried on and on, taking up space and holding up texts which could have been used by students capable of learning from them. We had to be rid of her. She was given the day and night to set her affairs, to collect her possessions and say her farewells. She was to leave in the morrow, but she left in the night instead… after setting the library alight. It was a story that was shared in the old man's usual dull tone, but even being as young as he was at the time, he could tell it was but a mask that hid the old magister's utter fury at the memory. *Alchemists brews she used to fuel the flames, and they ran so hot that the stone of the walls began to melt. We had to contain the section, forsaking the tomes it housed to the void.*

Despite the Citadel's expansive reach and resources, Mertle was never found –   a hideout in a Nurhdvalian swamp would explain that more than adequately. Knowledge of ingredients and technique would suffice for rudimentary healing, illusions and tricks, and that would be all someone would need to pass for a witch amongst the small folk. Mertle's time in the citadel along with the stolen books would have given her both. What remained a mystery were the murdering thieves. They weren't *his* murdering thieves – without explicit orders, they were likely still running through the woods – but they may have been the same murdering thieves who killed and robbed him. *Likely, very likely.* If not, they would certainly know the ones who did. He needed to find them, search them, and question them if the contracts were to be located – assuming they hadn't been burnt at the hands of unfathomable stupidity.

"I'm goin' to find her," huffed Guunt as if reading his mind. "I'm goin' to find her, and the bastards who killed my Bronie. And I'm goin' to cut 'em up, piece by piece, finger by finger, until there is nothing fuckin' left. Who will come with?" He rose on uncertain feet looking to see if anyone else would.

"Guunt. You don't even know if it truly was her," said Radwha. "And don't forget Rhena – how she helped her get better when the coughing wouldn't stop?"

"She helped her so good, the wee thing died three months after. 'twas just a cold before you took her to that old hag, before she fed her that green shit."

"What about Orik's leg," she said, pointing the peasant out with a flailing hand, "or Sigrid's fever when he could barely even stand. And don't forget your Bronnie when that nasty cut began to go foul – who did you go to?"

"And I paid for it too! I paid for it dear!" yelled Guunt. "She took my wife that same year, and now, she took my girl too."

"Guunt," said Sigrid with his deep voice calm and controlled. "The witch has powers – there is no doubt in my mind about it – but we don't know if any of this was her doing. Look past your grief and your anger and you will see that never has she tried to do us harm through the decades we have known her."

Guunt snorted in response but his lips remained shut.

"They were men who did this," Sigrid carried on, "frightening men, maybe even possessed – maybe even living in the same bog. If they are, who better to help us find the cunts than she?"

"And what if it really was her doing, Sigrid? Maybe you're too close–"

"If it really was her, we will do as you said," thumed the giant. "Piece by piece, arm by arm, and leg by leg, we will cut her until there is nothing left."

An ill-contained smile curled Sander's lips. "And surely," he spoke, "surely Knute would love to be a part of that too. After all, his brains has returned and he's a man once more – and what man wouldn't want revenge?" His eyes were propped wide open, hungry for the fear Knute was meant to betray. Refusal and cowardice was what he wanted to bring out in the half-wit, intent on shaming him for reasons unknown.

He gave Sander a response that the peasant wasn't expecting, "I will."

12

"Masters of their craft – masters of all craft, really. They gave all they could give to their creations, and when that wasn't enough, they gave what they could not." – Master August of the Citadel, as spoken during tutelage.

"Ffhuuugh," he sucked on the night air trying to force it into his lungs. His body fought against it – it wanted to die. *"Urhhh."*

"Ffffuuuugh." Each laboured breath carried along a wheezing whistle from somewhere deep inside his battered chest. He could feel his ribs, separated beneath the skin, moving in ways they weren't supposed to, screaming at him to stop. *"Urhhhh."*

Not today. He pulled on each breath in defiance, forcing it through the tightened opening of his throat. Every single one hurt. A slave, he had been beaten before – be it for disobedience or a slip of the grip – but never quite so. The shacklers beat slaves like trainers beat riding elephants. They beat them hard enough to teach while keeping their property undamaged. This wasn't so. This was a beating he wasn't meant to survive.

He flipped his head to the right. Pain, but the bearable kind, meaning his neck hadn't been wrung like a chicken's. His arm was at an odd angle though, thumb straight down in the snow, its edge to the night sky. *How odd,* he thought to himself just before his mind caught up.

It felt like someone had stuck wire heated white under his nails, all the way through his fingers up to the wrist where they merged to creep up the bones and up to his jaw to split again and burrow in his teeth. His gums went numb and mouth filled with spit. He wanted to close his eyes – *maybe it'll go away* – but he couldn't bring himself to as beyond his arm there laid something else.

My leg! It was deflated as if all of the meat and all of the bones were taken out for it to be stitched empty. It laid bare skinned and stretched across the snow, throbbing but unresponsive. He tried to kick but it wouldn't even twitch. Something else did, his leg, still inside the trouser. *What in the fuck?!* Then he remembered.

"I have something for you – a present if you will. I am showing you kindness," said the thing before it began to tear at one of its limbs with a rusted blade that materialised in its grip. The limb was firm, resisting each stroke of the blade, skin sticking to be pulled back and forth with the motion. Yet when it severed, it served clean, leaving but few trailing wisps to vanish in the air. The thing dropped the limb before him. "I will visit you again, my dear friend, to see if you like my kindness."

The memory was enveloped in dreamy ooze which stretched and melted like a lump of tallow placed on the tongue, yet, the image beneath was clear and unwavering. The thing he saw unconscious was the same he saw in his dream. It was an omen that a teller would draw caution from, and on a different day, it would have concerned him too. But the pulsating stretch of pale flesh was a far bigger worry.

It began somewhere underneath him, though where, he couldn't exactly tell. He assumed a stretch of it was under his back – the creature must have laid him on it. He couldn't feel anything other than snow but it was there. He could see it. It looked revolting, a severed limb that only belonged in nightmares. It must have been dangerous too. He had to get away from it, no matter how much it hurt.

And it did.

As soon as he moved, his ribs began to scream, wailing and crying, begging for him to stop. His arm joined in too. The pain overpowered all else within. Breathing stopped, vision too. The world was replaced by darkness filled with glistening forms. Everything was asking for him to stop, but instead he pushed through the darkness until his arse was sunken firmly into the snow. With a few agonising breaths, his vision returned. He looked down to see that the limb had moved too – it now laid nearer, curving about the base of his hip.

His instinct was panic at its mere proximity, to squeal and run. Yet, as much as its existence unnerved him, there was little to suggest that the limb was actually dangerous. It just laid there, pulsing rhythmically, winding about and past his feet, narrowing to a pointed end resting before a nearby tree. It seemed familiar.

When a child, Urkii and he used to swim in a water hole that only the highest of tides could fill. As waves washed over its lip, they would sometimes drop off a fish or a crab or something much more quaint from the ocean's depths. Most would leave with the next tide, if not, the one after that. That remained true for all but the red octopus. At first, he and Urkii thought that the creature couldn't make it out – that it was too weak or couldn't time the tides. They spent that entire day trying to catch it and it was a proud moment when they finally did, carrying it back to the safety of the sea. But the next day, it was in the hole again.

Four days they've spent catching the octopus then releasing it to sea, and each day, it washed back in. *Stupid thing – he's back in again,* they'd say before 'rescuing' the creature yet again. It took them all four days to realise that it wasn't the octopus that was stupid. Whether it was the warmer water or the easy picking of food in its rocky confines, the creature chose to make the water hole his home – all in spite of two pesky boys who kept on throwing him out to sea. Having realised, they left him to do just that.

The creature was skittish at first, hiding away between rocks as soon as the two plunged in, doubtlessly convinced they would carry on trying to throw him out to sea. It took a week before he would even dare to peak out of his hiding spots and another for him to attempt the shortest of swims on the other side of the hole. They left him to do so in peace. Soon enough, he realised he and Urkii meant him no harm, and so he approached them, grasping onto Erkii's leg with his long, red arm. It had suckers and spots.

The closer he looked at the strange limb beside him, the more he realised that it was the octopus' arm it resembled. He could see the suckers, he could see the spots but the colour seemed different. Or did it? Slowly, the pale skin began to take on shade. It was turning red, or had it always been so?

He recalled the sensation of the tentacle latching onto him, one he couldn't compare to anything other than being kissed in a hundred little spots – a startling sensation when swimming – and he began to wonder. *Will it feel the same?* He reached out to touch it.

His fingers never felt something so... vacant. At first, he thought it smooth, smoother than anything he had ever felt, smoother than the black blouse that they pulled off the sorcerer's corpse. He slid his fingers along it towards one of the suckers. Like worn boots on moist ice, there was no resistance to them sliding. It was as if they were moving over nothing, and yet, he felt something. He could feel his fingers – their warmth as they passed over the limb, the coarseness of cracked skin and the scars as he laid them to rest over the little suckers. He thought they would latch on like the little octopus did, grasp onto him like a thousand tiny lambs suckling a teat. They did not. Fingers and suckers just touched one another, getting acquainted as he sat there distracted from pain by the realisation that the limb he was touching was his own.

It cannot be, he told himself as his new limb throbbed atop the snow. He reached back to find its origin, patting the skin stretched taught by lumps and bruises. There was blood but he paid it no mind as his fingers tried to grasp the root of the octopus arm. He pictured a great fissure with the limb planted there, skin sewn about it to keep it in place. *Pain,* his fingers followed the pain, patting about in search of the hole where the thing attached. He found cuts and bruises and swellings, but there were no openings – certainly not large enough for the limb. He raced over his skin once more wincing with each new contusion but found nothing that would explain it.

It was attached somehow, somewhere, *but maybe not in this world.* Einsleigh and the doe – *it could be like it.* She was there but not there, only seen through his eyes, and only when the gods willed it. The limb may have been the same magic as she, given to him by the monster in his dreams. It would make sense, a gift from the other world that he has been visiting. *Mertle will know,* she had to, he needed her to. He had to see her.

With a heave, he rocked himself onto his feet. All went black. Vomit rose to the back of his throat and he began to wobble as scorching pain washed over him. *Fucking bastards*, he could see them in the black, stomping his body into the ground to frost over or be torn open by wolves. The day before he regretted going with Torgy, he regretted trying to steal a stupid shirt from the boys hut. Now, he regretted that he hadn't slit his throat.

In blotted pieces, his sight returned. Moonlight welled through the tree crowns, illuminating the forest floor and the scattered tracks of the chase – the tracks he had to follow to get back to the beaten path. It was time to walk.

Left foot then right, he walked with his air held in as his vision slowly faded to pulsing black. A few yards, then he had to stop. His lungs were asking for air yet he was afraid to let them have it – the first breath was bound to carry hurt he wasn't ready for.

"Fffuugh," the air came in without regard for his wishes. His rib cage screamed as bone grated against bone and stabbed at him from within.

The next breath came easier and the one after that even more so. He could still see. A few more, then he moved again.

The limb dragged in the trench of footprints he left behind, slithering like a snake through the gutter. He could feel the frozen crystals scraping its leathery outer, their chill working itself deep inside – it was cold but unlike any cold he had ever felt before. There was dimension to it, pressure, texture, and a flavour. The appendage must have been sunk deeper than his feet, and yet, it left no track of its own. If it touched the ground at all, it must have done so softer than a duckling's feather.

He managed three more yards before the pain forced him still. Mertle's home was less than a mile, and in his state, he was beginning to wonder whether he could even make it halfway. His body was fighting him once more, refusing to take another step in fear of another jitter to its splintered bones. Against its will, he forced it.

Shacklers, fucking shacklers, he cursed the two who broke him and left him in the woods to die. He could see their ugly, pale faces... the world began turning black again, but while his sight faded, the two only turned clearer – a wolf's grin on one and idiocy on the other. *Little Gharan slave boy,* they taunted with boots dug into his back. *Watch him try stand like man.* He felt his muscles resonate, heating up and buzzing like an ant nest being pissed on. It felt like it did at the river.

I will kill them, he droned, forcing each step through the hurt. He was angry – truly angry – and for once, not at himself. It was them, not what he was and not the things he had done. He didn't stop for breaths nor for his sight – by the time he reached the path, both caught up with his anger and so had the limb.

It began to move, or rather, he began to move it. He didn't know how – he couldn't know – because how did one ever move his own limbs? Without learning or a lesson, the appendage had become just another arm. He lifted it into the air, contracting whatever strung its inners as to bend them into tense arches that spiralled about his person, tension building as if the auctioneer was watching with his strap at the ready. Then, he released it.

A whip, it uncoiled at speed, swiping out at the surrounding forest. He cut right through the trees, but it wasn't trees that he was seeing. *I will kill them*. His mind filled with shattered bones protruding out of two bloodied corpses as helpless they wailed on the ground.

"*Aaaaagh!*" He began to scream as the limb lashed out. Snow and splintered timber dusting the surroundings was what he expected, but instead, the limb moved through without disturbing a flake. He whipped again, and again, each attempt quicker than the last. "*Aaaaaaghhh!*" The limb was powerful – he could feel it – yet had nothing to show for it. "*Aaaghhg*," his scream of anger turned to pain as his body refused to be pushed any further.

All turned black. Erkii dropped into a heaving heap as the limb curled up about him.

*

Weary of the pain, he shuffled down the road three steps at a time. The limb dragged behind him useless and deflated – he could move it, but what for? It could not lift, nor touch. It couldn't support his weight nor help his crippled steps. *Useless*.

By the time he reached Mertle's abode, the sun was already waking, turning the nights indigo to blue. Sitting on its slight hump in the swamp, the hut made for a fine silhouette against the blue – one he would have appreciated more in a different circumstance. As it was, the steepness of the approach forced him to take but a single step between breaths. Those breaths began to stretch as he neared the mouldy door, slowing him to a pace so pathetic that he may as well have been standing still. It was as if the path was growing under his very feet just to add to his torture – he was beginning to believe that. And then, he was there.

His hand slid up the green tinged timbers, its back dragging against the grain. Flipping it at the wrist, he gave the door a rasp with the knuckles. There was no answer as his leg began to give. He leaned forth in search of support, finding it as his shoulder wedged itself between the door and the frame.

A voice escaped through its cracks. "I swear by the gods, I am going to turn you into a bleeding mud-pit toad if it's you again, Torgy." The door opened but his legs weren't ready. "Boy, what in the world are–" Erkii's limp body came fell forth to rest on her crooked frame. "Stand yourself," she spoke, voice muffled by his weight. Her hands pushed against his chest.

"*Aaaugh*", he heard himself moan as Mertle's hand parted his cracked ribs, pushing itself into him. Air escaped his lips and his stomach jolted itself awake, spouting mucus into his mouth and down his chin.

"Erkii," she said, moving her hands with caution to support him at the armpit. "Stop being dramatic." Her hands were firm and surprisingly strong, holding his weight near entirely as she led him through the pulsating darkness to a bed heaped with tussled furs. "Lay here," she said, supporting him in his descent into the already warm covers and wedging a stuffed sack beneath his torso and head. She made a few adjustments to ensure support, then shuffled over with a stiff gait to search through a trunk sat obscured in the corner.

"Oh Erkii," sounded a familiar voice, "what happened? Who did this to you?" It wasn't Mertle, she was still meddling with the trunk. The voice came from the bunk across the room, from the doe laid within the unconscious Einsleigh.

"Bern," he murmured.

"But it couldn't have been – he's a good man. Maybe you're remembering wrong?"

"Beat me... leave to die."

"No, you must be mistaken."

Mistaken. How stupid did she think he was?

"He wouldn't hurt any of us, I promi– Erkii, what is that?"

He hurt me, he beat me, and left me to die.

"Erkii, are you...? Stop."

"You are stupid," he muttered through his teeth. *Stop, stop what?* He wasn't doing anything.

With a voice depleted of air, Einsleigh yelped, "Stop... you're hurting me." The tentacle was wrapped about her, trapping three of her legs to the trunk. Her one free leg flailed in aimless kicks as the limb tightened.

"You better be having delusions you're speaking to, boy," said Mertle from her table, spoon spinning about the rim of a little wooden bowl.

There was no way Einsleigh could escape the limb's coils. He watched as it squeezed the light out of the writhing doe. *What can I do? Maybe Mertle...* Surely the witch could help. But how? She couldn't even see her nor could she see the tentacle. He could. He felt them both – the struggling doe and the constricting limb. It was *his* limb. *I am choking her.*

He released. The doe fell heaving onto the bunk. She stared from there with bulging eyeballs, heaving as the limb obediently coiled and came to rest at his side. It rolled up precisely where he meant it – everything it did was precisely what he meant.

"Erkii, what… what is that?" she spoke with twitching legs, sometimes one, sometimes all.

What do I say? How do I explain? She spoke of seeing things – frightening things. *Maybe she knows the man with hundred legs?* If anyone did, it would be one who lives in this other world.

Before he had a chance to speak, Mertle tugged his lips open and shoved the wooden bowl against it. "Drink."

Thick liquid, smooth and cold, rolled over his teeth and down the length of his tongue coating the entirety of his mouth in endless waves. A never ending tide, surging gently down his throat, it was ready to carry him away in a little boat to a land serene and numb. Where the boat came from, he wasn't sure, but he felt warm and safe laid inside its womb. Einsleigh was there too but a few feet away, drifting in a boat of her own. The waves lulled them together as if they were babes in their mothers' arms, warm and safe and at peace, and between them in the middle of it all stood Mertle.

Hello, he tried to say but the words simply melted and slipped back down his thickly coated throat. *Hello, Einsleigh,* he tried once more, and again, the words washed away. *How odd,* he thought, giggling within at the humour of it all. It was truly amusing that he couldn't speak, and trying as hard as he could, he couldn't move either. *That's okay,* he didn't need to do that – he didn't need to do either of those things while laid in his little boat.

As content as he felt, Einsleigh didn't seem to feel the same. Laid within her boat, she continued to tremble behind the peaceful haze, eyes still staring at his new appendage. *It's wonderful, everything is wonderful,* he would tell her if he could, *let it be wonderful.* But she didn't seem to understand. His new friend was there too, from a distance peeking through a window. *Maybe he could help her feel better? I will ask... but later.*

Mertle emerged from the waters by his side. Her fingers fiddled with the knotted strap that kept his furs together. Once undone, she gently unwrapped them from about his chest. The touch of her fingers made the flesh beneath jostle and tingle in tiny blossoms. *She's beautiful,* he thought, *with creases and wrinkles carved into her by decades of life truly lived – the lovers she must have had.* The thought pumped heat into his loin.

She took a measured, downward glance and swirled her head as loose streaks of white hair trailed behind it. "Urgh, stupid boy," she groaned, "that's the last time you'll be getting any gurlyn." She folded the furs over his arms and began inspecting his chest. There was something she saw to the side, obscured it seemed. She gave the furs another tug, sending something to tumble out of their folds.

It came to rest against the inside of his arm, a tiny cold creature touching his skin. It felt lovely. He wanted to touch it so terribly much, yet, he wanted to remain without motion equally so. Mertle's fingers were still at the side of his chest, each touch causing pulsating tingles that filled his body with ecstatic warmth – a sensation he wished would never stop. *But what is that?* The creature was pressing against him, pushing into his flesh distracting his mind from the pleasure. What was pleasant at first began turning into a nuisance. It had to go.

Lazily, he reached for it with his appendage, patting with the suckered tip until he found the little, bronze ring propped against him. The limb entered into it. Everything began to spin, turning him about a point with no control as forces unknown began to pull on his entirety. It was a hole in the bottom of a bucket and he was the water being sucked through it. The serenity stayed behind to be replaced by immense clarity as his eyes opened to the sight of a man.

The first thing Erkii noticed was his stature. Standing at little over half Erkii's height, he was far shorter than most despite being as wide, if not wider. His unusual body was covered in dress to match, hugged by loose folds of gold and black silks, layered upon him and held together by a solid gold belt of elaborately inlaid, interlocking clasps. The hair on his head was wiry and unkempt, scattered into several, grey growths that seemed to be at war with one another, determined to never make contact. In contradiction, his face was shaven clean with nothing obscuring a symmetric collection of determined features, the most prominent being his nose. Its bridge was clasped by a metal object with two round, transparent crystals mounted in metal rings to either side. Through those crystals, he looked Erkii over with enlarged, amber eyes.

"Another visitor, I see. You kill the other one or did someone else do it for you?"

"I–"

"At least I hope you did – for your sake of course – because if he comes looking, I am absolutely certain that the little sprout you're dragging about on my floor will be no match for his power."

"Who are you?"

"*Who are you* – that's a little rude, don't you think? You stumble uninvited into a man's home and have the audacity to question him. I'm the one who will be asking '*who are you*'."

The man referred to the place as home, yet if it were, it was unlike any home Erkii had ever seen. They stood atop an obsidian floor polished to a mirror like sheen, its perfect uniformity broken only by circular trenches spiralling through its expanse. Out of the trenches protruded shards of translucent crystals, hundreds if not thousands of them, all in constant motion as they followed the trenches appearing and disappearing out of sight.

"I'm Erkii," he muttered, unsure whether to look at the stranger or at what was happening behind him. The little man seemed oblivious to his inattention.

"So it was you two days back who tried to harness the power of my creation. It didn't take kindly to you, did it," he chuckled. "That is what happens when an idiot lacking in both education and talent attempts to use a tool made for the Ngahdetyn. How truly amusing that is." But his amusement seemed to fade quickly in the way of curiosity. "You should have died. The mechanism should have sucked you dry or its torrent torn you into pieces. Yet, you survived – though I doubt we can credit that to personal merits."

"Urkii almost died!" he replied, somehow mustering a little indignation out of the confusion that he felt.

"*Urkii almost died,*" the strange man mimicked. "How? Did you drop the rafters on top of him? Flung him off a cliff? Set his bed on fire?" Despite the mockery, he waited for Erkii's answer like a dog for scraps.

"It broke a sheet of ice and he fell in the river."

"He had a cold bath! You should be grateful that's all it was. Oh, how it could have been worse you cannot even fathom." The crystalline structures carried on twirling and overlapping to the rhythm. He began to notice a repeating pattern in their movement as if they were dancers entangled on the floor of a noble's ballroom. Some moved fast and other slow, yet despite that, they all seemed to follow the same rhythm as if to the tempo set by an invisible ensemble. It was mesmerising. He couldn't stop his eyes from following them about the room. The man noticed.

"Fascinating, isn't it? My own creation too, yet even I – myself – often cannot help but watch them as they move. And when they're put to work – oh the magnificence of it – sparks fly between their tips, lighting up this place in a hundred different colours. Then the air begins to resonate, humming melodies so enchanting your little mind couldn't even begin to imagine. And then it stops and I have to wait."

"Wait for what?" he asked. Ever so slightly, the crystals seemed to be slowing down in their motion.

"For power of course! It cannot function without power flowing through it, a surge of incoherence to rearrange and reorder. Unfortunately," he said, turning back to Erkii, "that means that I am reliant on the outside, reliant on things I cannot control – reliant on the likes of you. At least Maximilian was likeminded – a scholar of an astute mind. You on the other hand... well, you might just have to do."

The man's words made little sense and the disdain in his voice was grating. *The likes of you.* He thought so little of him. And Maximilian – *who is Maximilian?* It must have been the wizard that he took the ring from. They were working together, and now, the man wanted him. He didn't really understand what this was, who the man was, and he disliked the condescending words, but he was certain that the little man was offering him something very few would have been offered before.

"What do I do?"

13

*"Cruelty borne of passion is easily understood by
anyone that ever loved. Have you ever loved? If
you have, you should set me free." – Burslov of
Ghmin, used to be father, the day that his
mourning was ended by the headsman.*

"He's a dangerous man," said Eadmunt, "a very
dangerous."

The provost's lips moved to a sound – Bear was certain
– but his words seemed little more than noise filling the air
between them. He couldn't shake last night's dream. Talons
sunken through flesh and wrapped about his spine, even at
midday it wouldn't let got. He could still see the sorcerer's
eyes, blue and piercing, stuck in his vision like two sun
spots. *Let me take him*, he spoke. *If he stays with you, he
will die.*

Joran will die, the thought wouldn't leave his mind.
And the fault would be his. A branch cracked in the
shrubbery to the right. He turned to find that Eadmunt was
no longer with him. He was three steps behind.

"Bear, are you listening?" he asked gristly.

"Yes, dangerous," he repeated the old man's words as
he waited for him to catch up. The provost did so slowly.

Suspecting that the brigands were still a threat, the Marshal decided that they would leave the sleigh and circle about the ambush site on foot. They have been trekking for over an hour. Bear has been keeping to Eadmunt's pace which, with the old man's hip, meant the two were weaving between the trees on their own, following in the patch carved by the Marshal and his men. As soon as they neared catching up, the others would carry on and leave them to fall behind once more.

"Yes," said Eadmunt, now yet again hobbling by Bear's side. "You've seen what his... dogs did to that boy and to his family. The torture, the burning, the maiming – they are bad men. Every one of them has hands that drip with so much blood that no river could wash them clean."

"They're soldiers – that's what soldiers do," he told him curtly hoping to give the old man a hint, but the provost wouldn't relent.

"Aye, they're soldiers, and so were you and so was Miska–"

Me and Miska? He cut him off, "Aye, I was. You were not. Don't speak what you don't understand."

Eadmunt grabbed onto his elbow, sinking narrow fingers deep into flesh. "Maybe I don't," he replied as sharp as Bear spoke, "but just think, Bear. Think! If they're bad men for what they did, then what does that make the one who made them do it? He's a monster – remorseless beast of a man who we need to stay far, far away from."

He doesn't understand it, none at all. It's a part of war – a part of being a soldier and a commander. But what does he know about that? Before he had a chance to retort, the others came into view.

The soldiers and the Karlkans were stood still by the foot of a hill, Marshal Obert at their head. He was looking to Bear, face a mask and lips motionless as he watched their sluggish approach. His silence was an example which the others followed. Eyes trailed their walk but with no sympathy, even from Miska. It was entirely annoyance. Eadmunt said he could walk, and he walked – what more did they want?

"Our dear guide," said the Marshal once Bear and Eadmunt stood beside him, "tells us that the site of brigands' ambush is on the other side of this hill. They might still be there. Sujr and Kettil will follow me and you will remain. Watch your step, keep your blades ready, and stay low."

"Aye, aye, aye," spoke Gorgie eagerly, "and from the top you can definitely see the cut down trees and the holes those bastards were hiding in."

The Marshal was already two steps up the hill but hearing the driver he spun on his heel. "Thought they were hiding *behind* the trees – which was it?" He spoke quietly but his words were honed sharp. Gorgie's weight changed from one foot to the other then back again.

"I... I... it was holes between the trees."

"You mean gaps in the tree line or holes dug in the ground?" The Marshal stared intently from beneath a furrowed brow forcing Gorgie's head into an awkward tilt. It seemed as if the driver was trying to turn away but his neck wouldn't let him.

"In the ground, they were in the ground... in holes... and those holes had trees around them." The driver's face turned as red as it did with wine.

The Marshal examined him a moment longer then turned, finger pointing to Sujr and Kettil. Released from his gaze, Gorgie's shoulders dropped as a sigh slipped his unlatched lips.

"To the hill top. We can asses it from there. Wyhltrem," he said, turning to to the soldier whose gaze was already awaiting his, "pommel's yours."

Wyhltrem nodded.

With orders acknowledged, Obert began towards the hill. His steps brisk and confident, he wove between the evergreens as if there was nothing underfoot. Sujr and Kettil followed. The Marshal moved to a tight rhythm, taking each mounting step at the exact same interval as the one that came before it. There was precision and efficiency to each movement that made it fascinating to watch as if seeing a master of his craft if the craft, bizarrely enough, was walking. The others moved far more jagged – far more human – but despite, they made sure to keep pace with their commander. All that betrayed their struggle was the irregularity with which the steam of their breath appeared. Then Sujr's leg was snatched backwards.

"There he goes–"

Leg caught by some invisible obstacle, Sujr stumbled, in a sloppy half-spin. Seeing it, Jahn let out a raspy chortle. "Still got milk in his mug. Little git."

"Drinks it straight out the teat, that one."

It took Sujr three knee twisting jerks to break free of the root which caught his foot, each one squeezing a hearty bout of laughter out of Jahn. Astir let out a couple chortles too.

"Alright, quiet now," whispered Wyhltrem.

Astir did promptly as told. Jahn chose to argue.

"Easy there, Wyhl – it's funny!"

"Did you not hear the commander?"

"Yea, yea, you got the pommel."

"No, you thick cunt," Wyhltrem hissed, "the part about the brigands still being here, over that hill. Don't wake the rabble with your yapping."

"Do you really think a brigand with half a brain would hang about the same place where they've killed someone? They're long gone. Most we'll find on the other side is pissed in holes and a body or two."

"The commander certainly thinks they would," Wyhltrem replied, "but I suppose you are the expert on what backwood rabble would do."

Jahn's face soured like milk spilled in the sun. "Careful now, gold diapers won't keep your arse safe from a whooping." He squared his footing, a shift that sprung the nimble Astir between the two.

"Jahn," he hissed, "chain of command you stupid bastard! Marshal sees you raise a hand and you'll be swinging from a tree before lunch."

Jahn took a moment twisting his head between the two men before giving them a narrow smile. "If I have to eat another stale oatcake, I'm hanging myself from a fuckin' tree... along with the peasants there," humbled by his comrades, he turned to the Karlkans instead, smile widening into a wolfish grin. "Show ya what a bad man I really am. Or do you think Obert will hang 'em himself?"

He heard – of course he fucking heard. Bastard. Now, he was threatening them with a hanging.

"What the fuck are you talking about?" asked Wyhltrem.

"Didn't ya hear? All that whispering behind our backs. *Bad man. Monsters.* That's what they call us."

"I didn't say anything! I swear!" exclaimed Gorgie, face losing a little colour with each word. "It was them! I heard it!"

"Will you dance nicely for us?" he took a step towards them, sending Gorgie two steps back.

"Eadmunt, Eadmunt," Gorgie's hand flailed in the provost's direction, "it was Eadmunt."

Coward, was the only thought he could spare for the driver as he slowly began to reach for the axe head hung off a ring on his belt. He all but forgot the argument they had, the frustration with the old man's self-righteous pompousness. Maybe deep within he even thought him right? Regardless, even if he were a moment from knocking the man's teeth out, Eadmunt was a friend – one of his own – and he would stand and die by his side. The thought of a fight was a thrill, an old heat come again to warm his inners. His muscles were ready and mind rehearsing, but as his palm cupped the cold steel, Miska grabbed his wrist. He looked over to see her head shaking ever so slightly, staring firmly ahead without sparing him a glance.

"Don't be thick," she mouthed under breath.

He looked down at the hand restraining him. *What is she doing?* Of course, he knew what it was – she was clear about it in the night – he was not to get involved, he was to *let him die.* But how could he? Even a woman such as Miska couldn't get her way whenever she pleased.

Her fingers were wrapped tight, pushing tendons right to the bone. There was no deceiving nor slowly slipping away – there was only one way out of her vice-like grip. He pulled hard. Miska dipped, letting go only as not to fall. Astir reacted in an instant, putting himself in Jahn's way.

"Ease up, would you? They're not the first to and won't be the fucking last."

Jahn looked at Miska who stood crooked with mouth heaving and at Bear whose hand now rested firmly on the gleaming head of his axe. Shadowing a smile, his face seemed set on stirring more shit, but instead, he turned to his comrades and grunted, "Ain't much fun today, the two of ya."

"I know a few girls who sell that by the Uslig docks – might be a bit pricy with a face like yours though," said Astir. He looked over the shoulder to meet Bear's eye. There were words in his, an apology mixed with a warning and a touch of plain old *you owe me*.

"I'd hold off with that," spoke Wyhltrem flatly. "Plenty of fun where we're going."

"Wha'? Where?"

"Up that hill – the commander signalled." Wyhltrem moved and in his step they followed.

With the path cleared and the hazard of the root clearly marked by numerous streaks left by Sujr's flailing the path promised to be easy – it was for most. The soldiers, with Miska scraping their heels, made prompt work of it. Even Gorgie, though his mouth gaped and steamed like a boiling kettle, wasn't far behind. The entirety of the struggle was Eadmunt's. Strained by the hill's incline, his left leg refused to take any weight. Bear had to take its place. Together, they struggled upwards, taking each step as carefully as a toddler taking their first, yet even so, there were missteps and each caused Eadmunt to wince into a clenched jaw.

By the time they made it, the hill top was already empty. The others were descending down a neatly carved path – Gorgie, Miska, and Sujr and Kettil before them – and ahead of all was Marshal Obert, already at the bottom, crouched inside a ditch at the paths end. Intently, he stared at the ground as Bear and Eadmunt tried to catch breath.

Fuck them. They didn't wait. He thought at least the Karlkans would have – if not Gorgie, at least his wife. *Bitch,* he cussed in thought, and the thought caused him a pang. It wasn't because he called her so rarely, but because it was rare that he meant it. With how far she was, he could have said it aloud and she wouldn't even hear. She wouldn't even turn.

"Let's move," said Eadmunt, gritting his few remaining teeth.

"You need a break," *a sit down, anything*. It was more so that he needed one. Heaving air through a gaping hole, he felt exhausted. The hill would have been little challenge were he alone but having carried another with him, his breath had gotten lost somewhere along the way.

"I will be fine, just keep moving." The provost pulled forward, his good leg leading the way. With most of the old man's weight on his shoulder, Bear had no choice but to follow. *Stubborn old bastard*.

While the climb was a constant push to make his legs move, walking down was a struggle to make them stop. His feet were trying to escape him – to betray him – wanting to move, to take longer, faster steps, each less controlled than the last until he and Eadmunt would tumble in a flurry of limbs into the crusty snow below wringing their necks on landing. He had to fight them, reign them in like a farm mule.

"She is right and you know that," he heard Eadmunt over the huff of his own breath.

"What are you talking about?" A loose rock shifted beneath the bowl of his foot. His chest turned vacant and his bowels near emptied as he slid two inches.

"Don't play a fool," the old man spoke between grunts, too focused on his lopsided steps to realise they came close to falling, "as much as people may take you for one, you are not. I saw that back there, the whole commotion – you reaching for arms and her trying to stop you. Don't get yourself killed to spare some old, mouthy fool a bruising."

"He'd be the one getting killed." He had no doubt about it – the pup would have been left pumping scarlet into the white.

"And after that?" the provost asked. "Are you going to fight the other two, somehow murder them, then follow up by murdering the Marshal too?"

"If I have to," he said crassly. He had saved his life, *thankless crooked cunt*. The old man was looking at him, deep set eyes watching too closely. He felt the urge to hit him, and looking in his eye, Eadmunt seemed to notice. The old man gripped tight on his shoulder.

"Bear, dear friend, we both know this is my last leg." Eadmunt's mouth broke in a brief smile. "A moon's time, and I will have withered away. Someone will need to care for Karlka and its people. And if war... You need to compose yourself. Think with your head, think again, then act. It's what you need to do to keep them safe. That goes for Gorgie too."

Care for Karlka. He wanted him to take his place. *Why?* They had talked, maybe even more than with others, but the others had lived there far longer. *And Gorgie,* "He's a bastard."

"A bastard who risked his health to bring you here, and yet you look at him like he is some moist dung stuck to your boot. He is scared, Bear. You can see it in the way he moves, the way he acts, the way he speaks – he is still in Guhdlval Keep. He brought the dead with him and now carries them inside his head. And their killers are around him, salivating at any hint of fear or weakness. He's not you, he's not Miska – don't judge him as harsh."

The rock he carried in his gut now seemed more of a sack of loosely packed pebbles and Eadmunt's words added yet another handful. The old man was right but to think though all that he had said was too much right now.

The slope began to ease into a flat. Obert and the others were already out of the ditch, and by the time Eadmunt and Bear made it near, the only thing waiting for them was a crumbled chunk of frozen faeces. Among the excrement laid arrows. They were fletched in white, identical to the ones he pulled out of Sassa, though these hadn't lost their heads in the boy's flesh. In a way, his quick death was a mercy. Was it not so, he would have needed the iron barbs removed, dug out by his mother's or father's inexperienced hand. He'd seen a surgeon do it, digging about with quills to stop the barbs from digging in, but that was on grown men. A boy, that would have killed him. If it didn't, the inevitable soldier's fever would. *The witch could have helped – she would have had to.* Living somewhere in these woods, they could have taken him to her and maybe he would have been fine... The two nights that passed since seemed an eternity as they travelled, but now, it was coming back. As they moved past the pit and towards the road, it seemed as if the arrows were beginning to fly once more.

Something moved up ahead, ginger and bushy, two foxes running to the safety of the trees – one carried a strip and one carried a finger. They stopped in the shelter of a nearby spruce, watching as Marshal Obert wandered the field of the ambush. The three brigands were sprawled out, opened, most their flesh missing with gnawed bones protruding out of the remaining skin and tendons. Their clothes laid in shreds to the side – though they could likely be sewn back together. He remembered their death, the surprise in their eyes as their swords turned mid air, each striking the other down, and he especially remembered the third. His skull was – for the most part – missing. Like a jug of distilled piss thrown into the fire, it exploded sending jaw, teeth, bits of the temple, and an eye socket into the tree line. The brain has been dug out from within.

Amongst the brigands laid Swallow. They stripped him of cloth, leaving the wizard bare as he came from the womb. *They beat him too.* The man's face was bludgeoned, bone beaten out of shape and flesh spread into a mush over it. It was frosted over. There was only one arrow in him, inch beneath the heart. *Would have been alive for it too.* He pitied the wizard but would have done the same in the brigands' shoes. Was the outcome different, he may have done the same to them – picked their pockets too. Not that they would have been near as full as Swallow's whose mere undergarments seemed precious enough for brigands to steal, yet, that wasn't a thought other scavenging beasts seemed to share. Olive skin intact, the wizard's flesh was unmarked by fang or claw.

Crouched by the corpse's head, the Marshal seemed to be speaking to himself, "The animals can smell it a league away – avoid it like death itself."

"Smell what?" Wyhltrem asked, frowning as he caught glimpse of Jahn out the corner of his eye.

Jahn was nudging a stripped jaw bone of a brigand with the toe of his scrappy boot. His mouth moved silently as he did. It was a puppet show, one that seemed to have the sniggering Sujr as its only audience. Astir shook his head, joining Wyhltrem in a show of distaste.

"The magic – its corruption is obvious to them. If only it were so for man." He knocked on the side of his head in salute to the gods. "If I were you, I wouldn't play with this one's corpse, Jahn."

Jahn stopped immediately, boots neatly together as if they were always stuck to their spot. He looked down at the ground, mouth clenching a grin. Sujr held onto his sniggers in kind, though they tried to escape out his nose. Wyhltrem crouched across the corpse from his commander.

"Likely," Obert continued, "the vermin already stripped it of curses along with the cloth but you can never be certain about a thing like this." He kept an arms distance from the body, inspecting it with eyes alone. "Magic is a fickle thing, stolen by those foolish enough to not know that it belongs to the gods. Considering the man's new found poverty, there is no need to take that risk – anything of value either died with him or was carried off by the vermin."

Vermin. Human vermin. Brigands. Their friends were sprawled out in the snow, three half eaten corpses... there were four – the woman. He cut her down, or so he thought. Maybe a lover carried her off for burial or maybe she still lived while his son laid dead. It wasn't right. He could see the tracks that the sled had left. Along them, he could point exactly to where Sassa's light went out.

"Is that it?" spoke up Gorgie. "Can we go back... back to Karlka?" His voice was louder than the others in an attempt to disguise a slight tremble. He couldn't disguise the one beneath his furs.

"Yes," replied Marshal Obert without as much as a glance towards the driver. "We're going to find the rats. Kettil, find their track."

"Yes, Marshal Obert." The slim soldier gave Sujr a hearty pat as he pushed past. The boy's grin trickled down his chin.

Gorgie seemed confused, eyes flicking from soldier to soldier, pausing a while on Sujr and Jahn but careful not to catch their eye. "Does that mean I can go?" he finally spoke, resting his gaze on the tattered cape clothing the Marshal's back. The hesitation was clear in his voice, blood for the wolves.

"But we were only getting to know you, weren't we?" Sujr's spoke, forgetting the apparent slight of having Kettil chosen over him.

"Aye," joined Jahn, "our lumptious strawberry – just getting to know ya."

"I just want to go home." There was defeat in his voice, a plea to something – anything – that would back him. It was sad and pathetic, so much so that even Bear thought to help. And though his eyes were still on the corpse, the Marshal did too.

"That's enou–."

"But how will we get to know ya if you go home?" Jahn spoke over his commander, only realising his mistake as the back of a mailed hand slammed into the side of his jaw. A swing driven from one hip to the other, it connected with a thump. Eadmunt and Miska recoiled. Jahn slumped over, lost his footing and fell as the Marshal's hand came to a controlled rest by his hip.

Fuck me, the suddenness of it all jarred even him. There was no hint nor warning. The Marshal spoke with measure and calm which made the sudden strike a surprise. Jahn's hands rose up in a desperate guard. He was ready for another, muscles tensed in preparation for whatever would come next. Obert's hand remained still.

"I am sorry, my dear Jahn," he spoke with his voice unchanged but eyes seeping at their edge. "But you have bound your honour into my service and therefore into that

202

of our king. There are expectations that come with that for both you and I."

"Yeth, Marthal Obert," lisped Jahn. The part of his face with which the mail connected was red, raw, and beginning to swell – probably what caused his new lisp. Regardless, he dipped his head in a bow. Gorgie stood by like a stump, as uncertain as before, though he seemed to know better than to ask again.

The Marshal bowed back, then turned to Kettil who stood patiently amongst the trees. "Have you found it?"

"They were pulling a harness – a well made one too. Not much left to follow."

"Are you able to?"

Kettil turned, glancing once more over the snow's surface. With his finger, he traced a path ahead. "There was a small gap in the branches – they didn't adjust them to sit proper. It's close, but still don't look quite right – there."

Marshal Obert approached closer, eyes following the path being drawn by Kettil's floating hand. "I don't see anything."

"It's the level – look close." The Marshal leaned in as Kettil's hand motioned towards something, a rise and fall – the subtlest of humps. "A little raise stretches on and on, no more than an inch high –it's hard to see. But as you look and see it, it keeps going on and on."

Obert continued to look, squinting as he did so that the bouncing light wouldn't stop him from seeing what Kettil was trying to show him. His brow loosened. "Yes, I see it. Are you certain it carries on?"

"No, ser, I am not. No way to know, ser, until we've followed them a while."

"And so that is what we will do," Obert declared before turning to address his men. "We will march silent and alert.

Expect them. Expect traps. Expect ambush." He turned to Kettil. "The lead is yours, Kettil – I fear your eyes may be finer than my own." With a flick of the hand, he gestured his men into marching order before turning to the Karlkans.

"And to answer your question – yes, you may leave. All of you may leave. I expect you will find your sleigh if you follow the track which we have left. You will return to Karlka, to your families, and rest yourselves for the trying times ahead." His eyes moved to Gorgie who flinched at their contact. "You will rest the gelding I leave in your trust, though, I do fear this gives away the favour I will ask of you – please return in two days time to where your sleigh now sits. Can you do that for me?"

Gorgie stayed silent as if not understanding that he was expected to answer. He took a moment to eagerly answer, "Yes. Yes, Marshal Ser, of course."

"I am pleased to hear that," he gave the driver a measured smile before addressing the Karlkans once more. "Take care now my good men and, of course, my good woman." He bowed to Miska before turning away.

His words were clear, *you may leave,* but it made no sense. Now that he had made it so far, he didn't want to leave. He wouldn't leave. The bastard dragged them out into the woods, had him carry Eadmunt for five miles, and now he wants them to just go make their way back. And the woman, she still lived. Sassa's killer, she was there, at the end of that track they found. The pebbles in his gut turned to rock once more. He thought he wouldn't need it, but now that it was so close, after having travelled so far, he was going to find his revenge.

"No."

Marshal Obert turned, movement measured and controlled. Jahn's cheek had swollen to the size of an apple.

Let him fuckin' try. He would hit back – beat him to a tender roast and then some more. There were the others too, but they were a worry for the after. He met the Marshal's gaze, minding the motion of his hands and hips in his peripheral. He was ready to bob. But the Marshal's hips remained fixed and his hands unmoving.

"I understand your grief," he spoke with a firm calm. "Take the advice I have given – write your memories – and by the time you finish, the men responsible will have met justice. You have my word." In a smooth arc, Obert's hand came to rest on his shoulder. Bear placed his own on the Marshal's.

"No, you fuckin' don't understand – I have to go!" He didn't truly understand himself until this moment, but now that he spoke, the words were coming out on their own. "They killed my boy. My boy! They took him right from under my arm like nothing. His father – meant to keep him from harm. I failed. I fuckin' failed him. Blood," he said shaking the man's shoulder, "blood is what my grief calls for. And not taken by you or any of these fuckers. Taken by me. By me. Do you understand that?"

Be it the shaking or the words, there was a flicker in the Marshal's gaze. *He's thinking about it.* Out the corner of his eye, he saw someone join his side, a soldier. It was Wyhltrem.

"I understand," he spoke quietly. "Marshal, ser, if he can keep himself, let him come."

Obert looked over his man in silence then slowly nodded. "You are his charge, Wyhl. Keep him to pace or I will need to cut him loose."

"If he's going, I am too," said Miska, standing taller than before.

"No," the Marshal cut her down. Bear was ready for an angered response, a violent protest. If it was he who told her that, a fist would undoubtedly have been hurled at his jaw. Instead, she gave a single, reluctant nod. "Someone needs to ensure that Provost Eadmunt – in his ill state – makes it safely back to Karlka. I want that to be you." They held each other's eye long enough for a slither of jealousy to make its way into Bear's heart. Before he had a chance to welcome it, the Marshal turned and, with a flick of the hand, set them all in motion.

Kettil went first with Obert treading the snow at his heels. Sujr and Jahn were a step behind. Bear followed the slack jawed brute with Wyhltrem at his back. He looked back to the Karlkans, trying to catch Miska as she turned – exchange a smile or the slightest of nods. All he caught was the back of her mane.

*

The pace was excruciating. As much as he struggled before, he had put it down to having the provost to mind and carry. It was only after they set off that he realised how much Marshal Obert eased the pace for the Karlkan's sake. There was no easing now. They walked at a scout's pace with no relent.

"Keep moving," Wyhltrem grunted yet again. It pissed him off every time. Jahn was five steps ahead now – one more than he was but a minute ago – too far as deemed by the grey specked soldier. They were falling behind. "Come on, man." The words brought up anger. He wanted to slap him. Instead, he put that thought into his next step. Maybe that's what the bastard wanted.

Fucker. He felt like one of his boys trying to keep up when they walked the Karlkan hills together. Their mouths would wide open, sucking up so much air that they had no chance to even complain. He'd tease them about it too, open his mouth wide then close it like a fish. It wasn't so funny now.

Trees parted for yet another stream – or maybe a bend in the same one that they passed a while ago. It was difficult to tell. The woods out here were unfamiliar to him. The brigands had made it their home a long time ago and few would ever have big enough of a reason to take on the risk of venturing into their home.

"Look at that," mouthed Sujr, pointing out what looked like a cracked eggshell resting on the ice.

Jahn scoffed. "Lost for luck."

Stripped of flesh and crushed, it was the head of a carp. Bellow the surface, its body was perfectly intact – nature's twisted jest.

"Got caught in the freeze," said Wyhltrem. "Killed just like that by something it couldn't predict nor understand. Poor bastard." The warmth of his breath dissipated on the back of Bear's neck.

14

"She made her choice moons before my blade parted her flesh, mind unwavering from birthing you no matter how much I plead. You would split her open, a moth tearing through the walls of its cocoon, then strangle yourself on strings of her flesh. Both of you would be dead – that is why I cut her. So do not be asking me that question again, boy." – The Witch of Sangen Swamp, speaking to the only son of the Great Giant Rundhier

A felled tree, Guunt dropped flat into the snow. It was a spastic misstep which sunk the tip of his left snowshoe into the powder. His right made no effort to compensate. There was no flail to his arms as he fell, no attempt to break nor cushion – his mind wasn't in a state to think such complex thoughts. Now he laid there, uncorked wineskin in hand dribbling burgundy remnants into the snow. He clutched it taught yet little came – most of it already filled his head and belly. Like many before, he hoped it would displace his pain but all it did was render him unconscious by midday.

Poor bastard. As necessary as its cause was, Sparrow took no joy in the man's suffering. He wished he could tell him of all the lives that the girl's sacrifice will save, the rape and robbery which she nobly prevented – not that he could understand. The small folk rarely could see the knots and chains of the events unfolding – their lives' simplicity saved them from it.

"We will take a rest 'til he comes to," thumed Sigrid before dropping his staff and kneeling to remove his oversized snowshoes. One foot at a time, he sunk into the snow, turning the leather pads into a makeshift seat. He then brought about his enormous rucksack and reached within to pull out a linen parcel that unwrapped to reveal six dried trout. "Eat," he said, handing each of them a fish. There were two left in his hand, one bigger than the other. Without thought, he wrapped up the bigger then plucked away a piece of the other, gently placing it in his mouth. His eyes were fixed on their heading.

As treacherous as it was to walk on, the snow was still packed too tight for the others to drop in as deep as the giant. Instead, they sat with knees at an awkward bend, tearing away at their fish. They were six – only six – for no reason other than that no others would come. It only took one to hold off their mob and most who were its part saw this excursion for what it truly was – too big of a risk for the sake of vengeance. Those who came were grieving fathers and brothers, Sigrid and Sparrow, still bound to a halfwit's body. It was three days since he made claim to it, and yet, he still struggled.

It was easier, far easier than before. He could feel the strain brought on by the long walk, the resistance of ill adjusted lungs as they tried to catch up on air, and the itch of seeping crust formed about the stitched wounds scoring his thighs. These were signs of progress. Yet, after so long, he would have expected more. The vessel was a horse with no bridle or saddle, obeying only if given undivided attention. Letting loose for even a moment could mean loss of control and detachment, and if it were so, he wasn't sure if he could make it back before a soul taker snatched him. Its memory alone set his teeth into tingles – nightmares only his mind could paint – and so, he held on in a deadman's grip. *I'm scared,* he held enough insight to admit and accept that truth. He was absolutely right to be. But only a moron would miss that it was that same fear which kept him from doing what he needed as to gain full control of this vessel. Without it, his chances of recovering the documents were near equal to those of the drunkard sprawled out before him making it back alive.

"We should reach the swamp by nightfall," said the giant, pulling a fishbone from between his lips.

"And what are we to do then, Sigrid?" asked the red haired Rolen, seeming genuine in his inquiry.

Sigrid plucked at the fish. "We're going to find out what she knows – what they know." He placed the dry clump of flesh in his mouth.

"They're going to kill us," said one of the others, spitting shreds of meat as he did.

"They're not going to kill us," Sigrid assured, still looking ahead, "there is no reason for them to."

"There was no reason for them to do what they did back there either, but they did." There was fear in the man's voice, and it made it twinge and pull, and run entirely too quickly through his teeth.

Sigrid turned from the woods to face him, the giant's eyes inspecting his for a moment. "Aundr, if it was them, do you really think Vas would be visiting *us* to get his oats?

The bastard may be an old crook but he's not stupid. And the gold he had to spend – he payed us double what any of it would be worth on the best of days – where did it come from? That's what has me worried."

The eyes of a tagalong youth sparked. "Maybe he was paid for killing our own – assassination," he said with brows arched high as if he was unravelling a grand conspiracy. The frightened Aundr nodded in agreement. Rolen looked between them and Sigrid with a pause in the middle to gauge Sparrow's thoughts – Knute's thoughts.

Assassination. Were he in better humour, the ridiculousness of that assumption would have been a grand amusement. *Do they truly think any man would spend such a substantial amount of coin just to be rid of a couple peasants?* Far more likely, they'd pay that to have them taken slaves.

"I doubt it," Sigrid spoke Sparrow's thoughts.

"But how can you be sure," the young man insisted.

"Because our lives aren't worth anywhere near as much as it would cost someone to hire one of those fiends."

"And the circles – the fires," added Rolen, eyes taking on momentary haze.

"Yes," Sigrid concurred, wiping greasy fingers on a fold of his wrappings. "Whoever they, whatever reasons they had... it's all beyond me. But Mertle may know. The outcasts might know. And they're not going to kill us because we're not going to kill them. We bring them no harm. We're going there to ask questions, nothing more."

"Tell that to Guunt."

"Guunt isn't in a state to harm anyone," he said with feet strapped back into the snowshoes, "and with the wine we brought, he won't be for a while yet. If he is, we will stop him." He approached the unconscious man and shook him from side to side. "Time to get up, Guunt."

Guunt's eyelids opened. "Yurh, mugh gil," he mumbled whilst scrambling back to his feet, taking a first step before he was even up. The others followed as his words continued to dribble atop a stream of phlegm overflowing his mouth. "Mugh gil."

Any minute and he will be out again. Sigrid seemed determined to ensure that, putting another full skin in the man's grip. Yet even as he carried on suckling, his feet continued more or less in the right heading. It was fascinating, the man's resistance to drink – a marvel of nature. *Years it took him to build that.* To still be awake would have been a feat, doing that and walking was an achievement not many would manage.

"Mugh gil."

*

Spruce and cedar, all but few, have cleared in favour of more resilient and invasive shrubbery. Most of it failed to rise above the snow, sitting disguised instead, covered by iced layers of snow to form sparse mounds over the largely flat ground. *Swamp, how typical,* a cliched choice if there ever was one, though certainly a reasonable one. Come summer again, it will become near impossible to traverse on foot and certainly so for cavalry, giving plenty opportunity for escape. If the attack was to be at the hands of peasant mob, those familiar with the area's winding paths and boot thieving treacheries could use them to craft a formidable defence. It was an ideal brigands' lair – a lair they were approaching exposed.

The giant didn't seem bothered by their vulnerability. His stride remained as certain as it was when they left the gates. Highly effective leadership on his part, and the more he looked between the peasants' faces, the clearer it became how much they needed that. Twitches and spasms plagued their expressions as their eyeballs raced and shuffled without purpose. Was it not for the giant, they would have turned back long ago – all but Guunt. The drunk would still be ploughing ahead, lips occupied by lament and intermittent drink.

"Em comin'," he mumbled, "em comin'."

There was a wisp of smoke ahead, trailing out the chimney of an abode as obscured as they were. Topping a prominent mound at where desolation met the woods again, it stood unashamed amid the swamp. Though looking at its shape, it was a surprise it was standing at all. Despite the layers of snow to smooth it, the irregularities of the roof were apparent even at distance. He could only imagine the crooked mess supporting it from beneath, the cracks and rot in its walls. There was no pretence of esteem nor any sense of shame from the hut's owner. *Must be Mertle*.

Sigrid lengthened two of his strides to catch up to Guunt. His arm came to rest about the incoherent farmer, palm cupping the entirety of his left shoulder. "Easy, Guunt. We're here to talk, remember?"

The farmer tried pulling away but Sigrid's grip was unyielding, containing the withered man in safe firmness. "Le' go," he mumbled agitated, arms flailing in harmless jerks like trinkets wrapped about a teller. With each flail, his resistance faded as he came to the inevitable realisation of his powerlessness. It was a sight seen all over, as if the giant was a father trying to prevent his child form bringing about futile harm. "I know, I kno', " Guunt's arms came to rest, "le' me fucin' go."

"I will, friend, I will. Just ease yourself." Sigrid's voice remained a soothing echo in the deepest of caves and the drunken Guunt seemed to respond to it, easing in his hold. With a hefty pat, the giant let go of the farmer's shoulder as they carried on towards the hut.

Is it stupidity or arrogance? Walking in the open with no fear or concern, the giant's approach was a worry, yet none of it appeared in his features. *He is either stupid or has been here before,* and if Sparrow was to pick between the two, it would have certainly been the latter. But circumstances change, prior arrangements alter, and relationships wither. *Who are they? How many? Friend or foe?* These are things he likely would have known if he had truly lived in that village. It certainly seemed the others did, or at least trusted Sigrid enough not to put that to question. He didn't share their peace. *I have left enough to chance already.* He had to see for himself.

Bracing all others for resistance, he released with a single feeler. It was wobbly, uncertain, and those in tether were reins but a slither away from slipping his clutch. And yet, that was more control than he had at any point before. That slither of control was enough for a minute's wander, and that was all he needed.

The feeler sprung outwards, flailing from side to side as it sliced through the air towards the cabin. Spring's chill slid at speed over the ethereal expression – a figment his mind assigned to a thing man could never truly comprehend. It felt cold, and with every tree and shrub it cut through, he felt a sear of pain. *Not real pain,* he knew that, but it still made him flinch at times. He felt a throb of a

214

minuscule heart and two more nearby – they were rabbits waiting out the cold beneath ground. Slabs of timber – he met the walls of the hut – and behind them there was nought. *Snowberry, the old hag must be burning the leaves.* Just like in the chamber of the academy, the feeler couldn't feel a thing. His vessel was beginning to buckle.

He left the hut a darkness, sweeping frantically as he entered the woods. Timber, branches, life forms so insignificant they gave him no pause, and beyond them violently throbbing hearts – they were moving closer. The vessel bucked, and he promptly retracted.

Four, he was certain of the count. *Humans,* he judged by their size, *agitated,* the rhythm gave away. There was steel on their backs and at their sides. Whoever they were, they were nearing the hut, bound to make it before the peasants. They would gain that advantage, then there was the unknown of the hut to consider. *It's risky.* Regardless of how much living in the outer lands of their kingdom had them hardened, the peasants were heading for a fight entirely unfavourable. If they were to have a chance, they had to be ready.

"I can hear something," he said in an exaggerated hush. "Ahead."

They all began to turn their heads about like startled hens, searching for the sounds which – as of yet – they had no way to hear.

"Can't hear anything," said Rolen, stretching his neck as he looked for a source of the claimed sound.

You will soon enough. "There's someone ahead, I'm sure."

"What are you, a fucking dog now?" scowled Aundr with nervous agitation, twitching as – once more – his voice projected much further than he had intended.

"I hear somethin' too," said Guunt, moving in exaggerated, bumbling motions, yet somehow managing to nearly look in the direction of the incoming men. *That should help.*

"We have to surprise them," he said, but Sigrid shook his head.

"As long as they know us to be no threat, we have nothing to worry about." The giant sounded as certain as if he believed that himself. Judging by the calm with which he walked, maybe he actually did. The others took his cue, all but Guunt whose hand groped the dried out hilt of a clunky, pig steel sword – if one could even call it a sword. *A drunkard with a cleaver.*

Four figures emerged from the woods up ahead. The peasants dropped to a crouch about the giant making for a theatrical display, yet somehow, it went unnoticed. Single minded, the brigands went for the hut's door.

"Get up," said Sigrid, pulling the peasants up by the scruff just as knuckles struck timber.

Violent, the knock echoed, followed by a woman's shrill, "Open the door!" A man tried pulling her back by the shoulder but his grip wasn't enough and she was right back to striking the door. "We're here for the bastards who killed my Vulf!"

"Mertle," said the one who pulled her back. His voice was aged but lacking in dignity that would usually afford. "They betrayed us. They hid pickings, then tried to murder a boy in the middle of night 'cause he no longer wanted to keep it quiet. Let us in and I promise we'll treat them fair." He recognised the voice from the village gate, men buying grain. It seemed Sigrid did too as his shoulders loosened and dropped an inch.

There was a moment's wait, then a mumble made indiscernible by distance and walls.

"Aye, they had nought to do with it," said the man, "the girls won't lose a single lock – I put my word on it."

A soft creak, draw of swords, and all at once, the brigands stormed inside. There were screams, shrieks and cries muffled by timber and mounds of shovelled snow. A thump and the structure shook. Powder dropped from the roof. Another thump followed by a crack and a piercing shriek, then all was quiet but for a single whimper. Sigrid continued walking them forward.

They reached the door as two brigands emerged grasping a man between them. A mess of blood and raw flesh obscured the left of his face, eyelid shut tight and hidden somewhere beneath. His other eye was wide open, stretched to the edge, frantically trying to look back inside. His neck wouldn't allow it and his body was locked tight, captive to the two brigands. "I'll be back. I'll be back," he wailed, making an attempt to break free of their grip. A brigand slapped his hand. He sucked air as his eye shut close and feet curled inwards. His forearm swung from a bend half-way down the elbow. While one on the left, far younger, winced along with the captive, the man who struck him gave up a smirk on his densely scarred face. The smirk disappeared once he noticed the peasants' approach.

"Stay where you are," he barked, shifting in the snow to face them, captive and a red headed youth forced to turn with him.

"Will do, friend," said Sigrid calmly motioning the peasants to a stop. "I am Sigrid of Sangelk and I mean you well."

"I don't fuckin'–"

"Bern," the aged voice cut sharp from within the hut, "calm yourself." Hair a bobbing grey braid, the old man came out the door walking toward Sigrid in disheveled steps. He extended a wiry arm to brace the giant's in a greeting. "Sigrid."

Sigrid reciprocated and the two held grip long enough to convey good will. "Vas."

"I suppose this has to do with your night outing," said the old man.

A thump sounded from inside, followed by a woman's voice, raspy and sharp. "He is in no state to move. Put him back on the bed, girl."

"Fuck off, you old hag," shrieked the same voice that ordered the door be opened.

Sigrid paid no mind to the commotion. "Aye, it is," he answered the old man, keeping his eyes steady. "They took six lives from us, six of our brothers, daughters, sons, and sisters."

"They killed my girl," whimpered Guunt, lifting his chin in a sudden moment of sobriety.

"Aye, they have." Sigrid put his giant hand on the grieving man's shoulder.

Vas looked them over, brow dipped in thought. "So you think it was us who did this?" There was caution to his voice, one Bern seemed to share as he dropped a hand to his belt.

Sigrid made no movements in kind, hands far from the staff slung on his shoulder. "I do not. Whoever they were, they fought like no men I've ever known. They fought like no men I ever thought to exist. And what they did to them – it was ritual – it was magic they were trying to do."

The shrieking woman's head appeared in the doorway, dragging something from within. Her face seemed doglike, elongated, and in manner she reminded him of one who had found a bone. There were boots beneath her arms, squeezed tightly into her sides as she leaned forward in the struggle against the mass. To the sound of scraping and occasional thumps, she emerged, letting go of the legs as soon as she noticed the peasants. With grimace and a flick, she bared yellow teeth and steel.

"Put that away now," said Vas, moving his hand over the slim blade which she pointed towards unflinching Sigrid.

A woman, wrinkled and crooked, stepped onto the doorstep. "Vas, I want the Gharan boys and – if clarification is needed – I want them alive." Despite her crooked back, she stood perfectly still, balanced and steady. She was in full control.

Vas paused on the ground, trouble painting itself on his brow before he even had the chance to look her in the eye. "They will be put on trial, Mertle. You know best that I cannot make any promises."

"I'm not asking you for promises, you daft old crook," she snarked, "I want you to do it, or better yet, leave him here. Just look at him, the poor bastard already got his share, and his brother... he would sooner step in a puddle than trample a worm – you know it as well as I."

The young woman spun on the spot, leaning forward with legs wound as if ready to pounce. "Get back insiiugh–" she winced as Vas clutched onto her wrist. Her blade dropped into the snow.

"It's not my decision to make," he gave Mertle a firm answer as the young woman contorted in his grip. He pulled her towards the others, free hand grabbing the prisoner's floppy wrist in passing to lead him out of the grip of the youngster and the brute.

The man whimpered. A little voice cried from inside. A tapper of feet followed. Mertle spun to clutch it still, her other arm swinging about and shutting the door closed. "Elia." The man tried to turn towards it but all he managed was a jerk before his broken arm stretched taught between him and Vas and his legs buckled.

"Stop it now," scorned Vas. "I made a promise, Torgy – the girl's aren't a part of it. Now, walk steady and I won't pull." The captive nodded, slowly coming to a stand.

Vas pulled him and the woman down the path that brought them here. It seemed that he had forgotten that he was still gripping her, taking one glance before letting her loose. She tore away from his hand before it opened fully. The captive followed meekly. "You two," Vas waved at the youngster and the brute, "carry him, and do it gently – if that is something you're capable of."

"Vas," spoke the giant, "I need to speak with you about our matter. " The peasants had become little more than observants to their spectacle, forgotten ones at that. Sigrid's words seemed a surprise, an unexpected nuisance which brought a flash of frustration into the cracks of the old man's face. In a clutch, he managed to compose himself.

"We have matters of our own to settle first as you can see. Come by in an hour's time – follow the path. We can talk then. Till then, bother Mertle." With all that he needed said, Vas walked on. The wolfish woman pushed ahead, wordless in her spite as she stiffly passed him. It wasn't long before the distance between them doubled then doubled again, but that seemed of little concern to the old man. Instead, he made sure to walk slow enough to remain near the brute, the youth, and the jet skinned man stretched between them.

He was sizeable, a load which certainly wouldn't go unnoticed even on the shortest trip. A slower pace would have been expected – even from men of their statue – but the pace should not have been that slow. *They're straggling,* purposefully attempting to fall behind with their prisoner. But it seemed that the old man, a captive of his own in hand, was more than aware and matched his pace to theirs. *Peculiar,* just as the man being carried. It was rare for a Gharan to end up this far north even when seeking escape from servitude. Nonetheless, it wasn't beyond the plausible. One was right before him, carried by the knees and elbows, feet and hands dangling like stuffed rags in a toddler's grip, a bronze ring about his little finger. It was his ring.

Realising that Vas wouldn't let them fall behind, the brigand's pace picked up, Sparrow's most treasured possession bobbing up and down between them. It was his ring – *his* – at least to the extent that any Ngahdetynian creation could ever be. The truth was that no man could ever fully understand, let alone poses the magnum opus of a ground dweller's life. He was a peasant merely borrowing his lord's plough, and yet he had held the plough so long he thought it his. Unwitting, the brigands vanished with it in the trees, walking to the place where the contracts must have been – the contracts he had lost his life for. But he was on the trail, and soon, he will bring an end to a war before it even had the chance to start.

Sigrid knocked.

*

The door rattled in its frame as the giant's fist hammered on the darkened timber. While gentle at first, frustration began to overcome him with each knock that was left unanswered by the crone. There was no pretence. They could hear voices inside, soft laments and attempts at comfort, Mertle's croak at times too. But the door remained barred. To her, they were pests she wanted gone – pests who wouldn't relent.

Sparrow's eyes traced the trail, etching it into memory in case it disappeared at the hands of some anomaly. It was close, *it must be, it better be*. Of course, in their ignorance the brigands may have burned it, lost it, or left it – the coat or the papers. They were hidden in a pocket sewn between layers of hide and accessed from the collar, near impossible to find even when looking. But if they did find it... *can they read?* Likely not, rendering them into little more than a great fire starter. He was near, so very near, and soon he would know for certain.

"Open the door," spoke Sigrid, the depth of his voice seeming to rattle the door as much as his fist which carried on knocking. The door unlatched and swung open.

"Boy, are you persistent." Nostrils flared and brows ruffled, Mertle made no effort to hide her annoyance.

"You should have opened."

"You should have stayed home, Sigrid. Now look at you, trying to knock down a witch's door." They faced each other in tension but their masks promptly slipped as the withered woman wrapped her arms about the giant's waist. She removed herself promptly to stare them down from the doorway. "I know why you're here – at least in part – the little they brought back with grain explained enough. You are looking for men who killed your people but you are looking in the wrong place – you know that as well as I."

Sigrid nodded. "Aye, I know. Vas knows better than to burn his last bridge. He needs us. He needs us to take his gold and needs us to feed his people."

"Bu' you don't," mouthed Guunt.

Mertle's head flicked towards him as if she were a bird of prey hearing a mouse squeak. "Speak up, boy."

"You don't," he repeated, hand fondling the grimy hilt of his sword in search of assurance. "You don't need us – witch!" he shouted the word in accusation. "Maybe it was you who–"

Sigrid looked ready to step in but Mertle was quicker. In a beat she vanished inside, reappearing with a piece of kindling in hand. Without a pause, she flung it at Guunt's head before he could finish his words. *Thunk*. The piece of timber glanced off the top of his skull, spinning out through the air until it embedded itself in a mound of white. Guunt sat, wincing as he nursed his scalp with his hand.

"Do not accuse me of anything I did not do, boy. Now," she said, turning back to the giant, "if you know it wasn't us, tell me what you want." Sigrid looked to Guunt whose arse was sunken into the white. He was checking on him, though it didn't seem to be out of concern for his well-being but rather to check if his fervour had eased. Looking at the way he sat, it seemed all of it had been knocked out of his head by the kindling.

"It was a ritual," he said, turning to the witch, "but not to any of our gods. It was like nothing I've seen. There was fire, and blood, and the way they were cut... they were all cut like pigs – to bleed slow as if they were trying not to spoil the meat."

Mertle's head tilted like that of a curious crow. "*Not to spoil the meat* – was it a cooking fire too?"

"I don't know, maybe–"

"And were any of them butchered?"

"They were all–"

"Not cut up, but butchered. Were they gutted and their finest slices of flesh removed? Were their limbs trimmed, brined, and twined for an even roasting?"

What a barbaric presumption. The thought of it made Sparrow uneasy, *eating human flesh*. He has known those who had, both out of hunger and yearning for forbidden pleasures. At least hunger he could understand, there aren't many things that those lesser would resort to when missing a few meals. Aundr and Rolen, the two peasants tending Guunt's bleeding scalp, were turning pale of face just hearing of it, but starve them for a while and one's teeth would inevitably sink into the other's flesh.

"No, they were not."

"So they were bled but not butchered," Mertle murmured mostly to herself. "And the fire – how big was it?"

"It was… big. Very big, all around them, and the smoke – we could barely see them through it."

"All around… smoke… what did it smell like?"

"I don't–"

"Was it sweet and wispy, cool as it entered your nostrils?" She was invigorated, mindlessly moving closer to the giant.

"I can't–"

"What did it smell like, Sigrid?"

The giant remained still yet his ever present calm was giving way to concern. His nostrils flickered, eyes widening ever so slightly. "It smelled like that, like your house."

"Snowberry leaves," she murmured once more, taking a step back into thought.

The wound in Sparrow's thigh began to weep once more. *She knows.* His heart took two beats in place of one. Whether he could or not was no longer a concern. He let a feeler loose.

Entry, he needed entry into her psyche. There was none. The witch's mind was encircled by a wall of tightly mortared bricks unyielding to even the hardest pushes he could muster. He tried again and again but the feeler only slapped against it – a weed in a child's hand as it tries to slay boulders. *There must be a way, certainly,* and nearby he found it. A keep in disrepair, embers glowing at its centre. *The drunk.*

"Did anyone survive?" she blurted, eyes once more on Sigrid.

"Yes," he said, head beginning to turn in time to be late.

For Bronie, he whispered into the embers. Before anyone made sense of the scraping, the rust spotted steel entered Mertle's side. Guunt let go of the hilt.

It seemed he expected it to drop, to fall and make a dent in the snow, but the sword remained where he left it. The bulbous pommel floated in line with the peasant's navel – an ornament central to the space in which they stood. There was something serene about its presence, as if they were brought here in tradition, jovial celebrants about to indulge on excess of last year's turnips. The pommel was a focal point at which they all stared.

"Fo' Bronie," he mumbled, the conviction of before no longer there. It was what drove him to plunge his blade into the old woman, it must have been – soon enough, that will be the reason his little mind will come to accept.

Mertle's eyelids flickered compulsively as she followed the pommel, the hilt, the blade, losing track just above her hip. Black folds surrounded the opening, pulled taught somewhere inside. It seemed the robes which wrapped her clung to the pitted steel and were pulled along into the wound. On the other side there was nought. She looked at the wound, she looked at Sparrow, then she fell.

The weight of the blade pulled her to its side, plunging first into the snow then – grating against bone – it made its exit on the other side just beneath the woman's ribs. Robes and steel pitched a pointed tent. Mertle's mouth popped open as if there was something urgent she needed to say but just couldn't remember. Her beady eyes rolled backward to try to catch fleeting words. They returned empty. It seemed no one else could find any either, all standing fixed to their spots with eyes on the dead witch and her killer whose fingers began taking turns to quiver.

Feet stamped quickly on wooden boards. "You fucking bastards!" screamed a woman, a haze of blond appearing briefly in the doorway before she slammed it shut. The narrow gap in its setting disappeared – she was leaning against it from within, pressing the door into its frame. A scrape, a metallic clacket, and the bar fell in place. Silence followed.

She must have known things after all. It was survival – he had to do it – and yet, there was pity within. He truly felt it as he looked down at the crooked corpse laid in a sanctuary of patchy robes that the peasant's fire poker wasn't sharp enough to pierce. The walls surrounding her mind were far beyond what even the most practiced of citadel's masters could construct, *all that with no aptitude*. She must have found ways of her own, experiments conducted within the safety of the bog or maybe knowledge found within the tomes she stole – those would be worth retrieving too. As things were though, the tomes were not a priority and the thick slabs of wood were enough of a hinderance to dissuade him from pursuing them.

Sigrid's foot lifted in a hesitant step towards the door. Half-way through, his mind changed, boot returning back to ground. He then turned to Guunt.

The man's shaky hand moved towards the witch's body. There was uncertainty to his movement and in his face a vacancy. No doubt his mind was writhing, desperately searching to understand what spurred him to do what he did. It would be understanding which he could never find and a search which he will soon enough abandon in favour of a cathartic delusion that he had made the choice himself. *Revenge.* As it was, regardless of whether there was a choice involved, the next actions were ones he could make on his own. He was going to flip her over and work the blade out of the flesh, rocking it back and forth through the suction, likely losing the worn out handle in the process.

Before Guunt's hand got anywhere near the corpse, the giant grabbed his wrist.

"You won't be needing it," he spoke a low rumble. Blue veins bulged on his paled hands, webbing over taught tendons of a hand gripping in excess of what was needed. Guunt was restrained with his arm forced into an angle it would have never taken on its own. The corners of the old man's mouth gave away pain. The giant didn't seem to care, or rather, it seemed pain was what he intended. His jaw tightened.

Will he break it? The intent appeared to be there and Sparrow's teeth clenched in preparation for the crack. Guunt's did too, whimpers escaping through gaps and vacancies of his bite. The old man's eyes were wide in their deep set orbits, beacons of muted fear – but he didn't protest. Whatever was to happen, he came to accept. A creak of the joint seemed to herald what was coming. The man's shoulder and elbow were a hand's width ahead of his wrist when Sigrid let go. He didn't want to let go – that much the tight fold of his brow made obvious – yet he did so despite. Impressive self-control, and amongst the rabble living on impulse and desire it was worth noting. *Will you be a target, pawn, or ally, Sigrid of Sangelk.* Though he held a prediction, it was too early to know for certain, maybe even too early to consider.

"I did it for Bronie," whispered Guunt, cradling his arm in relief for his shoulder and elbow. There was a recess between his eye and cheekbone, a little crevice within which tears began to pool. Soon, they were overflowing. "I did it for Bronie."

The giant's frost dried lips moved to a near silent, incoherent rumble. *What to do,* they read, *what to do*. Eyes drooped beneath a brow near collapse, he looked at the weeping Guunt. He then looked at Sparrow.

*

Sigrid decided that Guunt's fate would be up to Vas and his people. Allies, he called them – important for their future. That's where they were headed, following the fresh prints that the brigands left, to have a conversation about the man's fate and about the killings of their own. That was no worry to him – the likelihood of anyone besides Mertle knowing of the ritual was miniscule. No one else could betray what had truly happened. Of course, it will all be recorded by scholars, the difficulties he went through along with the sacrifice which the peasants had to incur. It would be beyond their comprehension – not that they would ever be granted the right to read the finely illuminated tomes – but the honour of having their contribution immortalised at least brought him some solace. They were Bronie, Alr, Stina, Kuarl, and Knute, who was the most important of them all. Yet, there seemed to be another problem in the making.

Despite her timely death, Mertle's question for survivors seemed enough to put undesirable thoughts in Sigrid's head. He was standing back now, walking last in their group as the other peasants led the way. His eyes were on him, on Knute's lumpy body, watching his every step. It was certainly a concern, one which he tried to address by reaching for the giant's mind, having a feel.

Suspicions and frustrations were indeed there, but they remained collected. They floated about in their bitter, ashy forms, circling one after the other refraining from frequent collisions. Collected thoughts were rarely an immediate danger. But the danger could still be elsewhere.

He reached out once more, sweeping outwards over the path and surrounding hills. Shrubs, trees, on the left, with more of the same in front. Atop the hill on their right, there were heart beats stuck close to ground. Seven, all men, coated in layers of fur, leather, and steel. The air vibrated by the lips of one.

"Aim for the big one," spoke a voice he recognised. Layers of bone and timber were stretched against their will by threads of hemp. Then, they were released.

Feathered bolts whistled through the air.

15

"All did it. Not all liked it – I didn't like it. But I did it. If ya' didn't, it's like you were judging them, like you're too good to be one of 'em. We were good, honest – had to be – so it couldn't be that bad if all did it, you understand? So when my turn came, I fucked 'er." – Captain Hujrlva, recounting the sacking of Pourtlin to his father.

Strings cut the air, squeaking like hatchlings calling for their mother. They were mounted to bows of horn bound in metal, laughably small, so much so he thought it some bizarre dream when the soldiers began pulling out bits and pieces out of their sacks and mounting them into tiny crossbows. *Children's toys,* he thought up until having watched two men struggle to bend the bows into place. They were killing tools. There was power which they held and, at the flick of the hand, released into the trunk of a man he was certain of knowing. He had no time to stop them. The mistake had already been made.

"Ugh." Sigrid of Sangelk dropped to his knees as four stubby bolts entered between his ribs.

The men in his company spun on the spot, searching to understand the sudden noise, looking to the giant in utter confusion. They looked at the pained expression, the gaping mouth, to the hillside, then back to Sigrid, mistrusting what their eyes were telling them. Goats shortened a head, their legs moved them in purposeless circles – all but a lucky one who took off seemingly before the arrows even struck. It was too late for others to run now.

The Marshal flicked a wrist. His men descended. Bear followed along uncertain as to why. *Maybe I can stop this,* he told himself, sliding down the slope in a white cloud with an axe in his hand. The young Sujr made it ahead, meeting a man – a boy – close his age before the other had the chance to draw. He sliced his throat then hammered the boy's head on return with the pommel sending him to ground. Sujr's mouth twisted in fulfilment.

"They're from Sangelk," he called to deaf ears, "I know them."

Astir faced a man who looked as young as the other. Unlike Sujr, he waited till the other had the sword firmly in hand – not that it mattered. There was frenzy reddening in the youth's eye and frothing his lip. All he had he put into the first strike, forfeiting his defence to deliver a killing blow which the soldier feigned with a subtle step. Swiftly, Astir closed the distance. His calm eye met the youth's gaped in panic. A man of red hair was now before Bear.

The man's blade came for his head. He ducked as the man went for another. *I know him. What's his name?* Whether the man knew him too, there was no way to tell.

The second strike came at Bear's hip, blade gouging his axe shaft as he parried. Then the third, a little higher, making a cut before he could react. The cold gave the pain a dull tinge. A wet warmth followed soon after. There was no time to consider. He stumbled backwards to avoid the next. *Fuckin' bastard. He* no longer cared for the man's name or his life.

The man's next strike was a lunge for his gut, one Bear managed to time. He leaned to the side and shifted forward to cut up behind the guard. "Yaagh," the man shrieked as the axe head cleaved into his wrist, sending his sword flying loose down the path. His fight was done but Bear pulled the stroke through.

The man's right hand abandoned its joint. In futility, he tried to put it back in place with his left as the axe arced about. Bear brought it about his head and, with all that momentum, sunk it at the end of his jaw. Flesh parted. Bone cracked. The man's head dangled loose at the end of a broken spine. He fell limp to the ground. All his teeth could have been counted through a gash that left his jaw detached.

Bear meant to stop this, he really did. None of them were the men for whom he came. None of them had part in Sassa's death. They were from a village not too far from his – neighbour he could have called them in circumstances not too different from the present. They could have called him neighbour too. He had bought a saw from Sangelk, had his hoe fixed there, and with the man he had slain, he exchanged grain for cured venison. *Rolen, that was his name.* The end which he met was undeserved.

Sigrid didn't have long either, the provost who could have well been the man he answered to. The bolts sunk in deep, doubtlessly piercing and tearing his inners. Death would meet him soon enough. A little puddle of scarlet sludge was forming at the giant's knees. There were no bolt shafts to be seen, no fletching nor loose yarn. They sunk deep and one ran straight through leaving but a single red spot in the snow behind. Before the giant stood another man, breath laced with drink. Bear had met him too – an old farmer who sold him radishes and yams one summer. *Guunt,* a widower and a father to a daughter so difficult for a man to forget. With wrinkled hands empty yet raised, he guarded Sigrid as the giant's life leaked into white.

"You bastards," he huffed to Jahn and Sujr who began a circling approach – wolves coming in on their prey, wound taut and ready to lunge.

"They're from Sangelk," he spoke once more, voice muffled before it even left his lips. It was quieter than he knew it ought have been. The two carried on without heed, and with blood misting his skin, stopping them felt a hypocrisy. But Marshal Obert heard.

"Stop." His voice an impassionate measure, clear as a rasp on the temple of one's head, Jahn and Sujr were quick to obey. "You're unarmed," he addressed the farmer.

Piss dribbled out Guunt's trouser leg. "Fuck yourself." A patch of yellow began to spread about his right snow shoe. Next to him, the giant mumbled indiscernibly.

"You're unarmed," the Marshal repeated, "and, hearing what my man is saying, from a place called *Sangelk*. What's your name?"

Lined face in twitches, the old farmer's eyes jumped between their faces, restless but for a moment when they stopped on Bear. "Guunt."

"Guunt, Guunt of Sangelk," Obert spoke back. "And behind you, who is that?"

"Sigrid, our provost," he named the giant who carried on murmuring all to himself.

Once stood so proud, Sigrid knelt humbled, brought to his knees on this backwood path. Clear mucus and yellowed phlegm had turned his beard into a sticky mess which began clinging to the furs covering his chest. A bulge started to form in his wrappings just above the belt, a pooling of blood which quickly found a point of escape in a parting of hides. All it took were five stubs of wood loosened with a hand's twitch to leave the giant dying, talking to himself, "I don' wanna die... I don' wan' die..."

"Sigrid of Sangelk." The Marshal became silent, body still as his eyes calmly assessed the clearing. He looked to the corpse before Bear and the one left by Sujr. He looked to the man who Astir fought, stood with a split lip but very much alive in Astir's grip, then back to Guunt whose hands gave up a tremor. "I know of him, and what I know would prove your words true."

"I don' wan' die..."

The Marshal took a step towards Guunt who immediately tightened beneath the skin. He was afraid, that much was easy to see as his eyes near shut in expectation – expectation which Bear shared too. Aye, he had travelled with the commander, spoken, eaten, and slept with him but none of that had endeared him to the man, nor did it convince him that he wasn't going to kill the old farmer who stood unarmed before them.

The Marshal's hand rose rigidly to the old man's shoulder. "I am in pain, my friend," he spoke with a voice meant to ease. "A mistake has been made, a mistake which I am bound to carry with me while I live. I hope that one day, you may come to forgive it. Tell me now, where is Sangelk?"

Guunt's resolve wavered under the weight of the hand which squeezed his shoulder in apparent compassion. "Home... there." Guunt's head flicked to the way from which he came. The Marshal looked to where he pointed.

"That's where you should go now, Guunt of Sangelk. You and your friend – I heard there is a great healer in these woods – take your provost to her and see if there is anything she can do. My prayers will be with you, though, I fear they may be coming too late." Obert removed his hand from Guunt's shoulder but his gaze remained fixed on the farmer's restless eyes. They jumped between the soldiers and the dead Rolen, to Astir, and to Bear himself where again they lingered. Then they shut. Despite how tightly he clenched them, tears still found gaps to stream through.

Poor bastard, he didn't deserve this. He pitied the old man who walked limp-legged to the side of a dying friend, he pitied the giant turned to a mumbling mess in his final moments, and he pitied the youth shaking in Astir's grip. He and the boy on the ground looked so alike, and when Astir was told to release him, he fell right on top of him. He dribbled clear ribbons out his nose and mouth as he grasped at the skewered chest. He screamed and pounded, and Bear's ribs caved in.

Earth tremored. Trees shook. All turned white.

*

Fuck, fucking fuck. His chest released leaving his heart to attempt an escape as it throbbed uncontrollably. Blocked by the snow, he couldn't see a thing past his own nose, and soon, he realised all he could hear was a loud ring.

Fuck, he said – he was sure he did – but he heard nothing. He shouted, desperate to hear his own voice but it was as if he were another man yelling from a distant hill top. *What in the fuck happened?* In his fifty years, he had never seen weather like this – no anomaly, no animal – nothing that could be blamed for this other than the gods. *The gods, it must have been.* Nothing else could explain it, nothing but maybe for the wizard. Yet, could he? He had seen magic men come along with the army to make themselves rich on the battlefield – to flail about their arms and mumble enough to convince the kings and lords that they have done something to win the battle. Doubtlessly, some even believed it themselves – made them better liars. He never did, not until he saw what that bastard did on the sleigh. *But he's dead,* and even if not, *no one* could do *this*.

"Call," a voice pushed through the ringing, dull and muffled. It belonged to the Marshal.

"Wyhltrem, sir," replied the soldier. One by one, the others did too. All five called in as their hazed shapes began revealing themselves in the white.

"Bear?" the Marshal's voice came a little sharper than before, and looking at the Marshal's outline, he seemed to be looking right at him.

What else was he to do but answer, "Here, sir."

The white that had surrounded them all winter had cleared to the ground leaving about walls of rich green.

Still on his knees, the giant remained as he were and Guunt by his side. He heaved, rib cage expanding slowly, face twisting as the air trickled into his lungs. His eyes remained on the ground, painting his thoughts on the newly ploughed snow. Next to him, the farmer had fallen to his knees, surrounded by a heap of snow that seemed to prop him upright. Judging by his face, it was a spot he wasn't ready to leave. The only thing amiss was the youth, likely disappeared somewhere down the trail of disheveled steps.

Bear's hearing returned – the wheezing of the giant's breath, Jahn's mumbled jest about his cock being the shaking's cause – all normal but for the ringing. The ringing remained though narrowed, higher in pitch, inconsistent. Within his gut, something churned.

"We're moving – restring, step quiet." As told, the soldiers moved. Legs in tremors, he moved with them. One after the other, they followed in the direction that the men of Sangelk were headed – or at least so he assumed. The path had disappeared. Shifted by magic and buried by the powder cleared from surrounding spruce, it was now buried, and where it used to be Kettil alone seemed to know. The snow was looser than newly ploughed soil and even with snowshoes their feet sunk. Each step was a squeak and a crunch threatening to swallow them up.

He could hear the crackles and creaks of the crossbows being bent – he could even hear Jahn's breathing – yet the ringing in his ear remained a continuing backdrop. It turned to more of a shriek. He hoped this was a step in its passing, but it only seemed to be getting louder. Its irregular pitch began sinking into the back of his ear drilling further and further in. The branches of a distant spruce shook suddenly as shapes moved through them – two – one large, one small. They were human shapes, their feet sinking deep in the snow causing them to trip with near every step. For the most part, they were moving on all fours.

"Loose."

Jahn, Sujr, and Astir raised. Strings squeaked. Bolts whistled a path ending in wet thumps. The small shape fell limp, the other writhed and added a noise to the ringing, though it added nothing new. It was the same, only an emphasis to what had been there from the start – a desperate wail. But this wail he could understand.

"Eali!" Her cry was followed by a wet, laboured cough. "Eali! She tried to crawl towards the little shape but the loose powder kept her in place shrieking and wheezing until Kettil sliced her throat. All of them moved past as if it were nothing. But it wasn't nothing to him.

Why? Why did they shoot? And the little one, face down in the white – some mercy from the gods – what could it have ever done? Wrapped in furs, just a tiny shape put down in the cold like a lame filly. It made no sense. There were but two and they were six, all grown, strong, and armed, and they still killed them without a question. *Why did you do it?* He looked at Obert whose face was unmoved. It wasn't right – the man wasn't right. Yet still, he followed. He followed the Marshal, feet sinking deeper with each step that brought them closer to the dreadful noise. The sky began to darken. The trees thinned out. His heart had sunken deep.

Mounds, collapsed and caved irregularly, he knew them to be homes – he lived in one before. Round huts of clay and woven twigs, shaped into domes, in winter they covered in snow which most didn't clear, not out of lack of will, but because it made them warmer. Now, the snow was only dead weight atop the collapsed structures. There was a sound coming from one of them, a muffled cry barely forcing itself through the mass – no one else heard and maybe it was but a noise he imagined. He moved closer to where the sound came from, leaning in towards a mound which seemed to be somewhat intact.

Someone's alive, he thought with his ear near touching the snow. He could almost make out their words as Wyhltrem tugged him away with a nudge to the rib. His head shook as he gave Bear a look.

One by one they moved past the mounds. There was more noise ahead, far louder and different than before. What seemed lone and incoherent was now a distinct chorus of piecing shrieks and pained moans. He could make out voices, many of them, high and low, each different to the next, each voicing their pain to a different pitch. The mounds cleared. Ahead, the evergreens were snowed over once more. There was a line dividing the bare trees from the others, on both sides, parting them a line so straight as if crafted with a guide rope. Beyond the line the snow remained firm, all seemingly the same. It was a partition and at its centre stood an enormous oak. Beneath the oak laid nought but suffering.

Arms and legs twisted, fixed to bodies cracked and caved. Most laid still, those who didn't heaved irregularly, expelling inhuman sounds out of rasped throats. Before the mass, they stood frozen in step.

The smell of piss filled his nostrils, there was shit too. The piss was his, he felt its warmth against his leg as it dribbled down the side of his leg.

"Find out what happened, then put them out of their misery." The words were calm and collected – pieces of certainty in whatever all this was. The men moved forward and so did he.

All their faces sat tight, desperately clinching onto thoughts they couldn't share. Astir, Wyhltrem, even Sujr and Jahn, walked tense – Jahn's eye twitching and Sujr's opening and shutting compulsively. Bear's hand began a dance he couldn't stop. *It's all the same, all of them*. The soldiers were just like men he had known before, those he had loved. They had work to do, work they didn't want to do, but work they did all the same. *There is no pleasure in this*. Duty, that's what it was.

As if to prove his thoughts wrong, Sujr and Kettil moved ahead, loosening all fibres of their being as they unsheathed their blades and dropped at the side of a man whose legs were bent in reverse. "What happened here, old boy?" they asked shaking him by the body wraps getting nought but pained grunts. Whether the man could reply or not, they didn't give enough time to find out. With a flick of the wrist, life began dripping in pulses out his opened throat.

Astir and Jahn questioned a woman of their own. They gave time, they coaxed, Astir even pled, but all they got was, "Don't kno'." By the time she was dead, Wyhltrem and he stood by a man too.

There was steam coming out of a hole in the snow to the side, streams of water flowing too. *How strange,* he thought, enjoying the respite this little moment of absurdity brought. Looking around there were a few of those, and a near empty fire pit beneath the oak. That's where he wanted to look, that's where he wanted to be. But Wyhltrem already began to ask the one question they could think to ask, "What happened?".

Eyelids unraveled from a pained clench revealing a cluster of spots red, white, and black. They stared right at him, twitching yet unmoving – they were eyes that knew the end was nigh. It felt as if the entirety of the old man's being was focusing on him. He had his attention undivided, unwavering, yet slowly it was slipping, soon to be gone.

"What happened?" Wyhltrem asked once more.

The man turned his gaze to the soldier. Cracked lips parted ever so slightly as he croaked, "I'm... gods." With a rasp, he suckled air into his chest then seemed to begin a cough as Wyhltrem's dagger sunk in between his ribs. The cough was never finished.

To the side Sujr was kicking the head of a spasming youth who managed to wedge Kettil's blade between the little bones of her palm. Wyhltrem seemed oblivious, eyes fixed on the next body. The question was the same, the answer may as well have been, but this time his dagger remained still. Instead he looked to Bear.

Me? It was a thought which Wyhltrem seemed to understand, hesitation and doubt he knew as well. But this wasn't the time. They both knew, they both understood. Stuck in this moment, neither wanting to – not that it mattered.

Me. It was his turn.

His fingers wrapped tight about the axe shaft. It had to be done. *Got seventeen at most,* that's how many winters he would have given the boy if asked. The axe rose to height with his shoulder. Frightened eyes stared into his. He wanted to think, to find cause to stretch the time, but thought was the enemy of action. He sunk the axe head into the centre of the boy's chest.

For a moment he let his eyes close in search of respite, in search of home, but as much as he wanted to he couldn't leave this place – they wouldn't let him. They moaned, shrieked, and screamed, and he could feel twitches crawl up the axe shaft from the dying boy at his feet. There was only one thing he could do to stop it.

He tugged, but far too gently – the axe head remained stuck. *Twist then pull, that's how you do it, boy.* Who told him so, he no longer remembered, but it worked. With the axe freed, they moved towards the next man whose writhing dug him deep into the white. At least this one wasn't his.

Men, women, children, their twisted bodies laid before him. But there was sense to be made of all of it. *Sassa, they killed him – they're here,* somewhere in the carnage they laid. *They deserve it. Fuckin' bastards. Fuckin' bastard,* he grunted inside as he dropped the axe once more. It nearly slipped his faulting grip. *She deserved it.* He believed it – he had to.

They reached the side of a brutish man who laid in undisturbed snow, propped up by the oak's root. Wounded he was, many times, but unlike the others, most of his wounds have long healed leaving him etched in jagged lines. Was it not for the shard of collar bone sticking out of a brown mess of crusted fluid and fabric, it would have seemed as if he were merely resting. As it was, he laid there grunting through a narrow gap between scar split lips. "Fuckin' ghr– cunt, fuckin' bast'rd"

Wyhltrem crouched beside him. "What happened?"

The brute looked down from the oak's crown, eyes two leaking wells. "Th' fuck it looks like to you? Gharan cunt could do magic – fuckin' bastard. I knew it from the day they got here – knew not to trust 'em. I said so, fuckin' said so. Now look. All dead, all of 'em – my family. My family." The beds of his eyes began to overflow, tears streamed down his face making the thick scars their beds. "They were gonna rob them, take it all, and I stopped 'em. Fuckin' cunts."

Wyhltrem studied the man for a moment before turning to where the Marshal stood. "This one knows something – says there was a Gharan mage."

Obert didn't respond, head motionless, stooped over parchments which stretched between his hands. Like the brute laid before them, he wept too.

"Ser."

Without lifting an eye, the Marshal murmured a response, "Does he know where the mage has gone?"

"Do you–"

"That way," the man cut Wyhltrem off, flicking his unaffected hand towards a spot in the tree line where a set of tracks ended.

"Ser, they went into the woods – should we follow? Ser?"

Obert didn't seem to hear a thing. His eyes had reached the bottom of the page, then flicked back up to start again. Racing from word to word, he reached the bottom once more, then frantically pulled the front parchment to the rear.

"Ser?"

"Kill him."

Wyhltrem's body jolted to a stand. "But ser, he might know more," he protested, "we can use him." The Marshal looked at the disgruntled soldier, then promptly turned back to flipping between pages.

"Not to us."

It seemed Wyhltrem thought to protest once more, even disobey as he stared between the man and the dripping dagger in his hand. If the thought was truly there, it was but a fleeting one in his commander's presence whose teary eyes continued their reading. Wyhltrem turned to Bear.

There was no fear in the brute, no plea in his eyes, no bargain on his lips. "Just kill that dark bastard," was all he said as he turned back to the oak's crown.

Deserves it. The axe fell.

16

"Now that you know what I know, will you still plough their fields? Will you still fight their wars?" – street corner preacher, two days before his execution.

Limbs, pale flesh, claws, and grasping hooks, they were reaching wildly, grasping in the chaos at the forms coming detached from the corpses. Wild shapes, some he knew to be real and some that must surely have been in his head, they clung to the bodies from which they emerged, desperate as the things of many limbs tried to catch enough purchase to pluck them out. He laid amidst a harvest.

An arm lined on both sides with clawed fingers grasped onto him – onto his being. The entirety of him was squeezed taught, bits spilling through the grip as it pulled. He began to twitch, trying to shake off its cold digits, but all he did was embed himself into the snow. The one he knew, the one with many limbs who gave him his own arm, he stopped him. He lunged at the thing – a star of crawling arms – and plucked it off of Erkii. He kept him safe.

He was there before the others – before it all happened. He waited. He helped pull the power, to funnel it into the ring out of everything. It was so much – too much – and when released it shook sky and earth with the kind of violence he had never felt. It killed them all, all but Bern – but Bern was the one he wanted. He was going to slit Torgy's throat, he was going to kill them, yet he was untouched. Urkii tried to get him, reached for Bern but the brigand slipped grasp and slashed. The coat slit open. Pages fluttered through the air, spinning about and falling to the ground. It was a strange sight, one which brought a pause to both men as they shared a moment of confusion and disbelief – neither noticed Torgy raise the sword nor drop it onto Bern's shoulder. The scarred brigand fell into the snow. Then more came.

Like paper moments before, they fell through the air, drifting from heavens in overlapping spirals. *La'Uth's servants*, he thought them – here to save them all from the surrounding chaos of grasping limbs. What he thought was wrong – they were but there to join in the harvest. While beating down the limbed creatures with their pale wings, they latched onto the beastly shapes, pulling taught on opposing ends threatening to tear them in half. Baskets, satchels, bottles and vials dangled from their fleshy torsos. He felt arms wrap about him from beneath – they were his brothers arms.

"This way, big man," he heard a familiar voice.

Urkii carried him like a newborn calf, straight through a shapeless torso of seven bulbous protrusions – they moved through it as if it weren't there. It wasn't, at least not in this world. All there was here was him, Urkii, and Torgy, and the remnants of those he had murdered. And there was pain, searing through the flesh of his little finger right down to the bone. He couldn't move it, he couldn't bend it. *The ring,* but it wasn't a ring anymore. It had melted, turned to liquid and cast his finger in bronze.

Up ahead walked Torgy, under arm he carried the ornate blouse of shimmering black.

Epilogue

The power, the burst, the swarm – he ran without shame. Still in the trees, fifty yards from where it was unleashed, and yet it still tossed him like a rag doll. By the time he got up, he could see the Gharan being carried into the tree line. Behind him dragged a limb he thought could only ever belong to the Takers. Nothing, no gold, no title, no land, could have convinced him to go after the sorcerer. Whatever power he had, wherever he got it, was far beyond what he could muster. And then the swarm. Staying there would have been a certain end for him and the kind of an end he wished on no one.

The contracts fell into Obert's hands, it was done. *Why was he there?* He asked himself after every league travelled, at every border crossed and with every carriage hired. It made no sense for Marshal Obert, the kingdom's zealot, to be scouring about a bandit camp in backwoods at the border. Bad luck was all he could write it down to. Bad luck – that's all it was. But how was he to explain it to the man he now kneeled before?

Draped in silks of white, black, and gold the Emperor looked over him with a measured calm. The fabric cascaded loosely down the cushions of his deep seated throne, down to his feet past which they were bunched and set by servants – as per tradition – to the left from where they carried on until the very bottom step of the rise. The servants stood to the side, watching the Emperor with undivided attention for any sign of movement which could indicate he wished to stand. If such was seen, they would rush promptly to manoeuvre the silks in such a way his walk was unimpeded. If he was ever needed to ask, new servants would be promptly found and the ones who failed would be found looking elsewhere for employ. Not all emperors of the past were as stern with their servants, some even choosing to avoid traditional robes entirely, others chose to execute them instead. Ardian was a ruler of just moderation.

"'Ink dries quicker than blood'," the Emperor's voice travelled down the steps in thoughtfully articulated cadence. He projected at the median of his range that he used in common conversations. "With me on his knee, that is what he would say as he etched, signed, and sealed documents I was far too young to understand. I understand them now. I understand the words – the nuance of their identity – I understand the reasoning behind the precise order and form in which they were placed, and most important of all, I have come to understand the many purposes they were written to achieve. My father never had that same privilege – a circumstance which contributed to his untimely death at the hands of his closest advisor. Of course, Teryys was right in his killing – not that it made his ends any more pleasant – but his act of objection was morally righteous. My father was leading us into the worst war of all – one that favoured both sides equally. Either if we were to win, we would be claiming fealty of a broken people in whom the rot of treason has been instilled deep by our own sword and spear. Our army would have suffered great casualties, leaving our expanse of borders and collection of dissenting territories ripe for either taking or rebellion. A brigand, a duke, a lord, or even a king could wage such warfare, but an Emperor must know better. He must use the tools he has to ensure that every act leads to ends which are more favourable than the beginnings. He must or the empire will fall... the contracts, tell me what happened."

"I made it," he told him, struggling to control the tremble which threatened to capture his foot. "He signed them all, but they were taken in my death. I attempted to retrieve them but failed to. They fell into the enemy's hands."

The Emperor's back straightened beneath the robes causing a slight shimmer to cascade down the length of the silks. He was listening, taking in Sparrow's words with care as he examined his every feature. Likely, this was where his life would end. Another spymaster would take his place before the day was over. Any moment, Ardian's fingers would snap bringing forth guards who would overpower him with ease, bind him, then lock him in a cage too narrow to sit and too short to stand. His barriers would then be broken – not at first, at first he would resist – but eventually, with time and persistence, they were bound to make it through. They would violate his mind, extract every thought, memory and idea which could be of use, then discard the rest.

"Show me."

He wants it all, every detail, the entirety of his recollection. Failures and fears served on a platter for his reverence to do with as he pleased. *What use will he see in me once the curtain has been lifted?* Ardian's eyes closed in focus.

The Emperor's vine sprouted, grasping near blind in Sparrow's search. It had taken him decades of tutorage and practice to do that, to develop a single, pathetic feeler – an effort which for anyone sensitive would have been an embarrassment. But not for someone born deaf and blind to the other side. For someone without an innate gift, this was near impossible.

The vine found him, the outskirts of his mind kept safe by layers of masonry. At their foot, it waited. The Emperor made no effort to break through – even if given centuries he couldn't have unless allowed in. His thoughts were still his own. He even contemplated keeping them so – he could refuse – but the end to that notion would have been certain death. And as moderate as Ardian was in his dealings, in cruelty he seemed to find an outlet. If he didn't want to lose all of his digits and limbs a joint at a time, there was no other choice but to let him in.

With a feeler of his own, he lifted the little vine and pulled it through the gaps in his masonry. He walked it through the passages, the hallways, and tunnels constructed in weeks passed. He let it linger where needed, at the recollections of his voyage, the butcher's disguise and his cliff climb to King Emett's chambers. The negotiation and Emett weeping as he signed were a particular point of interest along the naming of Jarls who would pose a challenge and those who would fall in line. The near slip on his return climb, the millers wagon, and the long walk on which he skewered a dire bear, even the ambush in which Sparrow died were all flittered over, insignificant in the grand scheme of things. The only pause was when the world shook, his linger on the outskirts – the fear that sparrow had felt permeated through regardless of how much he tried to mask it. On all sides, the takers tore at the dying, but their presence was only a figment of his experience. There was nothing of them that the Emperor could sense but throat clenching fear they brought on which coincided with the sight of the bodies and the Gharan. And even with that fear conveyed, the mage took the Emperor but a moment to consider. What truly occupied Ardian was the man who arrived right after, the one who had the dying executed and whose hands now held the contracts.

The Emperor's eyes opened. "Who is he?" His voice was firm, quickening in its delivery.

"Rhuan Obert, Nurhdval's Marshal."

The Emperor looked to him once more yet didn't seem to be looking at him at all. With eyes glazed over, the thoughts spinning behind them within the Emperor's mind could almost be seen. *I am done,* he thought, readying himself to hear a rustle of mail from the doorways at his hind and flanks. But the Emperor's mood seemed to suddenly lift.

"Good. That will be all."